The
Christmas
Glass

The
Christmas
Glass

Marci Alborghetti

Guideposts
New York, New York

The Christmas Glass

ISBN-13: 978-0-8249-4776-7

Published by Guideposts
16 East 34th Street
New York, New York 10016
www.guideposts.com

Distributed by Ideals Publications, a division of Guideposts
2636 Elm Hill Pike, Suite 120
Nashville, Tennessee 37214

Guideposts and *Ideals* are registered trademarks of Guideposts.

The characters and events in this book are fictional, and any resemblance to actual persons or events is coincidental.

Library of Congress Cataloging-in-Publication Data

Alborghetti, Marci.
 The Christmas glass / by Marci Alborghetti.
    p. cm.
  ISBN 978-0-8249-4776-7
 1. Christmas stories. I. Title.
 PS3601.L338C47 2009
 813'.6--dc22

                    2008042768

Cover and interior design by Thinkpen Design, Inc., www.thinkpendesign.com
Typeset by Nancy Tardi

Printed and bound in the United States of America

10 9 8 7 6 5 4 3 2

For God.

To Charlie.

The People of *The Christmas Glass*

In Italy

ANNA, a widow who operates an orphanage in northern Italy
CATERINA, Anna's mother
ELENA, Anna's grandmother
SARAH, one of the Jewish children being sheltered in Anna's orphanage
FILOMENA, Anna's cousin, living in southern Italy

In Connecticut

FILOMENA, now eighty-three and living in an assisted-living residence
PAOLO, Filomena's late husband
CATHARINE, one of Filomena's twin daughters
GREGORY, Catharine's husband
EVELYN (EVIE), Catharine's daughter
TOM, Evie's fiancé
JACK, Evie and Tom's son
OLIVIA, native of Ghana, executive director of Stonington Mills, where Filomena lives
CHARLIE, Olivia's nephew, also from Ghana
GRACE, Olivia's niece, also from Ghana
MICHAEL, owner of a B&B in Ogunquit, Maine
FRANK, Michael's father, now deceased

In Accra, Ghana

PAMELA, Olivia's sister; Charlie and Grace's mother
OLIVIA'S FATHER
CELIA, Olivia and Pamela's late mother

In Key West, Florida

LOUIS (PADRE LOU), a minister, native of Jeremie, Haiti
MARGUERITE, Louis' assistant
ISABELLA, Louis' adoptive mother
JIM, Louis' adoptive father

In Sausalito, California

MARIA, Catharine's sister, also from Connecticut
DANIEL, Maria's husband, also from Connecticut
ROBERT, Maria's first husband while living in Connecticut, now deceased

In Bodega Bay, California

MARK, Maria and Robert's son, also from Connecticut
SERENA, Mark's wife
BOBBIE, Mark and Serena's son
LAURIE, Mark and Serena's daughter
MELISSA, Mark and Serena's daughter
LUKE (PASTOR LUKE), Mark and Serena's counselor
ELINOR, Luke's wife
DAVID, a friend of Maria and Daniel
SANDY, David's wife
BLOSSOM, David and Sandy's adopted baby

In Fort Lauderdale, Florida

SARAH, now an elderly widow
BEN, Sarah's late husband
SAMUEL (SAMMY), Sarah's grandson
GUILLERMO, native of Cuba, a cabdriver
GUILLERMO'S MOTHER
CHRISTINA, Guillermo's deceased wife
CAROLINA, Christina's sister
CLEMENCIA, Guillermo and Christina's daughter, now living in Brooklyn, New York

In Jeremie, Haiti

JULIA, Louis' mother
PIERRE, Louis' father

I

ANNA

ITALY, 1940

How should she pack the fragile, precious glass for the long journey? The question nagged at her, though she knew it was foolish. She had seventeen children to protect, Italy had just joined Germany in war, and here she was anxious about wrapping a few ancient Christmas ornaments for their trip to safety. If everything weren't so wretched, she might actually laugh at herself.

Anna could hardly remember the sound of her own laughter. Nor could she even imagine the laughter of her newest wards, the solemn, silent children she was collecting one by one. The prospect of battle did not awaken in her three new children the same misbegotten excitement it brought to the other orphans in her care, local children too naive to understand what war meant. These fourteen Italian youngsters who'd been with her for some time in the orphanage she ran here in Varese could still laugh and play; the recent arrivals followed her every move and word as if their lives depended on it. Because, as she'd just begun to understand, they did.

Few Italians had been surprised when, more than a month ago, on June 10, 1940, Mussolini declared that Italy would wage war on the side of Germany against Britain and France. France, now occupied, had all but fallen by then, and Mussolini wanted to be on the side of the victor. Soon after, the shadow children began arriving. Anna could not ignore them even though there were barely enough beds and food for the Italian orphans she officially sheltered.

Her parents had left her the rambling old house on Lake Varese where she and the children lived; there'd been hardly enough money to add rooms for a school. Fortunately, she and her husband Giorgio had cultivated enough wealthy patrons to keep the place going on donations. When Giorgio died five years ago, just after their dream of opening a haven and school for the province's poorest children had been realized, the donors had not deserted her. Would these good people continue to help if they knew she was secretly harboring Jewish children?

Anna wasn't willing to test them by revealing her decision. Although Italy did not share Germany's animosity toward the Jews, fear could swiftly turn people to hatred. And Anna knew this would be true of even the kindest Italians if their own lives or their children's were threatened.

So she would not tell her contributors, most of whom lived in Milan, just south of Varese. There was no way to keep it from Isabella, the cook and housekeeper, and Carla, who helped teach and care for the fourteen children legally enrolled. Both women had accepted Anna's decision wordlessly, and she could only pray they would remain loyal—and silent. She was not afraid for herself; since Giorgio had died suddenly and so young, she'd feared nothing, certainly not the death that would bring them together again. Some days, God help her, she yearned for it. But she did fear for her orphans: What would happen to them if she were imprisoned—or worse—for sheltering Jews?

Yet how could she turn them away?

Many Italians nervously dismissed as mere rumors the stories leaking out of Germany that Hitler had a mad plan to murder every Jew in the world.

This sounded so ridiculous that the Italians, like the rest of the world, could dismiss the possibility.

But Anna believed. Her husband had never trusted the Nazis, and Anna, who discussed everything with Giorgio in the twelve years they had together, expected the worst. What she heard from the people who'd furtively brought the Jewish children to her door confirmed her fears. The first two brothers, who'd arrived two weeks ago, had been brought over the Austrian border by a former patient of their father, a prominent Innsbruck physician.

"A man I do business with in Milan knew of you, Signora," he'd said, mentioning one of Anna's most prominent benefactors. She must have looked alarmed because he immediately added, "I did not tell him I wanted to place Jewish children with you. No, no! I made up a story about a friend in Milan with an orphaned nephew he could not care for. I would never dare speak the truth . . . for your sake and for mine. But you must hide these brothers, Signora. For the sake of God! Because of Mussolini's pact with Hitler, Italy is safer than Austria, and the boys will be protected here. Their mother has given me this to leave with you for their care."

He reached into a bag he'd set down by his side and thrust an elegant leather case upon her, pushing it into her hands and then backing away, holding up his own hands as if to relinquish responsibility and demonstrate that she'd committed herself. *He can't wait to be rid of these children,* Anna thought, and at that moment she sensed a change in the two brothers who'd appeared to be ignoring the exchange between the adults. They'd both raised their eyes and stood so straight they seemed to be quivering, like hunting dogs on the scent, all their attention on the case in Anna's hands. It was, she realized, the case in which their mother kept her jewels, and the faint scent of her perfume wafted from the rich leather.

What did she tell them? Anna wondered. *How did she say farewell? With tears? With false smiles and hollow laughter? Did they know what was likely to become of her, of their father? Did they know what would become of themselves?*

As she looked at them, Anna realized the Austrian man was right: She had committed herself. He knew it too. By the time she returned her eyes to him, he'd picked up his own bag and was hurrying away.

Later, when she opened the jewelry case, she was stunned. These jewels must have been handed down through several generations: diamond brooches and necklaces; emerald pins; two sapphire-and-diamond bracelets with matching earrings; pearl hairpins and combs; antique rings, including a large solitaire diamond in a platinum setting; gold and silver chains.

Anna was dazzled, not only by the beauty but also by the bounty. The contents of this case would keep the orphanage running for some time. It would be easy to find buyers for such extraordinary pieces, she reflected, smiling sadly as she imagined her mother's voice: *"Those with money and a good eye won't care where these came from. Tell them the jewels were donated by a wealthy benefactor, and they'll ask no questions."*

It was the sparkling jewelry that had started her thinking about the Christmas Glass, her own small family's treasure. The dozen intricately shaped glass ornaments, which in their brilliance did indeed resemble the desperate woman's jewels, were shot through with translucent colors that shone like multi-hued stars descended to enliven the dull earth. Her mother, Caterina, had always made much of the ornaments. "Your father may have this old house from his family," she would say dismissively, "but we have the Christmas Glass."

§

Early each December 13, St. Lucia's Day, after her father had left for work, Anna's mother would ceremoniously lead her to the cupboard where her parents' wedding china and the good silver were kept. Anna didn't like the silver because it required frequent polishing, a ritual so tedious she shared it with her mother only grudgingly. But on the very top shelf, so high that her diminutive mother had to bring a chair to stand upon, was the box of Christmas Glass.

The box itself, crafted of beautiful fruitwood and waxed to a high sheen, lay under the shroud of dust that always accumulated during the eleven months it waited in its high niche. Before she'd even consider revealing the box's contents, Caterina would address the dust that was, to Anna's young eyes, a kind of protection in itself. Her mother would take a new cloth—not the same age-softened rag she used every day to dust furniture, but a fresh, slightly dampened flannel—and wipe the dust away. She used unusually gentle strokes as if she, too, thought that the dust deserved a measure of respect.

Caterina would carefully carry the box down the long, darkened hall and into the parlor, where a large window spanned the entire upper half of the wall. Normally the heavy drapes were kept drawn to keep the bright morning sun from shining directly into the room.

"It will fade the carpet and furniture," Caterina would respond implacably when Anna's father protested about keeping out the light. But on this day, Christmas Glass Day, Caterina would stride boldly into the gloomy room and set the unopened box on a square table between two chairs by the window. Then she would fling the drapes back, allowing the sun to flood the room with blinding light.

The early sun made everything look different. Caterina was a ruthless housekeeper, and there was not a particle of dust or dirt to dim the newly revealed colors of the carpet and the deep rose fabric covering the chairs. Even the dark wood of the furniture gleamed in the relentless light.

A side table held the family's collection of photographs, and Anna was always drawn to the gilt-framed photo of her parents at their wedding. Caterina appeared to be a different person then, smiling shyly beside Anna's father. There was a sweetness to the girl in the portrait that Anna did not recognize in her formidable mother. Anna could not imagine her parents young and in love.

Christmas Glass Day always found Caterina at her best. On that day she was the mother Anna wished for every day. After Anna had gazed to her heart's content upon all the familiar objects and furnishings that the sun made new, she'd return to where her mother stood by the wooden box. By that time Caterina would have turned the heavy chairs so that they faced the window, and mother and daughter would sit with only the table and the box of ornaments between them. Even today, Anna could remember holding her breath in excitement, waiting for what came next.

First, Caterina would recite the story of the Christmas Glass and how it had come to her family. Though her mother had been dead for almost ten years, Anna could still hear her voice.

"There is a small village called Lauscha, set in the mountains of Germany. There, for many years, have lived families who have just one job: to make beautiful glass. The grownups do the hard part, forming the hot glass and pouring hot silver into the shapes. The children dip the ornaments in lacquer and paint them. The women pack the ornaments into baskets that they strap onto their backs and walk long distances to sell the ornaments at markets.

"Many years ago, a glassblower in Lauscha and his family made our Christmas Glass. We do not know their names, but they fashioned the glass with a love for the Baby born on Christmas Day, and that love sparkles in every piece. When my mother—your Nana—got married in 1875, her mother wanted to give her a very special gift, an heirloom she could give to her own daughter someday. She wanted something different, something wonderful, something that would make everyone who saw it sigh with pleasure and envy. But she didn't know what such a gift would be. Until one day she saw the Christmas Glass.

"She was passing by a shop in Milan—not a particularly nice shop; in fact, it

was a shop where people sold their valuables because they needed money. The window facing the street was streaked and filthy, and your great-grandmother Elena probably planned to walk right by without a second glance.

"But just as she was about to pass the window, a glint of color caught her eye. She peered through the dirty glass and was frozen there by what she saw. On a table in the window lay the most beautiful collection of glass she'd ever seen. Each piece shimmered as if it held a small flame burning within. She could not help herself: She had to go in.

"The collection proved even more extraordinary up close. There were twelve pieces lying in an open box—this open box, Anna, this very box we have before us! It was covered with a layer of grime, and the gleam of the wood was nowhere to be seen.

"The ornaments seemed to be alive with light, and Elena fancied that if she touched them, she would feel their warmth. Each was a different shape, and their colors were so vibrant they appeared to glow. There was the Holy Family, with streaks of indigo coloring Mary's dress, while green marked Joseph's robe and the Babe shone with gold. Three were long and thin, each in the shape of a wise man, and their robes were marked with scarlet and purple and deep green, all flecked with gold. There was a crystal star with just the slightest sweep of fiery yellow lighting it from within, and an angel in joyous flight, his wings lined with silver. A starfish, awash with blue and green, winked from the box, and a long icicle, such as we sometimes see here in Varese but often appear in the German mountains where the glassmakers live, flared with a thin spiral of silver and gold. There were *two fish, symbols of our Lord: one spun with blue, green and silver and the other with red, orange and gold. And finally, Elena saw two perfect globes, crystal clear each, one with the merest sprinkle of red and gold, the other with green and silver.*

"Your great-grandmother reached out and cautiously lifted the red and gold globe to test its weight, to feel the delicate glass in her hand. A man came into the front room through the curtain dividing the shop and smiled at her. He gestured at the box and said, 'I see you've found my treasure.'

"Intrigued, she asked, 'Your treasure?' When he nodded emphatically and described the ornaments as 'the very jewels of my heart,' her own heart sank: Surely he would not be willing to part with something he held so dear. Unable to hide her dismay, she murmured, 'Ah, then they are not for sale.'

"'You mistake me, Signora!' he said quickly. 'I meant only to say that they came to me with a story that made my heart weep. They were brought in not a month ago by a girl, no more than a few years past twenty. The ornaments—the Christmas Glass, she called them— had been a gift to her when she and her husband married five years ago. But now she and that husband have two children, both girls, and the man has no work. She wanted to sell them to feed her family and to keep her husband from having to beg. I told her I could never pay her what these are truly worth, but she was fraught and anxious and wanted to take what I would give her. She could not bear to look at them as she left, and so they have become like jewels to me: both lustrous to the eye and cutting to the heart.'

"Hearing this, your great-grandmother was torn. The ornaments had been proudly crafted for joy, to celebrate a wedding, yet they were touched with such

sadness. Should she give them to her own daughter to mark her own wedding? Or
would they bring more sorrow? She knew that marriage was much more than just
the wedding festival. These ornaments had seen both happiness and pain, and
had served both. Hadn't she wanted something unique, something unforgettable?
She gazed at the glass, captivated by the life and light that blazed from within
each figure. Finally, she looked up at the expectant shopkeeper.

"'I want the box cleaned.'"

Every year on Christmas Glass Day, Caterina recounted this history. Then,
with great dignity, she would go to the long side table that held decanters of
the mysterious cordials Anna only ever tasted at Christmastime. Caterina
would reach up to the cabinet above the decanters and remove two impos-
sibly fragile glasses with tiny tulip-shaped cups atop slender stems. Slowly,
she'd pour a few drops of amber-colored liquid into each glass before handing one to Anna. Mother and daughter would face each other over the still-
closed box of ornaments and raise their glasses as Caterina proclaimed,
"To the Christmas Glass: May it reflect more joy than sorrow, and cheer us
through both."

After the trickle of hot licorice had made its way past Anna's heart and
into her stomach, Caterina would slowly open the box, and the daylight filling the room suddenly found a new home. It was as if the sun itself could
not resist the Christmas Glass, concentrating its rays on the translucent figures until the floor and walls and ceiling danced with shimmering lines of
indigo, gold, silver, green, red, purple and yellow.

Once Anna and her mother had gazed on this spectacle for some time,

Caterina would unfold the length of scarlet velvet that had covered the glass in the box and lay it on the table under the window. When it was precisely placed according to some pattern Caterina alone knew, she and Anna would reverently place each ornament on the velvet, arranging each to best catch the light. When they were arranged to Caterina's satisfaction, she'd return to the sideboard and retrieve five silver candlesticks of varying heights along with five perfect ivory beeswax candles, so that at night the Christmas Glass would have a source of light much softer than the sun but no less flattering to its beauty. Anna could not remember ever entering that room on a late-December night to find the candles unlit. Her mother kept the Christmas Glass illuminated as though each form was a beacon welcoming the Babe.

Nor would the heavy drapes be drawn again until January 7, the day after Epiphany, when the Christmas Glass would be returned to the fruitwood box and stored tenderly away for another year.

§

Now, on a hot, overcast summer day nearly a decade after Caterina's death, Anna opened the box of ornaments knowing she would probably never open it again on a bright, cool December morning. She would not cry, she told herself. She'd made a decision and could not falter now. She was sending the Christmas Glass to her cousin Filomena.

Anna was convinced this war would not end quickly, and she was determined that the most important thing that remained of her mother—of her family—would survive. Even if she ended up sacrificing her reputation or even her life—possibilities that had become decidedly more likely since she'd taken in the Jewish children—she would not risk the one priceless thing her mother had given her. Anna somehow felt that if the Christmas Glass survived this coming nightmare, the memory of her mother and of her own wedding to Giorgio would also remain untouched by the filth of war.

The glass would be safer with Filomena, who lived in Bacoli, a small seaside village just outside of Naples. She hadn't seen her cousin for more than three years, since Filomena's marriage to Paolo, but she knew the young couple, now with two-year-old twins, hoped to emigrate to America as soon as they could arrange passage. Even if the young family had to wait out the war, the Christmas Glass would be safer in tiny Bacoli, so far south of the Austrian border and Germany.

Anna couldn't help the sob that rose in her throat, knowing she might never see the ornaments again. Still unsure of how best to pack them for the journey to Bacoli, she went to her wardrobe, hoping to find something suitable, perhaps some fabric she'd never had time to make into a dress. Her eye fell on her wedding gown, covered in paper at the back of the wardrobe. Her mother had used an extravagant amount of material to make the dress; the ivory silk was heavy and voluminous. Anna took a deep breath and held it. Could she really do it? Cut up her wedding dress to wrap the ornaments?

There had been times, right after Giorgio died, when she would bury her face in the dress, twisting it around her in an agony of grief and yearning. Yet now it was the perfect answer: Not only was the heavy silk ideal for the purpose, but it was also somehow fitting that the dress she wore on the day her mother gave her the Christmas Glass would be used to preserve her family's treasure. Slowly releasing her breath, she reached for the gown.

Knowing that if she hesitated for even a moment she would talk herself out of it, Anna found her mother's sewing shears and got to work. First, she cut a square from the bodice, the part that had been closest to her heart, and, folding it carefully, enclosed it in the velvet from the Christmas Glass and put them both in a cedar-scented drawer of her dresser. That way she would always have a bit of both the Christmas Glass tradition and her wedding day. She thought briefly—selfishly, she told herself—of keeping one of the ornaments too, but she remembered her mother saying it would be a terrible thing to ever separate them. Anna had been eleven at the time, and old enough, she felt, to keep one of the ornaments in her room. But when she asked Caterina if she could have the angel for her bed table, her mother had been aghast.

"No, no!" Caterina had cried, shaking her head emphatically, "These belong together! They are like a family. If you take the angel, who will guard the Babe, hmmm? No, it is no good to separate them; if you do, they will always yearn to be together again."

Although Anna was old enough now to smile at her mother's warning, she was not about to ignore Caterina's wishes. All the ornaments would go to Filomena in Bacoli and later, she hoped, to America. She began cutting up the wedding dress methodically. She would double-wrap each ornament and use the heavy silk scraps to cushion the spaces between them. She worked in silence. The children were at their lessons with Carla in the opposite wing of the house, near where they slept, one large room for the boys and another for the girls. Isabella was in the kitchen below, preparing their lunch. Normally, Anna would try to eat with her wards and Carla, but today she was determined to finish the task at hand.

She glanced up from her work and was so startled by the thin, still figure that she almost dropped the shears. The child was so quiet Anna hadn't even known she was there. This third Jewish child, a girl named Sarah, was indeed an orphan. Her grandmother had brought her to Anna more than a week ago. Anna could see them now as they'd been that day: The visibly impatient grandmother, dressed in threadbare clothes that had once been elegant, standing apart from the little girl, who held a suitcase bigger than she was as her eyes fixed on something outside the window. The grandmother made no attempt to hide her frustration or soften her words.

"My son and his wife died last year in a fire. My daughter-in-law always insisted on too many candles—you don't need twenty candles to light the dining room when just two are at table, but did she ever listen? Never! We saw the fire from our house but could do nothing. This child—their only one, and you can be sure her mother spoiled her and let her run wild through that house—was visiting cousins that night, but the way the world is these days, it may have been better if she'd been in the house with them."

Anna had been unable to stop herself from giving the old woman a reproachful look and gesturing at the child who stood just a few feet away. This had the effect of aggravating the woman even more.

"Do you think this is easy for me? Do you think I planned to have an ungovernable six-year-old girl all but left at my doorstep?" she snapped, her eyes flashing. "She has not spoken since the night her parents died. She wouldn't eat until her grandfather—and he is not a well man—and I agreed to bring her every day to the ruined cottage behind the ashes of her old house. She sits there for hours. Just staring.

"And now, after we begged my niece in London to sponsor us and sold most of what we own to escape that murdering Nazi, this child refuses to leave. She flew into a rage when we told her we were going. She imagines we are taking her from her parents! Her parents who have been dead for nearly a year! We must lock her in her room to keep her from running away. The shame! And what do you think it will be like for us—two sick, old Jews—trying to get her quietly out of the country? The only reason she agreed to come here is because we told her this place is just across the lake from her old house."

Anna realized then that the girl was not staring idly but looking across the lake to where her home had been. From this distance it wasn't possible for the girl to recognize the precise place, but her stare unnerved Anna nonetheless. She studied the child, searching for signs of the violent and inconsolable grief her grandmother had described. None were visible; the girl appeared utterly detached.

But her stillness and self-possession were not signs of calm or acquiescence; rather it appeared that she was in another world altogether. Small and nearly emaciated, with large, dark eyes like coals smoldering in her thin, pale face, she was intensely focused on something that existed only for her, and Anna did not want to be the one who took her from it.

The grandmother watched Anna with a mixture of hope and hostility. "I can't pay much," the old woman said, reaching into an embroidered bag and pulling out a small sack weighted with coins.

"Keep your money," Anna said coldly, her own voice surprising her by how much she sounded like her mother. For the first time, the grandmother looked abashed, and Anna suppressed a small rush of triumph. Certainly the old woman had experienced great loss—and was about to lose her granddaughter as well—but Anna was convinced that this was a woman who would have managed to be unhappy no matter what life brought her. "I'll try to keep her safe," Anna said turning away.

"You can send her to us after the war. Perhaps by then she'll appreciate what we've done for her," the old woman said with a hard glance at the child. "I'll send our address when we're settled."

Anna watched the girl, her eyes still unwavering on the distant point across the lake, as her grandmother took a step toward her. "Well, Sarah. I'm leaving. Come here and kiss me good-bye," commanded the old woman waspishly.

The child remained still, her eyes unmoving. Her grandmother stared at her for a long moment, and Anna caught a spasm of longing in her age-worn face. As if to herself, the old woman murmured softly, "You are so like your father," and then she moaned, a strangled sound halfway between fury and despair, and walked away, her heels clicking hard on the tiles in the hallway. She dropped the bag of money on a table as she left.

Now that same child stood in the doorway, watching Anna destroy her wedding gown. Sarah had given her no real problems, but neither had she spoken to Anna or to any of the other children. She hadn't even glanced after her grandmother when the old woman left, much less shed a tear to see her go. When the Jewish brothers approached her shyly, she ignored them just as she did everyone else. She endured her lessons with Carla and ate Isabella's food without appearing to care what she was doing.

She spent every free moment staring across the lake where she believed her home had been. Anna worried she would try to run away, to go back there, but Sarah seemed satisfied with fixing her gaze on the place. There was an obsessiveness to Sarah's solitude that Anna didn't know how to approach, much less break.

Gesturing at the squares of white silk and the open box of ornaments, Anna asked, "Sarah, do you want to help me?"

The girl's eyes moved from Anna to the silk and the ornaments on the table. Without answering, she walked slowly toward Anna. When she reached the table, she stared at the Christmas Glass as if mesmerized. Continuing to work Anna explained about the Christmas Glass, how her great-grandmother had found them and how Caterina had given them to

Anna on the day she married Giorgio. She spoke of Giorgio, about how much she missed him, how much the Christmas Glass had meant to both of them. She was pouring words into the air, words she'd thought would crush her if she ever gave them voice, but they simply filled the room gently, creating images she loved, and then dissipated, taking with them the heaviest part of her grief and fear.

By the time she was finished talking, she'd cut up the dress and wrapped most of the Christmas Glass. Taking a deep breath, she looked at the silent child who'd been the catalyst for this outpouring. Sarah met her gaze.

"You are like me then," she said. "Alone."

Careful to show no emotion at the girl's first words in more than a year, Anna thought swiftly about how to respond, about all the things she should say. She should assure Sarah that she was not alone, that she had family waiting in London. She should say that neither of them was alone, that they had the other children, Isabella, Carla. That they had each other. Anna looked into the cavernous eyes of the child for what seemed an eternity and finally answered.

"Yes. I am alone. Like you."

And then she handed Sarah the glass angel to wrap.

II

AMERICA

DECEMBER 2000

1

Catharine

I t was still too warm on the ground for the light snow to amount to anything, but it would soon draw the shoppers to Mystic. *Nothing motivates Christmas shoppers like the prospect of a white Christmas,* Catharine thought. Not far from the Rhode Island border in Connecticut, Mystic was considered the quintessential New England village and a retailer's dream come true. Sometimes Catharine, who lived close to the center of town with all its shops and restaurants, wished it wasn't quite so quaint. Visitors from all over the world clogged the streets in summer and again during the Christmas season, making it impossible for everyone else to go about their business. Already this December—and it was only the fourth of the month—tourists and shoppers had blocked her driveway with their cars three times. *That's what happens when Thanksgiving falls so late in November,* she thought. *Everyone panics about not being ready for Christmas.*

After looking outside her bay window to make sure the driveway was still clear, Catharine returned her gaze to the fragile Christmas ornament. Her mother claimed it was well over a hundred years old, but that information was secondhand, coming from the cousin who'd sent this and eleven ornaments like it to her mother sixty years ago. Catharine had only been two years old at the time, recovering from rheumatic fever, and she'd never actually seen Anna, this mysterious cousin of whom her mother spoke with such reverence. Every Christmas as far back as Catharine could remember—and Catharine didn't forget much—Filomena had insisted on talking about Anna.

Each December when she took out the box of Christmas Glass, as she called the collection of twelve glass ornaments, Filomena would tell Catharine and her twin, Maria, all about Anna—again. It had started when they were toddlers, and by the time the girls were teenagers, they could have recited the story to each other, but they always let Filomena tell it her own way. Behind their mother's back, the twins called this recital "The Story of Anna." Catharine would silently roll her eyes or stare at their newly lit Christmas tree, a wonder they'd never possessed before coming to America, but Maria—always the perfect little actress—had actually listened attentively to "The Story of Anna" each year as though hearing it for the very first time.

The twins only knew Anna through a photograph that had arrived at their cottage in Bacoli along with the Christmas Glass at the start of World War II. Catharine had a fleeting memory of the photo, a slightly out-of-focus, sepia-toned portrait of a plain-looking woman with her hair fastened in a knot on the top of her head. As a child in Bacoli, Catharine had always been relieved that her mother, with long, thick hair, a quick laugh and lively eyes, was nothing like this dull-looking older cousin. But by the time the war ended and they'd made the difficult, frightening trip to America, Filomena seldom laughed anymore.

At sixty-two and now much older herself than the woman in the lost photo, Catharine wondered what had happened to it. *Maria probably has it,* she thought sullenly; her sister had managed to collect just about every other thing of value in their lives, why not their mother's treasured photo of Anna as well? As a child, Maria had loved to hear their mother say, "Remember, my girls, Anna was a widow." Maria's own eyes would fill with tears at Filomena's mournful proclamation long before the girl understood what a widow was, long before she became one herself and learned to play the role to the hilt.

Catharine sighed and tried to push away the bitterness. It wasn't doing her any good. She stared at the delicate ornament in her hand, the worn glass so thin she feared she'd shatter it with a breath. Threaded through with blue, green and silver, the fish seemed to swim through her fingertips, flickering in the lights of the half-decorated Christmas tree. This was all she had left of the Christmas Glass; Maria had the other fish. "The sign of Jesus," Catharine remembered Filomena saying. *Yes,* she thought now, *Jesus, who taught forgiveness, which I can't seem to do.*

She heaved herself up off the couch and got to work on the tree. She needed to finish in time to get over to the rest home before Filomena had dinner. She reminded herself not to call it a "rest home" in her mother's presence. "Assisted living!" Filomena would bark every time someone dared refer to her residence as a rest home or a convalescent home or, God forbid, an old folks' home. Filomena, who'd retained her Italian accent—deliberately, Catharine was certain—was a great favorite at Stonington Mills, the assisted-living facility just ten minutes from Catharine's house. The staff loved Filomena. "She's such a card," one of the aides had told Catharine just last week.

Sure, Catharine reflected as she hung the glass fish near the gold filigree star that crowned the tree, *easy for them to be amused by my nosy, stubborn, overly pious mother, because she's not their mother. They get to go home at the end of their shift, probably to a normal family with a nice, normal little old lady for a mother, who babysits and doesn't turn every conversation into an opera. They undoubtedly have mothers who don't manipulatively lapse into tearful Italian, turning their eyes heavenward with long-suffering glances of reproach at the Almighty Who'd sent them such wayward progeny. And their mothers probably don't believe that food is the answer to everything from cancer to family rifts.*

Maybe if I had a mother like that, I wouldn't be eternally battling these extra twenty-five pounds, she thought, placing the ornaments precisely where she'd placed them the year before and the year before that back to the time when her daughter Evie was just a baby and the extra weight had crept on.

Naturally, Maria had never been overweight, not even after her son Mark was born and certainly never in the thirty-plus years since.

How old would Mark be now? Evie was twenty-eight, so Mark must be thirty-one. It was hard to keep track.

Even though Catharine hadn't seen her twin for almost ten years, she knew Maria remained fit and trim because Evie insisted on showing her photos. The last one displayed Maria with her latest husband, a familiar figure Catharine couldn't bear to look at, presiding over a Thanksgiving table just a week ago at their mansion in Sausalito. *Probably they had tofu instead of turkey, that's how she stayed so thin.* They were on the porch—*Who has Thanksgiving dinner on a porch, anyway?*—with the San Francisco skyline in the background.

"It's not a mansion, Mom," Evie groaned when Catharine snidely commented on her twin's pretentious house. "It's just a small house with a great view." Evie was another one who never gave up. Just like her grandmother.

And now Filomena was playing the food card again. Never mind that everyone—for once, Catharine wasn't alone in this—thought it was past time for Filomena to move from the assisted-living apartment complex at Stonington Mills to the long-term care wing—a sleek new white-brick structure that Filomena insisted on calling "the dying building." The long-term care building was on the same property, just a few hundred yards from Filomena's current apartment, but she was acting like they wanted her to move to Siberia. The long-term care rooms, each with its own spacious handicapped-equipped bathroom, were newer, brighter and had a gorgeous view of Long Island Sound, but what was Filomena concerned about? Giving up that cubbyhole of a kitchen she had in her old apartment! Filomena insisted she would not give up her kitchen, completely ignoring the fact that she needed more attention than was available in the independent apartments.

"I can't leave my kitchen," her mother wailed whenever the subject was raised, always throwing in a few Italian imprecations for good measure. "Where will I cook for my family?"

As if any of us care, thought Catharine, wrinkling her nose at the thought of the small, dark kitchen with the perpetual odor of tomato sauce and frying onions, which seemed to hang in the air and cling to the dishtowels. Olivia, who'd been Filomena's caregiver at their old house in New London, had tried to persuade her to move. Olivia had risen through the healthcare ranks to become executive director at Stonington Mills, and she normally wielded a great deal of influence with Filomena. But not even Olivia could get her to budge.

Olivia's straightforward, sometimes stern manner was somewhat softened by an irrepressible sense of humor and the music of her Ghanaian accent. Though that was another thing: Don't call it an accent in front of Olivia! It was like saying "rest home" in front of Filomena. "Accent?" Olivia would say archly, her eyebrows shooting up, "It is no accent to me. It is no accent in my home in Ghana, among my own people. It is no accent in Jamaica or Haiti or the West Indies. You Americans! Everyone who does not sound like you has an accent!"

Honestly, thought Catharine, *between my mother and Olivia, you can't win!* Someday she'd like to point out to both of them that women with accents seem to be particularly touchy. She'd like to, but she wouldn't dare.

Every year until this one, Olivia had spent three weeks, from early December to New Year's Day, in Ghana, visiting her father and sister and brother-in-law, the parents of the niece and nephew who'd lived with Olivia in America for nearly four years now. This year, for some reason, she hadn't gone. Catharine was just grateful that Olivia was here to help with Filomena and, she hoped, to convince her to move.

So far, though, nothing had worked. Olivia, God bless her, had agreed to meet Catharine late this afternoon for a strategy session. Afterward they would go together to Filomena's apartment and launch a dual offensive.

Shaking her head, Catharine took one more cookie from the plate her mother had given her yesterday, "for decorating the tree," she'd said, invoking yet another family tradition that kept Catharine buried in those extra pounds.

When Catharine and Maria were children, starting with the first Christmas and the first tree they'd had in America, Filomena had baked dozens and dozens of Christmas cookies during early December. She'd seen a story about a December cookie swap in *Ladies' Home Journal,* a magazine that she'd adopted as her instruction manual on how to behave in America. Catharine could remember the stacks of back issues piled carefully in dated order in her mother's New London bedroom closet. In happier times, Catharine and Maria had joked about how if it weren't for *Ladies' Home Journal*, Filomena would have never bothered to learn English.

That particular article had encouraged young housewives to "Meet New Friends While Saving Time During the Holidays!" by baking ten dozen of one kind of cookie and then having a "swap party" with nine other women in the neighborhood. Each family would end up with dozens of cookies of different varieties without having to spend the whole month baking. The magazine had offered recipes for ten kinds of cookies. But, of course, Filomena had her own version of the plan.

"What do I need to do with other women? New friends? Bah! I have my family, don't I?" she would mutter as she buttered cookie pan after cookie pan, "Besides, some of these wives around here? The way they keep house? I wouldn't eat anything out of their kitchens! Germs and dirt!"

Then she'd spend the entire first week of December baking dozens of cookies—just as the article suggested—except she had no one to swap with. Soon her small family had a mountain of cookies to finish "before they get stale, they don't keep forever, you know!" By Three Kings Day on January 6, Catharine and Maria were so sick of cookies that they felt they'd scream at the sight of just one more. Meanwhile, their poor father, Paolo, just kept chewing dutifully through the whole month, stoically putting on at least ten pounds, which he would just as easily lose before planting the early peas in their spring garden. *Why couldn't I have gotten his genes,* Catharine wondered.

But the nicest part of the tradition had been the first plate of fresh cookies her mother put out on the afternoon they put up the tree. It was early enough in the month so that cookies weren't coming out of their ears, and she and Maria had been as excited about eating cookies all afternoon as they'd been about decorating the tree their father had cut out of Mitchell Woods behind their house in New London. He'd drag the freshly cut tree home, on a sled if there was enough snow, set it up in the cast-iron stand in their living room by the bay window facing the Thames River, and drape the large colored lights over the branches. Then he'd get out of the way.

It was always, Filomena had insisted, "a perfect tree!" Even the year they had one that was so dried up and dead by Christmas Eve that you could see the ornaments in back while you were looking at the front, it was "perfect." She refused to remove old bird's nests or strip pinecones from any of the trees, instead sprinkling silver and gold glitter on them and turning them into natural decorations, "the way God made them." In many ways their mother had been like a child herself, especially when it came to Christmas. Truly, Catharine reflected, if she'd given them anything (and she'd given them plenty, that was the problem!), it had been an absolute and utter joy in the holiday she invariably called "Jesus' birthday."

It was a joy that lived in Catharine to this day, no matter how much she tried to grow out of it. *Look at me,* she thought, half-embarrassed, *how many other sixty-two-year-old women insist on a freshly cut tree*—from Holdridge's in Ledyard, a trip her poor husband Gregory made uncomplainingly each year—*and then spend an entire day decorating it?* It's not that it took the whole day to put up, it's just that once she was finished, Catharine, like her mother before her, spent another couple of hours rearranging the ornaments and lights so that everything showed to its best advantage.

I used to tease my mother, she thought, *and now I do the same thing. Surely Maria doesn't spend this amount of time on a Christmas tree, if she even* has *a tree. Not that she doesn't have all the time in the world to decorate a tree out there in California, a lady of leisure twenty-five hundred blessed miles away from her demanding mother. She probably buys a swanky designer tree like the ones at Saks in New York.*

Those Christmas trees at Saks! Each year, Filomena would make one trip and one trip only into New York with her girls, though her dislike of the city made it a tradition fraught with anxiety. From Thanksgiving weekend on, the girls lived with the constant fear that their mother, who never went to Manhattan even when her church group chartered a bus to see a Broadway musical ("Broadway! Broadway! What do I care for Broadway?"), would cancel.

If it snowed or sleeted, or even threatened to storm, she'd warn, "If the weather is like this, we're not going. I don't trust those train tracks in slippery weather." If one of the twins got a cold or the sniffles, they'd do their best—impossible!—to hide it from their mother, who would declare, "Ah, that's it! I'd better cancel right now. If you're sick already, can you imagine what you'll be like after the germs in that city?" And, of course, if one of them didn't feel like finishing a meal, that particular catastrophe warranted an outburst of, "No appetite? No point in paying all that money for the train and a fancy lunch at Saks. We'll stay home. I'll make soup."

Through all of this, their father would smile patiently and wink at the girls when Filomena wasn't looking. Paolo knew that his wife would never deny them this holiday outing. Catharine and Maria always passed those weeks caught between excitement and dread. But their father had been right: She never did cancel the New York Christmas trip, and from the time they were eight years old to the last Christmas they spent together a decade ago, the three had spent a day in Manhattan each December.

From those first years when Filomena tightly gripped their small, eager hands in hers through the whole trip, only releasing them while they ate at Saks's lunch counter, to the years when Catharine and Maria had taken their own children along, the tradition had a rhythm of its own. They would board the early train out of New London and arrive in New York by mid-morning. Then there was hot chocolate (espresso for Filomena) and fancy pastries at the coffee shop in Penn Station; the teeming streets with a policeman on every corner to keep innocents like them from being lost in the whirl of people, cars and incomprehensible traffic signals; the cabs that Filomena grumblingly paid for rather than risk her precious children on "that grimy underground dragon," as she called the subway; the colorful shops lit and decorated so lavishly that Catharine and Maria would stand mesmerized on the sidewalk while irritated and occasionally amused strangers streamed around them; and then, around noon, Saks Fifth Avenue itself!

It was always at this moment, when they reached the magnificent department store, that both girls prayed for the one thing they'd been praying against since Thanksgiving. Now that they were safely in the city, now that Filomena couldn't possibly cancel their trip, now that they were at the place where the thrill of Christmas lived, they prayed for snow. Even on those days when there wasn't a cloud in the sky and a weak December sun tossed scant light into streets already shadowed by towering buildings, Catharine and Maria prayed for snow. As they lingered outside, transfixed by whatever Christmas fantasy Saks had created in its windows, they wished only for a sparkling flurry to make the moment perfect.

It only happened once. Despite predictions of "wintry weather" that had Filomena threatening dire consequences for two days before their trip, they'd left Connecticut under clear skies. But when they emerged from the train station, blinking and following their noses up into the light like three moles, what little sky they could see was overcast. Maria and Catharine, twelve that year, had all but yanked Filomena along, chattering nervously about nothing in the hopes of diverting her attention. For one awful moment on the street outside the train station, she'd stopped short, raising her head in a way that proved her not a Manhattanite (as if her old-fashioned coat and long, thick braid weren't enough), and searched the sky.

Catharine and Maria stopped tugging on her and held their collective breath as only twins can. Desperate, they silently marshaled their arguments, each later assuring the other that they would have refused to turn back into the station and accompany Filomena home.

As it turned out, they didn't have to. Filomena, not bothering to even glance at their upturned (she'd always been taller than the two of them and still was), beseeching faces, tightened her grip on each of their hands and stepped into a waiting cab. By the time they'd reached Fifth Avenue, the sky was positively glowering, and the crowds seemed to be moving even faster than usual, as if to outrun whatever winter was about to cast down on them. This gave the twins an advantage: They didn't have to wait in line to see the Saks windows, and they were spectacular that year. Catharine could still remember one scene: the foolish wooden Pinocchio, his nose grown long from lying, with Gepetto, the kindly old carpenter who'd fashioned him. The two life-size figures were shown at work in a perfect replica of a carpenter's shop, and there was a small crèche with beautifully carved figures of the Babe, Mary, Joseph, and an angel watching over them from a nearby table.

Even Filomena had nodded happily to see depicted in the window the story she'd frequently told her girls as a lesson in honesty. Catharine had looked up to see her mother smiling with a simple delight she'd seldom displayed since Bacoli.

And while they stood there, silent for once, hand in hand, it began to snow.

And then, two more miracles: Her mother didn't panic and drag them back to the station, and the people who'd been racing along the sidewalks and streets so single-mindedly slowed down; some even stopped. Faces that had been masks of concentration softened, and smiles appeared.

One tall man in a fine camel hair coat and elegant fedora, so incredibly handsome that Catharine and Maria gasped at the sight of him, stood still and looked up at the snow filling the sky. Then he slowly lifted his hat and swept it in a wide arc as if saluting God for creating something so wondrous. He moved so deliberately, so eloquently, that the scene had stayed with Catharine all her life. Even now she remembered how beautiful he was. Filomena and the girls were still talking about him when they visited the Christmas tree at Rockefeller Center, where they always watched the skaters before catching the evening train bound for Connecticut.

The twins usually fell asleep about halfway home, but this time they were too excited, trying to guess who the handsome man might have been. Catharine imagined he was a dashing foreigner from some exotic country where it was never truly winter, and so he was swept away at the sight of snow. Maria (naturally) insisted he was a Hollywood star, going so far as to say that he looked just like Gregory Peck. But when they'd had enough of bickering and turned to Filomena for a final decision, she had a dreamy look on her face.

"He is no foreigner or movie star," she'd said softly. "He is an angel."

§

atharine was startled out of her memories by the sound of a car door, and a moment later, her husband Gregory came into the house. She looked hurriedly at her watch. After four! Could it be that late? At least the tree was finished.

"I thought you were going to Stonington to plot with Olivia and then have it out with your mother," he said before pressing his lips firmly against her cheek. For more than thirty years, he'd never failed to kiss her good-bye when he left and hello when he returned, and for that, she was silently grateful every single time.

"I was, and I'm late," she said, starting to gather the empty decoration boxes.

"I'll put that stuff away," he said. "You should get going. The snow isn't sticking to the roads yet, but it's not stopping either. Should I drive you?"

"No, I'll be fine. I hope it won't take too long." Actually, she did want his help, but not just on the drive. She wanted him to take care of the whole thing: make her mother see reason and cheerfully move into the long-term care residence. He'd do it, too. Well, not the making-her-mother-see-reason part because, after all, who could? But he would definitely get his mother-in-law to make the move. Yet Catharine knew from experience that Gregory had little patience with Filomena's histrionics, so even if the result was a move, it would leave Filomena infuriated and resentful, Gregory aggravated, and her being blamed by her mother for callousness and by her husband for being too easily manipulated.

By the time she gathered her coat, purse and keys, he'd turned off the lamps. The short December afternoon was far enough gone that the tree glowed in the darkening house. Her husband stood beside her, his arm around her, and they gazed at it together. "Looks nice, Cath," he said. "You always do such a good job on the tree."

Though not on much else, she added silently, thinking of ways she'd hurt this good man over the years and dreading the confrontation with her mother. Moving reluctantly out of her husband's embrace, she kissed him and headed for the door. Just before she went out, she turned to see him facing her in front of the tree. "Go get her," he said, with stoic good humor in his face. She rolled her eyes in acknowledgment of how unlikely that outcome would be, and left.

The drive was easy despite the snow, and she found Olivia waiting for her in her spacious office. Catharine realized with a small pang of conscience that Olivia had probably rearranged her demanding schedule just for this meeting. Olivia was so essential to them, they often forgot she had her own life. "Mom," Evie would scold, "Olivia doesn't *belong* to us, you know."

Catharine was ashamed of how little she knew about Olivia's family in Ghana. Why *weren't* Olivia and the niece and nephew who lived with her going to Accra, Ghana's capital, where Olivia had been born and the children's parents lived? Still, the gap in her knowledge about Olivia wasn't entirely Catharine's fault. Something about Olivia kept her from asking too many personal questions. There was a wall that Olivia kept carefully between them.

It wasn't there so much with Evie. She'd visited Olivia's home in New London many times, once observing to Catharine how different Olivia's tastefully decorated, bland office at Stonington Mills was from her home near Ocean Beach with its gorgeous woven rugs, vivid colors, and books in every room. The few times Catharine had been to Olivia's home—usually to drop something off for Filomena so she could avoid visiting her mother herself—she hadn't paid attention to the house. She vowed to get Olivia a really spectacular Christmas gift this year, though she couldn't imagine what. Usually the family just gave her money, a practice that now struck Catharine as ridiculous. Olivia was probably making more than any of them. She'd ask Evie for ideas about a good gift, maybe get her and Maria's son Mark to chip in. And, of course, Evie would ask Maria, so Catharine wouldn't have to.

"What shall we do about Meme?" Olivia said. Catharine found herself relaxing. Olivia always called Filomena by the nickname for mother. In some ways she was more a sister to Catharine than Maria was.

"I was hoping you'd have some ideas. She refuses to listen to reason."

"That's because it's *your* reason, not hers. Her reason tells her to stay in her apartment where she feels in control of things."

"Whose side are you on?" Catharine complained. "I thought you agreed she belongs in the long-term wing. Even Maria admits it, not that she's going to do anything about it."

"Let's leave that be and concentrate on your mother," Olivia knew all about Catharine and Maria. "I *do* think Meme belongs in long-term; I'm just saying you won't have an easy time convincing her of it. She doesn't want to give up her place. I see it all the time with our people here."

"You mean she doesn't want to give up her kitchen. Can you force her to move?" Catharine asked.

"Me? Force your mother? No, thank you!" Olivia said, her eyes wide.

"Well, what then? You run the place!"

"And you *don't* run your mother!"

"All right, then, will you at least come with me to see if together we can talk some sense into her?"

"You know I will, but don't forget that we *can't* force her, Cath," Olivia warned. "Short of her doing something that's dangerous to herself or others, there's nothing we can do but try to persuade her. Besides, I think she has ideas of her own on the subject of moving."

"Oh great, what's that supposed to mean?" Catharine asked, her eyes searching Olivia's face, "Do you know something I don't?"

Olivia pressed her lips together and exhaled. "Let's go and get this over with."

On that unhelpful note, Olivia took her coat and briefcase, and they walked out into the cold, crystal night. Although the snow had barely dusted the ground, Olivia's maintenance people were throwing rock salt on the paths connecting the buildings. Closest to Water Street, the village's main road, were the assisted-living apartments where residents lived independently—theoretically, at least—taking advantage of social, medical, and nutritional services according to their needs.

In Filomena's opinion, she didn't have any needs, nor did she "have to bother with these nosy old people who live here; I have my family, don't I?" It was a constant refrain that made Catharine want to weep with rage and weariness. Because, for the most part, "my family" amounted to Catharine. Naturally, Gregory did his part, poor man, and Evie, now that she'd finally come to her senses and returned from Key West, was always ready to help. Still, Catharine didn't like to ask Evie now that Evie's son Jack had become a toddler in constant motion. So Filomena's endless and often unspoken needs—Catharine was supposed to read her mother's mind and God forbid she get it wrong—fell to her. And if she even hinted that she had her own life—a husband who'd retired so they could spend more time together, a marriage that needed attention, even a grandson of her own to dote on— Filomena would claim she needed no one.

So Filomena did her own cooking, sorted her own medications, and vigorously resisted becoming involved in any of the social events such as holiday meals, summer picnics and excursions, and just yesterday, the Stonington Mills Annual Christmas Tree Decorating Festival. Maria had even called her mother from Sausalito after Evie told her that Filomena was refusing to attend the party again this year. Apparently, Maria's plea had been to no avail, a fact in which Catharine took a secret, guilty pleasure.

It was the fourth annual Christmas party she'd missed. Not to mention what else she'd missed that year: the Fourth of July Fireworks Spectacular, the Easter Egg Hunt for Grandparents and Grandchildren, shopping trips to the Crystal Mall in Waterford, the Book Buddies Discussion Group (though Filomena, an avid reader, followed the group's booklist and read every title so "those old ladies won't think they know more than me"), and Ladies Who Lunch restaurant outings.

It was probably her mother's refusal to go to the Christmas party—again—that had been the last straw for Catharine. Even though Filomena loved decorating for Christmas, she dismissed the idea of having her own little tree in the apartment. Instead, she expected to be included in every one of Catharine's Christmas traditions, from shopping to decorating the tree to wrapping presents. It had gotten to the point that Catharine couldn't tell the difference between what she wanted to do for Christmas and what she did simply because Filomena expected it.

But this year Catharine had rebelled. It was her tree, and she was going to decorate it when she wanted and how she wanted. She wasn't going to get up at the crack of dawn to fetch her mother so Filomena could supervise everything, beginning with Gregory's pre-breakfast ritual of putting the tree in the stand and winding the lights around its branches. Nor was Catharine about to spend the rest of the day being told what to do and how to do it.

As they were walking down the carpeted hall to Filomena's room, Olivia said, "You know that Meme loves you."

"And that's a good thing?" Catharine asked, and then the two were laughing so hard they hadn't completely stopped by the time they reached Filomena's apartment. Catharine knocked, called out, "Mom, it's us," and turned her key in the door. An old and tattered wreath, which Catharine remembered from her childhood, hung on it.

"Why don't you buy your mother a decent wreath?" Olivia whispered, provoking a fresh burst of laughter as they entered the apartment. Filomena was seated regally on the old couch she'd insisted on having moved from the New London house. She wore a look of martyred patience and a freshly pressed black housedress; through the open bedroom door, Catharine could see the ironing board still set up.

Filomena was a tall, big-boned woman who could carry a good deal of flesh without looking overweight, and at eighty-three, she was still striking. Her eyes, more black than brown, were large and bright, and she was vain enough to use her glasses only when reading. Her hair was completely white now, and though years of sun had taken their toll on what had been flawless skin, she looked fifteen years younger when she smiled. She was not smiling now.

Empty packing boxes were stacked all around her on the couch and floor. They appeared to frame her in brown cardboard.

"Mother," Catharine asked warily, "what's all this?"

Filomena looked straight at the space between Catharine and Olivia. "I will move to the dying building," she intoned, using her own name for the long-term care residence.

Catharine gaped. "You will?"

Slowly, Filomena turned her sharp eyes fully on her daughter, ignoring Olivia, who was staring at the floor as if wishing she had indeed gone to Ghana.

"I will move only after Christmas. And only after you and your sister eat Christmas dinner together with me here."

2

María

aria was appalled at how fast time was passing. It was the first Saturday of the month, December 7 already, and she hadn't picked out Christmas gifts for her niece Evie and her two-year-old grandnephew Jack not to mention her daughter-in-law and grandchildren. Shopping for her mother was always a lost cause because Filomena invariably responded to gifts by demanding to know how much they cost and then lamenting "such a waste."

Then there was Olivia; Evie would know what to get her. And Evie would also be the one to talk Catharine into changing the insulting tradition of handing Olivia a Christmas card full of cash every year. Maria didn't envy Evie the task of convincing her mother: Catharine wasn't any easier to talk to than Filomena.

But she'd have to talk to her sister eventually, Maria thought, sighing as she grabbed her bag and headed out the door, determined to spend the afternoon Christmas shopping in town. Catharine had left a message on their machine that had combined iciness with a hint of panic. Maria had been astonished; she hadn't heard her sister's voice in a decade, and if Catharine hadn't identified herself, Maria might not have known who she was. Of course, it was just like her sister to demand that Maria call her back "at your earliest convenience." *That would be never,* Maria thought. Almost as an afterthought, Catharine had mumbled that their mother was fine, but there was something in her tone that made Maria wonder.

What else could make Catharine call her if not their mother? Maria had long given up the dream that one day she'd pick up the phone to hear Catharine forgive her or, better yet, acknowledge that she had nothing to be forgiven for. That fantasy had worn itself out years ago, when she'd finally married Daniel two years after they'd "rediscovered" each other and more than three years after her first husband, Robert, had died.

Maria tried not to worry about her mother or Catharine as she strode down the boardwalk over the bay, which served as the street to their house, a Thai restaurant and a half-dozen other homes built on stilts at the shore of Richardson's Bay. The view from their bedroom window alone made her pause every morning to offer a prayer of thanks. In this she was like her father, who had taught his daughters that thanking God for blessings was as important, if not more important, than constantly asking Him for them.

Every time she, Catharine, or even Filomena had claimed they'd been lucky about something or other, Paolo would quietly correct them. "Not lucky—blessed. We should be thankful."

And this house in this place was a blessing every day. People traveled from all over the world to Sausalito to gaze over the rippling bay at the San Francisco skyline, past Alcatraz Island, its powerful spotlight still revolving through the night, and undeveloped Angel Island, where a single tiny light glowed mysteriously on the beach.

Maria walked rapidly, her boot heels *thunk*ing solidly on the wooden slats as her eyes swept the panorama. The familiar view still took her breath away. This afternoon it was clear, but a fog dense enough to obliterate even the waves a few yards from her feet could descend in minutes. Maria knew she was one of the few Sausalitonians, as some politician had airily dubbed the residents, who reveled in the cold fog as much as in the sun. There was something about how the fog, rolling over the hills from the Pacific or creeping under the Golden Gate Bridge, consumed and concealed everything, that thrilled her.

To her left were the sloping Sausalito hills, known for lush gardens and spacious, elegant homes that seemed to be built right into the hillsides. She'd been surprised at first at the diversity of the city, but as Daniel said, "Sausalito doesn't discriminate: As long as you have money, you can live here."

Despite the beauty all around her, Maria couldn't help spending the short walk to the downtown shops wondering what was going on in Connecticut. She'd talked to her mother last week, talk being a relative term for the verbal sparring they'd engaged in over the Stonington Mills Christmas tree decorating party. Her mother had tried to dismiss the topic, reminding Maria that "these long distance calls aren't cheap, so don't waste time on such nonsense." When Maria, breathing carefully the way she'd learned in yoga class, had summoned her most pleasant tone to remind Filomena that *she* wasn't paying for the call, that Maria had called *her*, Filomena hadn't lost a beat, snapping, "Just because you have money now doesn't mean you should throw it away."

Before Maria could respond, Filomena continued. "And don't give me your silent treatment. You're a million miles away, even at Christmas, and when you do call, you criticize. What kind of a daughter criticizes her mother, eh? If you would ever come to visit, we could talk over a plate of spaghetti, but no, that's too much to hope for. When my own daughters won't have me in their homes to decorate for Christmas, why should I bother with these old people and their skinny fake tree?"

Maria hadn't bothered reminding Filomena about her last visit to Connecticut when she'd left Daniel behind in Sausalito to avoid any trouble, only to spend the entire time being harangued by Filomena to "make up" with the sister who studiously and coldly ignored her. Maria had been so happy to see Daniel at SFO when she got off the plane that she'd wept.

Needless to say, last week's conversation with her mother had changed nothing. Had she really thought it might? Could she imagine, in her wildest dreams, having even an iota of influence with the cranky old woman whom she loved just a little more than she hated? She'd hung up the phone that night sympathizing with Catharine despite herself. How did her sister do it? How did she find the patience to spend so much time with their mother, cajoling, pleading, even trying—and invariably failing—to manipulate her?

There were times when Maria literally ached for her family, but she knew that what she really missed was her memory of them. There was nothing to miss in the brittle present, and Maria had long since stopped thinking of Connecticut as home. Her home *and* her family, she told herself as she walked up Bridgeway past the Horizons restaurant jutting over the water, were here with Daniel and up the coast in Bodega Bay with Mark, Serena and her three grandchildren.

But then why did she feel so bereft at this time of year? Guilt was one thing; that, she'd learned to banish. But she couldn't seem to banish this sense of loss, of incompleteness.

Maria considered phoning Evie before returning Catharine's call so Evie could warn her about what she was in for. Evie and her mother were so different, thank God! Her niece was open and talkative. Evie had her own troubles, and she was more likely to bring them to her aunt than to her mother. Catharine, as both Evie and Maria knew, was judgmental, and Evie had kept a lot from her mother over the past few years. But since Jack's birth, things seemed to have calmed down. Now when her lively niece called, it was to report on some family matter or just to chat.

She'd definitely avoid an ambush by calling Evie first, she decided, walking into the Beach House. She liked the store; it carried quality merchandise, and it was far enough away from the teeming downtown block where tourists and other shoppers made it almost impossible to move this time of year. The Beach House was doing a brisk business in bars of Soapsup, this year's biggest Christmas item. Knowing that by Saturday afternoon they might well be sold out, she'd reserved her soaps in advance. When she told Daniel that she'd ordered four bars of seasonally scented Apples 'n' Spice for her mother and four more of Bayberry that she'd send to her sister with no hope of a response, he said, "Given the recipients, they'd be better named Sour Grapes and Prickly Ivy."

She also hoped to find something today for her daughter-in-law Serena, another one she never seemed able to please, though Serena's displeasure was much more subtle than Catharine's or Filomena's. Mark claimed, when she could get him to talk about it at all, that it was Serena who felt she couldn't please her mother-in-law.

"Just let it alone, can't you, Ma?" Mark would say plaintively when she'd ask what she was doing wrong. Maria couldn't figure it out. She never made any reference to the fact that Serena was Mexican and truly didn't care where she came from as long as Mark was happy. So why did Serena resent her? No matter what Mark said, she knew her daughter-in-law did resent her; the more she lavished Serena and the three kids with gifts and attention, the more Serena withdrew. Though Bodega Bay was only a little over an hour north, Serena was so adept at keeping a polite distance that Maria felt she needed an advance appointment to spend time with her son and grandchildren. It was one of the few things she and Daniel had ever argued about.

A year ago just around the holidays, she'd been complaining to him yet again about the situation, saying, "They might as well live in Mexico for all I get to see them. And I hate her passive-aggressiveness. Why doesn't she just explode and tell me what the problem is?"

Daniel had given her a mild look and probably would've let it go, but she was in a mood—something the holidays brought out in her—and she stared back at him defiantly. "What, you think it's not true? When in the past ten years has she once said what she thinks? Where's the fiery Latina temper we hear so much about?"

He'd carefully set down the Sunday *Chronicle* he'd been reading and said softly, "Maybe she knows what you think of her."

"What's that supposed to mean? Are you saying I'm a bigot? *Me?*"

"When you talk about a 'Latina temper' and say things like they might as well be in Mexico ... well, do you really think she doesn't sense your feelings?"

Maria had been incensed by Daniel's maddening ability to get at the truth. "No, I don't think she senses anything at all about me, because I don't think she cares even a little about what I think or feel," she shot back. "And if you think she'd give her own family the silent treatment she gives us, I beg to differ with you!"

"I absolutely agree," Daniel said. "But Hon, she doesn't really get a chance to, does she? When's the last time she's been with *her* family? She probably resents us to some degree simply because we're not her family; we're just the one she's stuck with. Have her parents even seen the baby?"

Maria hated arguing with Daniel; he never raised his voice, and he was usually right. Serena's parents had never been to Bodega Bay, even for the wedding. Whether it was a matter of money, she didn't know and didn't dare ask. And in the ten years they'd been married, Serena had traveled to Mexico only twice: once in 1993 when their eldest, Bobby, was fifteen months old and again three years later, right after Laurie's first birthday. Mark hadn't accompanied his wife and children on either trip and had never even met Serena's parents. The baby, Melissa, was now fourteen months old, and there had been no talk—that Maria knew of, anyway— of a visit to Mexico. Although Mark made a living from his fishing boat in Bodega Bay, Maria knew there was not a lot to spare. Maybe they couldn't afford the trip south this time.

"Do you think we should offer to pay for them to go to Mexico?" she ventured tentatively.

"I think that's the last thing we should do. Imagine how she'd feel if we made it clear that we thought both her family *and* her husband were too poor to afford a visit."

"See, that's exactly what I mean!" Maria said, her voice rising again. "How am I supposed to know what she's thinking, what she wants?"

"Sweetheart, you can't make everyone happy, and you can't be everyone's friend, especially when it comes to family. You, of all people, should know that."

Though he'd meant to end the discussion gently, tears had formed instantly at his words. He'd said more than he knew. The truth was, she wanted Serena to love her so she'd have evidence that someone in her family *could* love her. If Serena treated her like a mother, or even a friend, it would mean that she wasn't the selfish monster Catharine thought she was. It would mean she wasn't unresponsive and distant the way her mother claimed. It would mean she wasn't a failure at everything to do with family.

And here it was a year later, with Serena still cool, courteous, and mostly silent in her presence. What times they had together, Mark arranged, and he dutifully called Maria every week. She was trying to resign herself to the situation. But she couldn't help wondering if the perfect Christmas gift might make her seem a bit more worthy in Serena's eyes. She rejected the casual leisure clothes and oversized floppy hats at the Beach House. Serena wasn't a leisure type person, and Maria could just imagine the look of polite disdain on her daughter-in-law's face at the sight of one of the goofy hats.

A gift pack of Soapsup was also out of the question: It might seem too indulgent, or worse, that she was telling Serena what kind of soap she should use. When Serena and Mark had first gotten married, Maria had given her daughter-in-law a set of rose-colored Egyptian cotton sheets with a ridiculously high thread count, only to have Serena smile slightly and say, "Thank you. These are so much better than the plain white ones I got at Wal-Mart." Since then, Maria had been all but paralyzed when trying to select gifts for her. It had gotten so bad that Maria even worried over presents for Mark and the children, fearful of getting something Serena might interpret as a criticism.

"Christmas shopping is like a minefield with my family," she murmured under her breath as she left the store, her Soapsup bag clutched firmly in one hand like a trophy. She fought her way downtown, skipping the clothing stores and cafés. Merchants had strung tiny white and colored lights on the trees lining the sidewalk, and many of the shops had their awnings and windows cheerfully lit. The large tree at the Inn Above Tides was covered with white lights, and the fountain on the town square glittered in spotlights as weary shoppers gathered around it to rest or snack on the fudge, cookies, and waffle cones they'd bought with—or instead of—Christmas presents. Though it was only 4:30, the sun was dropping into the Pacific behind the hills, and a sparkling twilight reigned in the busy downtown block. The sight raised her spirits, and she even smiled when she saw the ferry disgorge another mass of shoppers and tourists. Among strangers, she could at least get a little into the spirit of things.

And she did have some gifts: the easy ones. Daniel was a pleasure to shop for. His delight in Christmas was one of the things she loved about him. He insisted they have all their presents to each other wrapped and under the tree at least a week before Christmas, and he wouldn't let her open even one until Three Kings Day.

"After all, that's when Jesus opened the very first Christmas presents, and they weren't from Santa!" he'd told her when she'd protested waiting so long. At first she'd balked at a new tradition that required so much discipline—as a girl she'd always torn open all her presents before Catharine had finished admiring her first gift—but Daniel was a firm believer in the Twelve Days of Christmas, and he'd convinced her. Now she felt sorry for people who had to go to sleep on Christmas night with that melancholy feeling that Christmas was over. She and Daniel always had an open house on New Year's Day, and all their friends had come to envy their still beautiful tree with the carefully wrapped presents in a tempting, undisturbed pile next to the crèche Daniel set up every year after Thanksgiving.

Daniel was so easy to please, it was hard not to go overboard. This year, she'd gotten him the complete *Tales of the City* by San Francisco writer Armistead Maupin; a CD of *The Messiah* performed by the Cleveland Orchestra; a set of ridiculously expensive chef's knives—which she considered more an investment than anything because keeping him happy in the kitchen meant she didn't have to cook—and a red all-weather jacket and wool hiking socks that were supposed to "wick away moisture" from L.L.Bean's winter catalogue. And then she'd really splurged. There would be a Big Gift, something he'd been wanting but hadn't managed to justify buying for himself: a sleek Zhumell telescope.

Most of their neighbors had them; if you lived on a boardwalk where everything from the unobscured night sky to the amazing bay and its bordering cities was right outside your window, surely you should be able to gaze out at it all using the best possible technology. But whenever she suggested buying a telescope, he would tell her his National Geographic binoculars worked just fine. Daniel took such pleasure in the bay and the night sky; now that he was semiretired she thought it time for him to indulge his passion.

Besides, the royalty check from her latest book had been generous, and what she hadn't donated to Doctors Without Borders or deposited into their retirement account, she'd decided to spend on Christmas presents. She wouldn't put the telescope under the tree; instead she'd "hide" it at her neighbor's. Cal, a computer programmer and self-proclaimed "techno geek," was thrilled to have the chance to assemble, program, and use the beautiful instrument for a few weeks. On January 6, just before they opened their presents, Cal had promised to bring the contraption over, festooned with ribbons because it was too awkward to wrap. She couldn't wait to see the look on Daniel's face.

She'd also planned for her mother's gifts, an exercise in futility, but still, she felt she had to give Filomena something. Once Olivia e-mailed her the booklist for the Stonington Mills reading group, Maria would buy the books online and have them shipped to her mother right before Christmas. Last year she'd had the twelve books sent to Sausalito, where she'd lavishly wrapped each and mailed them to Filomena early in December, thinking her mother might like to have the pretty packages out on a table even if she refused to have a tree. Filomena made a rare phone call to Sausalito.

"Why you send these books?" she demanded querulously, slipping into the broken English she used when upset.

"Mom, you were supposed to wait until Christmas to open them! Didn't you see my note telling you to wait?"

Ignoring Maria's question and the hurt in her voice, Filomena barreled on, "Why all this wrapping? Now I have more trash! You couldn't wrap them together? And why hardcovers, the most expensive? I give your sister the list and she goes to the library. All free! You don't have libraries in California?"

Maria had actually cried when she hung up the phone. Not a few angry tears, but deep, rending, pity-party sobs. It was only later in the year that both Olivia and Evie reported how Filomena kept the books displayed on her coffee table, occasionally even turning up in the dining room to sit alone and read so that everyone could see her "most expensive" hardcover books. This year Maria would skip the gorgeous wrapping paper, and when her mother called to complain, she'd clamp her mouth shut.

It was a shame, really, that her mother had become so grouchy about Christmas; she used to take such pleasure in the holiday, in the whole month of December. It was true, she'd changed after the war and their immigration to America, become less joyful and more anxious, but even then, she'd always made a big deal of Christmas. In those days, Filomena not only wrapped all their presents but even saved the paper afterward, urging them to "open careful!" The next day she would meticulously fold and iron the leftover paper and store it away for the following year. It was how she justified using good-quality, store-bought wrapping paper, but then Filomena had always been willing to spend a little more to make Christmas beautiful. Although she was sternly frugal most of the time, they'd always had what seemed a mountain of presents at Christmas.

Then there was the Christmas Glass. When they'd arrived in America, her mother had all twelve of the exquisite ornaments. But to everyone's consternation, one of them, a slender oblong shaped like an icicle, had disappeared the year they moved into the New London house. Filomena had been beside herself with panic at first, then anger, and finally grief.

Caterina, Filomena's aunt, had warned that the Christmas Glass collection must never be divided. When that ornament went missing, it was as though Filomena had lost her family, her history, and everything she had brought from Italy. She spent days tearing the newly arranged house apart, so anxious to find it that they were all relieved when anger replaced her panic. She was furious at everyone, not least herself, when she finally concluded that she must have misplaced it.

For a week she barely spoke. At last, Paolo rose from yet another silent dinner and drew his wife gently to her feet. The twins watched in shock as their father put on his coat and then bundled their mother into her own coat, buttoning it up to the chin as if dressing a five-year-old. He led her out the door and across Pequot Avenue to the beach, where the December waves beat on the shore. Maria and Catharine raced to the window and watched their father pull their mother down beside him onto a stone bench and then put his arm around her shoulders. They sat that way for a long time, not seeming to move, though the girls were certain their father was speaking by the way their mother's head slowly inclined toward him as if drawn in spite of herself.

When Paolo and Filomena finally rose, hand-in-hand, to return, the girls scurried away from the window and began to carefully clear the table so they would appear busily productive when their parents came in.

Maria didn't know why, but as the years passed, Filomena began distributing pieces of the Christmas Glass to people she considered important to their family. Whenever she'd announce a new recipient, Paolo would simply smile and incline his head approvingly in her direction. Once, right after Maria married Robert, she'd asked her father what he said that night on the beach to cause such a change in Filomena's attitude.

"What do you think I said?"

Giddy with her new status—married, and before Catharine!—she declared, "I think you told her she needed to stop moping and pay attention to her lovely young daughters and handsome husband! I think you told her that Christmas is about so much more than a few glass ornaments, and that she should be grateful for life in America with her family …"

But her father was not laughing anymore; instead he gazed at her with a small, sad smile. Embarrassed, Maria let her words fade into the silence. She was about to apologize, fearing she'd angered him, when he said, "I told your mother her family would always live in her heart, and that something as beautiful as the Christmas Glass should be shared for all the joy it might bring. Perhaps one day all the pieces would come together again."

And her mother had shared them. Those she hadn't given away herself, she'd given to Maria when she married Robert, and to Catharine five years later when she married Gregory. The twins in turn had given pieces away, and now Filomena, Catharine and Maria each had one remaining ornament. Filomena had insisted that each sister keep one of the extraordinary glass fish: Catharine's was blue, green and silver, while Maria's was a brilliant orange, red and gold. Each year Maria hung hers on the tree before any other ornament, even before putting on the lights, and she never forgot how she and Catharine would discover that each had hung her fish in precisely the same spot. It was a memory she savored, wondering every year of the past ten whether Catharine's fish swam on the same branch as hers.

Last year Maria had given away another piece of Christmas Glass. David and Sandy, a couple who owned a popular gourmet food shop on Princess Street in Sausalito, had been friends since the year Maria married Daniel. Last October, after an excruciating two-year process, they had closed the store for two weeks and flown to China to meet their new daughter, Blossom. The baby, underweight and sickly for the first weeks in her new home, finally began to gain ground in mid-December. When David asked Maria and Daniel to be Blossom's godparents shortly before Christmas, Maria knew she'd found the right home for the Nativity ornament.

Though only seven months old at the time, the silent and watchful baby had seemed to know the ornament was hers. Sandy hung it low on their small tree, and Blossom, lying on a blanket amid the presents—most of which were for her, and none of which interested her—kept her wide, serious gaze fixed on the glass form as if it explained everything. Even after David took the tree down in January, Blossom's eyes would search for the glass manger every time she was in the room until finally Sandy unwrapped it again and placed it near the baby's crib. It stayed there all year until they'd put up the tree last week and placed the glass crèche on a table of its own beside the tree.

It was the only thing that hadn't changed for the little girl, Maria thought, walking into the crowded shop where Sandy and David were both working to keep up with the holiday rush while Blossom, tottering around the playpen David had set up for her, spotted Maria immediately. Her small face, formerly wan and thin, now round and hectic with color from all the excitement around her, became a crinkling wreath of smiles when she saw her godmother. She immediately raised her arms to be lifted from her plush prison. For a twenty-two-month-old who rarely spoke and almost never cried, she could be quite imperious, instinctively aware that no adult in her sphere could resist, much less ignore her. Maria was no exception, and she swung the toddler into the air, only to be rewarded with a whispering giggle.

This is why I came in here, Maria realized, *not to buy more stocking stuffers or the Riesling Daniel loves. I came in here to hold this living bit of love wrapped in soft flesh and a red and green cotton jumpsuit. To hold her, to make her laugh, to smell her sweetness. To know that this child, at least for now, thinks I am one of the finest parts of her life, a happy slave to all her needs. If only it could be this easy with my family.*

After briefly greeting David, typically calm in the face of the shoppers' storm, and Sandy, typically harried by the chaos, Maria decided to skip buying more stuff that she didn't need. She gave Blossom the kind of loud, smacking kiss that the little girl loved, reluctantly put her back into her fenced kingdom, and escaped without looking back at her goddaughter's reproachful stare. The baby didn't cry, but oh, what a stare! She could break your heart without making a sound.

It was fully dark now, a diamond-clear night, and she could easily see the Embarcadero Christmas lights across the water in San Francisco. Lights also shone from the homes in the hills, and a giant tanker with a line of blue lights glided into the bay from the Pacific. Almost too soon she reached the boardwalk and the turn-off to her home. Daniel had returned from his Saturday routine—a large, sloppy hamburger at Patterson's in mid-afternoon, followed by an hour in the library and then a rigorous work-out at the Marin Nautilus "to make up for my carnivorous indulgence." She had to give him some credit for that; most people, enticed into Patterson's by the grill smoke cleverly fanned out into the crowd, never bothered trying to work it off. Now from the darkened boardwalk she watched Daniel through the bowed front window. Still frazzled by thought of her family and knowing she'd have to call Evie and then Catharine before it got too late back East, she drank in the sight of him as if he could fill her emptiness. So often, he had.

At sixty, he was two years younger than Maria and looked ten years younger than that. With closely clipped copper-colored hair that now had a little silver mixed in (he called it "salt and red pepper"), Daniel was very tall and tended to bend over a little when listening, as if to reduce the distance between him and the rest of the world. This added to the impression that he was a mild, kind man, and though it was true, Maria also knew he could be immovable when he felt he was right. She'd seen four or five displays of his Scots temper over the years, but never directed at her. It was usually ill-functioning technology that brought on his ire, though it was a standard joke among their friends that the user, and not the technology, was most often at fault. Once she'd been with him in the car on the Golden Gate Bridge when his cell phone malfunctioned during a vital call with one of his clients. As soon as they'd exited the bridge, he pulled into the Baker Beach overlook and, without saying a word, got out of the car and flung the phone into the ocean. Watching it arc through the air, glinting in the sun, she'd been consumed with laughter, and it took another hour of tight-lipped silence before he apologized for his antics.

His face, wonderfully mobile and covered with freckles, was beautiful to her. His smile animated his entire face, darkening his light blue eyes and waking the laugh lines around them. He laughed more than any man she'd known, not loud, boisterous laughs, but small sounds of pleasure and amusement. He made her feel brilliant, greeting her small witticisms with an appreciative chuckle. Many years ago Catharine had called him "a long, lean man," and she'd been right; Maria never felt so protected from the world, and herself, as when he wrapped himself around her. She couldn't imagine going to sleep outside the circle of his arms. *I love everything about him*, she thought, still watching in the dark, keeping her presence secret.

How had it happened that this wonderful man had caused her sister to hate her?

Daniel's family had lived in New London for several generations before Filomena, Paolo, and the twins came to America. Though Daniel was two years behind them at school, both girls noticed him right away. Actually, he claimed *he* was the one who'd noticed *them*, the new girls—twins! Most of the notice they attracted was unwelcome. They were teased unmercifully for their Italian accents and old-fashioned clothing; Filomena had not yet spent enough time with *Ladies' Home Journal* to know that American girls didn't dress like Italian girls.

Daniel became a sort of protector just by not paying attention to them— or pretending not to, for in truth, the gangly boy found the girls exotic, with their olive skin, their dark hair and eyes. He could tell that they were mortified by the teasing of the other children. He was the most popular boy in school, and anything that he wasn't interested in soon lost its attraction for the other kids. So when Daniel studiously ignored Catharine and Maria, their classmates eventually followed suit. If anyone was being particularly cruel, Daniel would saunter over and ask their tormentor to join a game he'd started. Instantly, Catharine and Maria would be left to themselves; no child would turn Daniel down.

By the time they entered New London High School, the twins had learned to fit in with their classmates, but they didn't forget what Daniel had done for them—especially Catharine, who was, even then, sensitive to every slight and insult. A talented student, Daniel had skipped seventh grade; by the time the twins were juniors and he was a sophomore, Daniel and Catharine were dating. Of course, "dating" when Filomena was your mother was not exactly what most girls in the fifties called dating. But even Filomena was not immune to Daniel's considerable charm, and Catharine was allowed at least a little freedom. By then, Maria had met the boy she would marry. Robert, a year older, and she were classic high school sweethearts, and often the twins and their boyfriends double-dated.

Daniel was the only one of them who couldn't be content with Connecticut. Like many of the boys, Robert planned to work after graduation at Electric Boat, the submarine manufacturer across the river in Groton that employed a good number of the area's men and women. The subs usually went right down the river to the Naval Submarine Base. But a career with Electric Boat or the Navy that used its products was not for Daniel. The West was his objective, and he had the grades to be accepted at the college he dreamed of—the University of California, Berkeley.

By the time Daniel graduated from New London High School, Robert had been a welder at EB for two years, and the twins were attending Connecticut College in New London, a situation that satisfied Filomena because they could live at home. "This going to college is not so bad," she would say after cooking a huge breakfast before they left for classes, and the girls would sigh in unison, wishing they'd at least picked a college far enough away to allow them to live on campus.

But the young foursome had a plan, one they carefully kept from Filomena. The night Daniel learned he'd been accepted at Berkeley, they'd piled into Robert's old aquamarine Chevy with a cheap bottle of champagne and headed to Ocean Beach. The boardwalk of the beach and amusement park was deserted at that time of night, and they sat on a blanket, Robert popping the cork into the darkness. Maria remembered how the cork had disappeared into the night and how Catharine had clung to Daniel as if he might vanish with it.

By the end of the night, they'd made their plan. They would not be separated for long: Daniel would go to Berkeley and study architecture, spending every school break working part-time in New London so he could be near Catharine; Robert would continue to work at EB, saving as much as he could so that he and Maria could marry when she and Catharine graduated.

Both girls would have teaching degrees; Maria planned to get a job in the area and work for a year or two to add to their savings; Catharine would move to California, find a studio apartment, and teach while Daniel finished college. As soon as he graduated, he and Catharine would marry, and when he'd established himself as a brilliant San Francisco architect ("Should take me about a month," he'd say with a grin), Maria and Robert would move to San Francisco. There would surely be plenty of work for a welder and a teacher, and the four of them would buy a two-family house somewhere in the city. They would have bags of money by then, they told themselves gleefully, and could probably buy a rickety house with a bay view and fix it up together.

We thought it was a perfect plan, Maria remembered, staring out across the bay at the twinkling San Francisco lights. *And we were perfect fools. Or perfectly, painfully young. How else could we believe we'd triumph over Filomena?*

Maria and Robert had indeed married when she graduated from Connecticut College and rented an apartment in Groton just as they'd planned. She got a job teaching in Groton City, near EB, so they both could walk to work. That first year, they saved money and held onto the dream of a two-family house in San Francisco. But when Catharine, Maria at her side for moral support, told their mother she was moving to California to be near Daniel, Filomena exploded, first with recriminations, then with self-pity, and finally with anger, forbidding the move. Catharine held firm, though Maria felt her sister's hand trembling in hers as they stood before their furious mother. When Filomena stormed off to call Paolo at work and demand he come home right away, Maria thought they might have made it. Surely, her father's reason would prevail.

It hadn't. After Maria finally left the house that night, Catharine was forced to shut her bedroom door against her mother's weeping and raging. After the second night, Catharine moved in with Robert and Maria, sleeping on the couch in their tiny living room. On the fourth night, Paolo came to the door, rang the bell, and stood in the dingy hallway, his head down, until Maria pulled him into the apartment. For a long time, no one spoke. Finally Paolo started, and for the first time in their lives, he did not look at his daughters when he spoke.

"Your mother . . . Your mother is very upset. She makes herself sick. She shrieks that her daughter will go to California to play the whore to a boy who will never marry her. I told her that is not true, that is not how Daniel is, she knows Daniel. She will not be comforted. She fears losing her daughters. When her cousin Anna died, that was the last of her family. Now she thinks she will lose both of you, for she knows, Maria, that you will follow your sister. You two will not be apart. You have never been apart. She thinks she will be alone. She does not think of me, her husband, as a comfort, as her family."

It was this final statement that broke their hearts—and their will. They could harden themselves toward their mother; they'd had to to survive. But to hear this soft, sorrowful admission from their father, who'd given everything for Filomena and for them—that they couldn't bear. When he asked them to delay their plans for a year or two "to let her get used to the idea," they agreed.

Had any of the three bruised souls who sat in silence afterward at Maria's kitchen table that night really believed they were only deferring their plans? Maria doubted it. Of course, in the end, Filomena had prevailed. Catharine's delay caused a rift between her and Daniel, so full of his new life and of San Francisco in the early sixties that he couldn't understand why his fiancée and his best friends weren't doing everything possible to join him. Catharine kept assuring him it was only a matter of time, and in the end, time did resolve everything; she took a job teaching first grade in New London, and Daniel's visits to Connecticut became fewer and shorter as time passed. Eventually he stopped coming altogether except to see his family for holidays.

By then Catharine had given back the diamond-chip ring he'd put on her finger the night she graduated and had started to withdraw into herself. She lost weight, her skin stretching inward as if a great vacuum was sucking her flesh back into her body. Maria held her sister for many nights as Catharine wept, but when the tears finally stopped, it was a different Catharine who emerged from the wreckage of their plans. She was somber and anxious, more willing to be alone and separate from her twin. She became humorless and solitary, her life revolving around her classroom and her room at their parents' house. Hard as it was to accept, Maria realized one day shortly after they'd read the announcement of Daniel's marriage to a San Francisco socialite, Catharine had become like Filomena.

In some ways, Maria thought, feeling the cold December air off the bay, *our relationship cracked all those years ago. The final break was just more obvious. Or maybe inevitable.*

Robert hadn't minded the change in plans as much as Maria had thought he would. He was content with their life in Groton City, and when it became clear that San Francisco would never really happen, he seemed almost relieved. Maria nursed a resentment toward him until she realized that he'd been willing to sacrifice his own comfort for her and Catharine's dream. By the time Mark was born, she, too, was content.

She hoped her sister would feel the same when, three years later, thirty-year-old Catharine finally gave in to what she called the "pesterings" of the handsome principal at her school and agreed to marry him. But Maria knew her sister's love for the man was mere warmth, not the kind of heat needed to forge a marriage. Filomena, of course, exulted; she'd been pushing Catharine to accept Greg's attentions for some time. "What, you think you're too good for him? You think many men want an old lady like you? How long before you can have no children, eh? You want to live here forever with your parents?"

Ironically, it was probably the last part of her mother's harangue that moved Catharine to accept Greg's proposal. Had Filomena understood the damage she'd done by manipulating Catharine into giving up the man she loved and pushing her into the arms of a man she did not? Maria hoped not, but watching Catharine on her wedding day, Maria wondered if her sister was marrying this strong, taciturn man simply to flee her mother's house.

Evie was born two years later, and Catharine seemed settled in her life. A very real affection had grown between Catharine and Greg—and Evie, a handful from the very start, diverted her parents' attention from what they didn't have to what they did. When Mark and Evie were children, the sisters regained some of what they'd lost, spending time together and plotting to outmaneuver their mother at least on the little things.

When Robert died of a massive heart attack at the terribly young age of fifty, Catharine had been an island for Maria and Mark. Catharine and Gregory were living in Mystic by then, and Catharine spent months in Robert and Maria's renovated Victorian overlooking the river in Groton City. And now it was Catharine who held Maria through long nights of tears and despair, sleeping in the same bed as they'd done whenever one of them was distraught as a child.

Filomena had been little help, acting as though her daughter might as well have crawled into the coffin to be buried with Robert. She reacted more dramatically to Robert's death than when the sweet, long-suffering Paolo had died four years earlier. At the time, the twins, having lost their lifelong ally and first love, had been more distraught than their mother.

Maria was devastated at Robert's death, too deep in grief to worry over how Greg felt about his wife's absence, but later she wondered at how easily Catharine had left her husband on his own for all that time. Evie was attending college in Rhode Island and often came home on weekends, but essentially Gregory was on his own. When Mark, who'd started at EB mostly to follow in his father's footsteps, quit his job two months after the funeral and told his mother he couldn't stay in Groton City with his father gone, Maria again turned to her sister. Catharine was still there the day Mark kissed his mother good-bye and started on a cross-country ramble meant to end in California. Through all that time, Catharine never tried to talk Maria into moving in with her and Greg, and much later Maria came to realize Catharine was as happy living with her in the old Victorian as she was in her own house on the Mystic River.

It wasn't until Daniel showed up, five months after Robert died, that Catharine moved out.

He'd heard about Robert's death and called Maria during the Christmas holidays to ask if he could visit. Catharine wanted her to refuse, but Maria didn't feel up to being rude, so Catharine spent the evening of his visit at her own home. When she left, cool anger in her wake, Maria was startled at how free she felt. Immediately she'd been ashamed. After everything that Catharine had done for her, all she could feel when her twin left was relief.

The visit was pleasant. She'd heard that Daniel and the "society lady," as Filomena gleefully called her, using her as evidence of Daniel's falseness, had divorced after only a few years of marriage. There were no children. Maria was surprised to learn that night that he'd never remarried.

She asked him if he'd bought the house in San Francisco they'd all dreamed of decades ago, and he said that he'd found a pretty cottage on a boardwalk in Sausalito, the first town off the Golden Gate Bridge. He commuted to his office in San Francisco by ferry; on nice days, he sometimes rode his bike to work over the bridge.

He stayed longer than she'd expected and, as he was leaving, asked her if they might spend New Year's Eve together. She refused, imagining Catharine's reaction and thinking it impossible to celebrate a New Year without Robert, but later she felt vaguely regretful at rejecting his friendship. When her sister returned the next morning, Maria told her that she'd never hear from him again.

But she did. He called periodically from Sausalito, and they talked about everything but the past. Once in late January Catharine answered the phone when he called, and though Maria, painfully aware of her sister's presence, only spoke for a few moments, Catharine moved out the next day. No angry words were exchanged, but everything was different from then on.

It was Filomena who took up Catharine's cause. "How can you do this to your sister, your twin," she'd shout, "talk to this traitor like he is a friend? What are you made of? Where is your heart? What do you think Robert would say?"

Maria assured Catharine, whose feelings she tried hard not to dwell on, that it was just conversation, just a long-distance acquaintance from years ago. Catharine said nothing. Their conversations became stilted. After Daniel's second visit in April, the sisters stopped their daily phone calls;

when Maria made her first trip to California fifteen months after Robert
died—as much, she claimed, to see Mark, who'd met "a nice girl" in Bodega
Bay—Catharine stopped speaking to her altogether.

Over the next two years, almost against her own wishes, Maria fell in love.
She'd not been deceiving her sister and mother by telling them that Daniel
was simply an old friend. She'd needed a friend, a man who'd known Robert
as long as she had, and she welcomed Daniel's easy talk and memories. She
hadn't intended to love him, hadn't thought it was possible to love anyone
again. But there was something in Daniel that was new to her despite their
long history. The sensitive, popular boy had become a successful, powerful
man who had not lost himself in his achievements. She'd not thought it
possible for a man to be so nurturing. He encouraged her to send some of
the children's stories she'd written to a publisher, and when she received a
contract for the first one, it felt like the first step into a new life.

In the spring of 1993 they married. She sent the last of a series of pleading letters to her sister on the eve of their quiet wedding in Bodega Bay.
She apologized repeatedly; explained her yearning for peace and a new life;
described what she'd found with Daniel, not realizing fully how she was
salting her sister's wound. Their mother had relented only upon realizing
that she would lose Maria completely if she continued her clamor against
the union. Lately, Filomena had focused her efforts on a campaign to bring
the sisters together "before I die." *As if,* Maria thought, turning finally
toward the cottage and Daniel.

He'd taken a phone call while she'd been staring out over the water, lost in memories, and now she stopped abruptly, watching him. There was something about his body, the way he seemed to hang in the air, holding the phone as if it might crumble in his hand. He listened for a moment, said a few words, put the phone down, and stood unmoving. Maria hurried to the door.

"Who was it?" she asked breathlessly, her heart speeding.

"Your sister," he replied, worry in his voice.

"Is it my mother?"

He smiled ruefully. "Well, in a way. . . ."

3

Evie

vie couldn't believe it. Tom had waited till today, December 8, to tell her that his submarine was leaving on a six-month duty patrol—starting December 20! Their first Christmas in Connecticut as a family, all the plans she'd made, and now he'd be gone.

"Look, Evie," he'd said, "You're the one who wanted to be near your folks, remember. The only way to get here was for me to transfer to submarines. And when you're on subs, you go when your boat goes. You know that."

The thing that really galled her was that he almost seemed relieved to be leaving when most of the submariners from the Groton sub base would do anything to be home with their families for the holidays.

And he wondered why she wouldn't, after all this time, marry him? He wondered why they'd been engaged off and on for five years and had a son together, and she still didn't feel sure enough of him? Well, this was a perfect example. His immaturity, his refusal—or maybe incapacity—to act like a husband and father, stopped her cold every time she started to think they might marry. Evie couldn't imagine her father even considering being away from her and her mother over the holidays, not to mention for an entire miserable New England winter, Evie's first since they'd moved back to New London from Key West. And if Gregory ever *had* considered such an outrageous thing, her mother would have made quick work of it!

And that, Evie knew, was the real problem. Tom wasn't so much leaving her and Jack for the holidays as he was leaving her family. She could tell herself it was his immaturity—that's what she got for falling in love with a man four years younger than herself—until she was blue in the face, but the fact was, Tom chafed under what he called their "smothering ties to Evie's family."

He'd grown up a Navy brat, never staying in one place too long and never growing close to his often-absent father and cool, efficient mother. He hardly spoke to his two sisters, one in Toronto and the other just under two hours away in Boston, and none of the three seemed bothered by the lack of real contact. In the nearly four years she and Tom had been stationed at Key West, just an hour and a half south of Tom's parents on Key Largo, Evie had seen them twice: once when they'd carted down some old furniture they no longer wanted, and again when Jack was born and they'd come for the baptism and stayed three hours. "They spent longer driving back and forth than they did visiting," Evie told Tom after they left.

And they'd treated Jack as if he was some mildly interesting novelty she'd trotted out for a bit of diversion. Tom's mother seemed to hold her newborn grandson only grudgingly, and his father refused to touch Jack altogether, muttering, "Don't want to hurt it."

As soon as they were gone, Evie turned on Tom. "What is *wrong* with them?" she snarled, all her pent-up resentment flowing out at full volume. Fortunately Padre Lou, who baptized Jack, had left by then, not that his presence would have stopped Evie. She didn't care if every other family on the base heard her. "They ignore us during the whole pregnancy, never calling, never visiting, never *helping*, and now that he's born they act like it's a major sacrifice for them to spend a few hours with their grandson— with us! Do you know, this is only the second time we've seen them in three years?"

"Unlike your family," he responded sullenly.

"What's that supposed to mean?" Evie asked, knowing full well what was coming.

"In three years, not a very long time for most *normal* people, we've seen your family eight times. *Eight. Times.* The holidays and birthdays that we haven't spent in Connecticut, they've come here. We ought to buy stock in American Airlines. And the only reason they're not here today for the baptism is that your father got the flu. Poor guy, I can't imagine what punishment he's getting for that bit of bad timing; your mother's infamous silent treatment, probably. You call your mother and your grandmother every week. And your aunt. And Mark. It's like being trapped in a huge spider's web; no matter how far you stray, you're still stuck."

They hadn't spoken for the rest of the day. Almost a week went by before things got back to normal, and during those days she'd cried on Padre Lou's shoulder, with Jack howling in her arms in solidarity. Evie and Tom's problems weren't news to Padre Lou, and his words and prayers had calmed her enough so that she was ready to face Tom by the weekend.

She hadn't been sure how to start the conversation she knew they had to have. Tom was twenty-two at the time, and she concluded at the end of that miserable week that he was simply too young to be a husband or a father. Crazy as her family might be, she'd get plenty of help raising Jack on either coast, though given all the drama she'd already endured, she was leaning toward her aunt and cousin in California. Besides, she couldn't stand listening to the many versions of "I told you so" she was bound to hear in Connecticut.

She steeled herself to tell Tom all this, but he came home that Friday night with his own announcement. "I've volunteered to train for submarines. They're going to transfer us to the sub base in Groton. You'll be closer to your folks. We won't be able to go until next year, but I love you, Evie. I want you to be happy."

And thus it has always been, sighed Evie, today's fresh anger turned to a dragging weariness as she hauled out the Christmas decorations. Tom had set the tree up while she was at church—probably because he knew he'd have to tell her about the December 20 patrol when she got home. She'd been right in being cautious that Friday night over a year ago when he told her of the transfer. How often had this frustrating pattern repeated itself in the six years they'd been together?

She'd met Tom when he was nineteen. She was a twenty-three-year-old marine biology graduate student, visiting Key West because she'd heard so much about the endangered coral reef around the tiny island. Like so many before her, she fell in love with more than just the reef. She became infatuated with the city, its light and heat, its raunchiness, and most of all, its astonishing freedom. Evie hadn't ever known such freedom, though she'd spent her childhood and teenage years in violent quest of it, much to the dismay of her parents and grandmother. In Key West she found it, and when her week was up, she stayed.

"Evelyn, what do you mean, you're staying?" her mother had said on the phone after a long silence. Tom was right about one thing: Catharine was particularly good at silence. Evie's grandmother was a screamer and whiner, but Evie would take that any day over Catharine's freezing, emphatic silence.

"Mom, I love it here. You can't imagine how wonderful it is! It's a place where people come to truly be themselves. It's wall-to-wall people, and everyone's from somewhere else."

Another long pause. "You mean, everyone's running from somewhere else. Abandoning their responsibilities."

Evie had known it wouldn't be easy. The "Evelyn" was a bad sign; her mother was the only one who ever called her by her full name, and when she did, it was the kiss of death. Evie soldiered on, "No, I don't mean that at all. People come here to take up their lives, sometimes for the first time ever, not abandon them. I've been offered a job with a local environmental group."

"What about school?"

"Mom, what I can learn here, what I can *do* here, is so much more than just books and classes. This is life! This is making a difference."

Catharine had simply handed the phone to Evie's father, not bothering to say good-bye. She knew her daughter would get the message, and Evie had. But as usual with the two of them, Catharine's cold disapproval only strengthened Evie's resolve. By the end of the day, she found a cottage to rent on Fleming Street and had moved in. When Filomena called later in the week, weeping and shouting into the phone, Evie wasn't even fazed.

She met Tom that first week in an outdoor Mexican cafe where people ate warm, thick, restaurant-made tortilla chips with three kinds of salsas and sipped margaritas under a banyan tree strewn with so many tiny white lights that no one noticed the stars. She was drinking a strawberry margarita, making a dinner of the chips and salsa, and reading Pat Conroy's *Beach Music*. Tom asked her politely if he could sit by her at the counter, and she assented, smiling coolly to show she wasn't interested.

Neither, it appeared to her slight annoyance, was he. He ordered a club soda with lime and pork *carnitas*. She couldn't help but notice when her young, handsome neighbor pulled a copy of Sebastian Junger's *The Perfect Storm* out of his backpack. That was a surprise. What had she expected? *Sports Illustrated*? Probably, she was slightly ashamed to admit. Whether she was embarrassed by her assumption and felt the need to make it up to him, or whether it was his serious, dark-blue eyes and black hair cut so short it made him stand out in this city of aging hippies, she said, "I'm from there."

He looked up from his book quizzically. "I'm sorry?"

"I'm from there," she repeated, gesturing at the book, "you know, where the story takes place—New England. I grew up in Connecticut. In Mystic. You know that movie with Julia Roberts? *Mystic Pizza*? And there really is a Mystic Pizza, believe it or not."

"Okay, I believe it," he said, showing a spark of amused interest.

"You know, your book? *The Perfect Storm*? Now *that* was a great movie. My cousin Mark fishes for a living, but in Bodega Bay, not the Atlantic. I was crying my eyes out at the end of that movie. Did you see it? Is the book as good?"

He considered for a moment. "Yes ... better."

"Oh." Evie could take a hint. "Well, okay, then."

She picked up her book again, chagrined, but he said hastily, "No ... wait ... I mean, sorry. I'm not a good talker."

"You can say that again."

"I'm not a good talker," he repeated, and they both smiled at the weak joke. They discussed their books a while, but Evie, irrepressible, soon took over the conversation, telling him about her minor epiphany on seeing Key West, her unfinished degree, and her new job. He listened carefully, watching her. Finally she asked, "And what about you?"

The question seemed to stymie him. He raised his eyebrows in what was only partly mock alarm and shifted a bit in his chair. She laughed. "Okay, let's make this easy for you. Are you from here?"

He smiled in relief. "No one's from here. I grew up all over, my dad was in the Navy. He's about to retire out of Newport Beach, the last place we lived."

Realizing that was the end unless she prompted him, she asked, "And you're here because …?"

"Well, I guess you could say I'm like you—my work is the ocean."

It was Evie's turn to raise her eyebrows. He looked too young to be a marine biologist. He grinned at her surprise, revealing a smile so infectious she'd later be convinced she'd fallen in love at that moment. She recovered from the smile and asked, "You're studying to be a marine biologist?"

"No." The perfect grin widened. "I'm studying to be in the Navy."

So that explains the haircut and the muscles, she thought, wishing she'd never started talking to him. She should have known: like father, like son. The last thing she wanted was to get involved with some military drone, no matter how handsome he was and how sweet he might seem. Because in her vast experience as a sheltered student from Connecticut, Evie was sure that anyone who chose the military could not truly be sweet. And as her grandmother said, "Handsome is as handsome does," whatever that meant. Nor could he be someone she wanted to be involved with. How could he even suggest they were alike in their work? She wanted to save the ocean, not use it for killing.

She glanced rather pointedly at her watch and said, "Well, I really need to get going. Nice meeting you."

"Not really."

"Excuse me?" she asked, irritated at his rudeness.

"You don't think it was nice meeting me, although you probably did a few minutes ago. But now, you want to forget the last half hour because you think you know everything about me. And you don't. Not a thing."

If he'd spoken in a raised voice, with a hint of aggression, or even with that mischievous grin he'd flashed a moment earlier, she would have walked off in a huff. But the boy was looking at her earnestly with a small, sad smile. Evie sat back down.

And it's been that way ever since, she thought, tossing the colored lights on the tree in a haphazard fashion that would have given her mother fits. That's the way it had always been between her and Tom. Back and forth, point and counterpoint, never quite leaving and never fully staying. She thought Jack would change everything, and for a while it seemed he had. Things had been good once Tom arranged for the transfer. She'd put away all thoughts of leaving him, hoping that once they got to Connecticut, life would be more stable. She'd even refused her parents' offer to rent them a little cottage at the beach in Niantic, knowing Tom would feel trapped and beholden. Not that she'd ever have to worry about feeling obliged to *his* parents; they'd never offered anything unless you counted that old, used living-room set. Escaping that ratty beige furniture—his mother's leftovers— almost made up for having to move into Navy housing in Groton.

Almost. Because their new apartment had certainly been no cottage on the beach in Niantic. Standard Navy, it was a well-used, serviceable two-bedroom, one-bath duplex apartment with dull wood floors and more windows than she'd expected. It really wasn't bad. She tried not to show any disappointment at the dated kitchen and bland colors, pointing out the good morning light and fresh paint job. Tom had barely noticed, saying, "It's enough for us."

Just enough, Evie thought as she surveyed the small tree Tom had set on an end table to prevent Jack from tearing it down. Not yet two, he was scrambling around like a little maniac, grabbing for whatever was in reach and chattering to himself in a language only he understood. Everything he saw, he wanted, and he was nimble enough to go to surprising lengths to get what he wanted. Evie had finally given up chasing him all day long, putting locks on the kitchen and bathroom cabinets and repacking all the baubles and knickknacks she'd arranged around the apartment to make it more of a home. The first time her mother came over after she'd child-proofed the place, Catharine looked around and asked, "Evelyn, where are the crystal candleholders we gave you and Tom for Christmas? Where are all your things?"

When Evie explained, her mother said, "When you were a child, I never put away one thing or locked one cabinet. Teaching discipline is much better than removing temptation."

"Yeah, Ma," Evie drawled, "that discipline thing sure worked great with me."

That was the thing that really killed her, she thought. In a way, Tom was absolutely right. Sometimes even *she* didn't like her family. Sure, she loved them, but like them? Not always. Except for her poor, long-suffering father. Him, she liked and loved, but her mother and grandmother were enough to drive a person nuts, and she knew Tom was beginning to think she fit right in with them.

Do I? she wondered.

Certainly she'd jumped back into the middle of things with a speed that had taken Tom aback. They hadn't been in Groton long enough to unpack before she was refereeing yet another squabble between her mother and grandmother, trying to spare her father some of the weight he'd carried for too many years. There'd been some crisis about Filomena refusing to keep a doctor's appointment that Catharine had made for her. Evie ended up taking her grandmother to the rescheduled appointment and Catharine had been miffed with both of them.

Tom had been amazed at the dramatics. As soon as they moved back to Connecticut, he realized that those relatively brief visits in Key West would prove to be a picnic compared to having all three generations of women living within a few minutes of each other.

Now there was this new catastrophe, engineered by her grandmother. Evie had to admit Filomena had topped the charts with this one: holding Catharine and Maria hostage to a family Christmas dinner in her cluttered little apartment before she'd agree to move into long-term care at Stonington Mills. The thought of Filomena's machinations brought a guilty smile to Evie's face. How did the old woman do it? How did she manage to cast four families into absolute chaos only a few weeks before Christmas? Evie knew her Aunt Maria and cousin Mark were also in on the act; Maria had e-mailed her last night asking if they could talk this afternoon.

And now Evie was smack in the middle of another family drama at the very time she should be focusing on her own relationship. Had it been a mistake to come back here at all? Yes, she'd wanted Jack to have a family, but had she placed an unbearable burden on her relationship with Tom by moving to Connecticut? Was she subconsciously hoping that being near her family would change him into the kind of husband and father she needed him to be? She prayed that that had not been her hidden motivation. She, of all people, after watching her family crash up against each other for years, should know that you can't change anyone. Maybe that was why she spent half her time wanting to be married to the only man she'd ever loved . . . and the other half grateful she wasn't.

If anything, Tom communicated less here than in Florida, though he wondered, occasionally aloud, whether she missed the environmental job she'd loved so much in Key West that she'd continued working during her pregnancy and after Jack was born. Unspoken was his concern that she wouldn't get a job at all, that she'd become so entangled in family issues that she'd lose interest in the work that had meant so much to her.

She defended herself against his unspoken criticism, telling him, "You know it's not easy being a full-time mother. Have you happened to notice how much energy your son has? It's no stroll in the park keeping up with him all day and night. You're gone so often that everything's left to me."

"I just asked if you missed working, that's all," he responded.

"And I just answered you. We've only been here a few months, I've only just unpacked and gotten the apartment set up. And what am I supposed to do when you go out on patrol? Leave Jack in daycare all day?"

"You could leave him with your mother or grandmother if you wanted to get a part-time job. God knows you spend enough time with them as it is."

"Okay, Tom, what is it you want to say?" Evie's voice became dangerously low. "It would be nice if for once you could spit it out without me having to yank it out of you like a rotten tooth. Are you worried that we won't have enough money, that you're not making enough?"

That was a harsh shot, and Tom had flinched. If she'd been trying to goad him, it had worked. "No, Evie, I'm not worried about money. We all know that your parents would be more than happy to support you and Jack for the rest of your lives. Your mother makes it obvious in more ways than I would've imagined possible what she thinks of me having seduced her brilliant daughter. That has been made very clear."

She'd opened her mouth to deny it, but Tom was just getting started. "So

I'm not worried about money, and to answer your real question, I'm not worried about myself or my ability to be a man, a husband, or a father. Maybe I'm worried about your ability to be a wife and mother as opposed to a spoiled daughter. Maybe I'm worried about how quickly you seem willing to give up your career, your independence, even your sense of joy, to cater to your screwed-up relatives. Maybe I'm worried that you're so tangled up with *your* family that you have no time for *our* family."

"Tangled up?" Evie had echoed, her outrage trying to block out the truth of his words. But Tom had banged out of the apartment by then. That had been right after Thanksgiving, and things had been cool between them since. Then, today at lunch he told her about the December 20 patrol and, after her initial outburst, said quietly, "I'm going to work for a few hours. I'll be back for supper."

The tears finally came as she unwrapped the ornaments, one by one, until she found the delicate red and gold glass orb that was her piece of the Christmas Glass. She hung it on the top branch, using it in place of a star or angel. The colors shimmered through her tears. Would she have to choose between Tom and her family? Or was it too late even for that? Would Tom slip away from them? And what about Jack? Tom couldn't get another transfer for a while, but he could easily join as many patrols as possible and live apart from them. She knew of enough unhappy military marriages that worked that way.

Jack started babbling from his room, something he'd taken to doing when he finished napping. Sometimes he was hilarious, talking on and on, stringing together incomprehensible words along with a few that Evie and Tom recognized. If Tom was home during nap time, he and Evie would sit on the hall floor outside Jack's door together, holding hands and trying to stifle their laughter at his nonsensical conversations. Sometimes he would repeat entire phrases he'd heard from them, and they would look at each other wide-eyed, proud of his progress but also wishing he'd never heard certain things they'd said.

"Livy" was one of his favorite words since Olivia had become his new best friend. Every time Evie visited her New London home, Jack was mesmerized by the colors and mobiles and books in the house. From the very first, he went as easily to Olivia as he did to Evie and Tom. It had taken Jack longer to become accustomed to his grandparents and great-grandmother than to Olivia, who treated him as if he were an equal, not a toddler to be hauled about and penned up at the will of adults. Jack's eyes gleamed in her presence.

Now he was going on about Livy, though much of his monologue was in his own language. Evie couldn't help smiling at what she assumed was a two-year-old's song of devotion. She continued decorating the tree, letting him chatter on, knowing that all too soon he'd be clamoring for release from the crib.

By the time the phone rang at three, the appointed hour for her aunt to call, she'd finished decorating, changed Jack, and put him in the playpen under the tree. Fortunately he seemed so astounded at the very sight of the brightly lit Christmas tree that he wasn't planning to destroy it—yet. He was staring up at it with his mouth open, one way at least to get him off the pacifier. She hoped his delighted paralysis would last throughout the phone call.

Maria wasted no time. "What am I going to do? And why didn't you warn me?"

"Hey, don't blame me. I just found out yesterday, and that was from Dad. Apparently Mom has been letting it simmer, trying to figure out a way to refuse Nana without letting anyone know. Guess she's given up on that."

"You'd think she'd have given up on that years ago," Maria replied. "Your grandmother is like an irresistible force. A natural disaster. There are two ways to deal with her: escape or submit."

"So which are you going to do?"

"You know, Evie, I don't really appreciate the humor you seem to find in all this. You're as bad as Mark!"

"Okay, but you have to admit, it's nice for me not to be the center of attention for a change. Besides, I'd love to share the pain over Christmas. Why don't you come?"

"Like it's that easy! I've made plans. My tree is up. We're supposed to go to Bodega Bay for Christmas, and if you think that was an easy invitation to finagle out of Serena, think again. I do have a life, you know."

"Congratulations. I didn't think having a life was allowed in this family."

"Exactly! Which is why I ran away from home. It only took half a century. But, look, even if I *wanted* to come, what about your mother? Am I supposed to leave Daniel home? No way. Not at Christmas. So how will your mother react?"

"Didn't you ask her?"

"Evie, I haven't even *talked* to her. Daniel was here when she called, and she told him."

"Wait—she talked to *Daniel*?"

"Apparently at some length. It seems she's desperate. And I can't say I blame her this time. She even asked for his advice."

"Well, since Daniel and my father are the only sane ones among us, what *is* his advice?"

"He won't give it," Maria answered, "and I'm ready to kill him!"

"Maybe that's the answer. We'll kill all our good, patient, loving men and move into the long-term care wing with Nana. We could share antidepressants."

"Ah. Sounds like things are going well with you, too."

"Tom's going on a six-month patrol starting December twentieth."

There was a long silence. "Oh, Evie. I'm sorry. And I think I have problems."

Evie swallowed her tears. "You know, I kind of wonder if we all don't have the same problem."

They talked for some time. Evie, knowing of Maria's difficulties with

Serena, asked whether Mark and his wife had weighed in on the decision. Apparently, like the other wise men in the family, Mark didn't want to touch the situation with a ten-foot pole, but Maria had finally gotten him to agree to at least ask Serena whether she would spend Christmas in Connecticut. "After all, your grandmother has never seen Mark's two youngest kids. And I'm sick of being afraid of my own daughter-in-law. She can at least consider it."

Eyeing Jack, who'd sidled up to the side of the playpen and started reaching his greedy little fist out to the lowest ornaments, Evie said, "I wish they would come, but it's a lot to arrange in a short time, especially with little kids.

"Maria, do you think we're *tangled up*? As a family, I mean."

There was no hesitation from her aunt. "Evie? Is that a trick question?"

4

Sarah

Sarah hung up and stayed very still, her hand on the phone for a long time, thinking about the request Filomena had made. It was a lot to ask, and Filomena knew it; she'd said she would understand if Sarah refused. Sarah didn't even know if she could do what her friend wanted, even if she wanted to; it was already December 10th, and getting a flight from Fort Lauderdale to Connecticut during the holidays on such short notice would be no easy task. Not that Sarah worried about the money or about missing Hanukkah with her family. The holiday had come early this year; she'd celebrated it with her son Jacob and his family last week. Two days ago Jacob, his wife Sharon, and Adam, their youngest son, had flown back to Israel. Jacob and Sharon both worked at Tel Aviv University and lived in the city.

Her oldest grandson, Samuel, had spent Hanukkah with them, flying down from New York where he was a graduate student at NYU. He wouldn't leave until tonight, and though she was always secretly a little relieved when her family left after a visit, she was glad to have her practical grandson with her now. He'd be home soon from the beach, where he'd spent much of the past week. Sarah knew the beach was a convenient excuse for Sammy to absent himself from his family; there was a reason her oldest grandson had chosen the US for his education, and it didn't have everything to do with NYU. She knew she wasn't supposed to have favorites, and she'd never admit it in a thousand years, but Sammy was hers.

It wasn't that she didn't love the others; of course, she did. It was just that she found it easier to be with Sammy than with her son and daughter-in-law, who could talk of little besides the university and its politics, or Israel and its politics. And while Adam was a sweet, solemn boy, Sarah felt he'd been limited by the academic world of his parents. It was no surprise to her that Adam planned to go to the university where Jacob and Sharon taught. Deeply attached to his parents, he was so unlike Sammy, who'd struck out on his own, attending NYU as an undergraduate and falling in love with New York. She wanted Sammy to come home for lunch so she could ask him what he thought about Filomena's plea that she spend Christmas in Connecticut.

He'd understand her conflict. He knew how much she loved her solitude, how she had insisted on it after her husband Ben died five years ago. It had been her and Ben's plan to live on the seventeenth floor of this high-rise on a Fort Lauderdale beach overlooking the Atlantic. They'd only been here two years when Ben had died, but they'd enjoyed every minute. She didn't want to leave the place that had been theirs, not to move to Israel as Jacob and Sharon thought best, not to move back to New York as Sammy might have wished, not to move to a place less vulnerable to hurricanes, as her old friend Filomena had suggested more than once.

She missed Ben every day, every minute, even after five years, and since they'd sold the house in Brooklyn, this apartment was the only place where his memory remained. She would never leave it. Oh, she didn't mind the occasional visit to Israel. And she positively enjoyed the long weekends she spent in Manhattan with Sammy. But the truth was that if she couldn't be with Ben, she'd rather be alone. She'd been alone before she met him, and without him, she'd be alone no matter where she went or who she was with.

That's why, as much as she enjoyed the Scrabble games and dinners with other single people in the building, she was always ready to come back to her apartment and shut the door behind her. She liked having the option to socialize, but she treasured her solitude. And while she looked forward to visits from her family, she was never terribly sorry to see them go.

When Sarah was alone in this home they'd chosen so carefully and furnished themselves, excited as a young couple just starting out, she felt that Ben was with her. That was the greatest comfort she could hope for.

Now, just when she'd been looking forward to a few quiet weeks before the tourists and winter residents returned en masse after Christmas, Filomena was all but begging her to come to Connecticut and help defuse the explosion she'd set in motion. If Sarah was the kind of person who feared boredom—and she wasn't—Filomena's invitation would have been welcome, for there was no doubt that the Christmas ultimatum she'd issued to her poor family would produce spectacular fireworks. As Ben used to say, "Never a dull moment." But Sarah was not sure she was up to the excitement. Nor was she as convinced as Filomena that her presence would bring a degree of peace. Peace did not alight often in that family.

It was just like Filomena to take such a dramatic step and then immediately fret about it. They were so different, Sarah and this friend whom she'd known, mostly through letters and phone calls, for nearly fifty years. Five decades, and she still shook her head over Filomena. Ben once said, "If the woman would be as honest with her family as she is with you, she'd have a lot fewer problems," and Sarah had known instantly that he was right. It wasn't that Filomena was dishonest with them; indeed, she'd caused no end of trouble by telling them frequently and in no uncertain terms what she thought. Her lack of honesty, as Ben termed it, was in not telling them what she felt.

Sarah and Ben had often wondered what might have happened all those years ago if, instead of hysterically forbidding Catharine to follow young Daniel to California, Filomena had told her daughter what she'd told Sarah at the time. When Sarah had chided Filomena for her harsh demands on Catharine, the older woman had been quiet for a time and then said, "This way she will only go if she has a deep love for him. If she does not love him enough to go despite me, she does not love him enough for a life together.

I loved Paolo enough to leave my home. That is the kind of love Catharine must have for this boy, or it is no good."

Frustrated with her friend, Sarah had said, "Mena, you must tell her that! When she was a child you never taught her the independence she needs now to decide against you."

Filomena had refused, certain that she was seeing to her daughter's happiness, not ruining her life. But as Catharine's life grew bleaker, Filomena had questioned whether she'd done the right thing in forbidding her daughter to leave. Still, Filomena never really learned. When Gregory had come along, instead of letting Catharine decide at her own pace, instead of letting her be drawn into loving this stolid, persistent man, Filomena had relentlessly pushed her into the marriage.

"She's trying to make up for her error, but in the process she's just compounding it," Ben had said, and he was right. Catharine had never loved Greg the way he loved her, and when Maria and Daniel had come together, the whole family was plunged into a crisis that the twins' relationship had not survived.

Filomena, Sarah knew, had been devastated by the break between her daughters. She'd come close to blaming herself—and admitting it to Catharine and Maria—but instead she continued trying to manipulate them into a reunion. When her machinations failed, she'd blame them rather than herself.

And now Filomena had outdone herself, making a demand that Sarah guessed had driven every member of the family into a corner. Separate corners, probably.

Not to mention me, Sarah thought. "Anna's Sarah," Filomena had begun the phone call, using the name she'd given Sarah long ago, as if Sarah couldn't have existed without Filomena's cousin, which wasn't far from the truth. Sarah was oddly touched by the name, and Ben had used it when he wanted to tease her. Jacob disapproved, feeling the name was demeaning, but Sarah ignored him; it was in his nature to object.

"Anna's Sarah, if you could come for Christmas, it would help," Filomena had continued. "I know this. You are quiet, good, like Anna. My children, my grandchildren, they know all about Anna's Sarah. They would want to see you." And then, typically, she added, "It will be good for you to be with a family, to eat."

Sarah couldn't repress a smile of disbelief at her old friend's audacity. Even when she knew she'd done everything wrong, she still acted as if she knew what was best for everyone.

"Ah, Ben, could she possibly be less like Anna?" Sarah asked softly, speaking to the chairs he'd sat in, the books he'd read, the table they'd shared. As she gazed around the room where they'd been so content, the bright midday light streaming through the window caught fire in the glass angel, his wings threaded with silver, and she remembered the first time she'd seen him, long before Filomena had given him to her.

Without really knowing why, Sarah had never told Filomena that this angel was the one piece of Christmas Glass she'd wrapped with her own small hands sixty years before as she stood at the table with Anna, her wedding dress sheared into soft scraps. Although she couldn't remember it, Anna later assured her that she'd spoken her first words in nearly a year that morning.

§

What Sarah knew of that day, almost a year after her parents had died and just weeks after her grandmother had abandoned her to the care of the soft-spoken Italian widow, was that her life had begun again over a box of Christmas ornaments. There was something about Anna, a sadness or a depth of empathy, that the child had never recognized in anyone else. As Anna wrapped each ornament, she spoke softly to Sarah as if to a bird she feared to startle away. When Sarah finally answered, Anna gave her this angel to wrap in the wedding-dress rags.

That Sarah did remember, as much with her fingers as with her mind: the feel of the extraordinary thing in her hand, both smooth and sharp; the way he caught the light, appearing to glow from within; her wondering which of the angels he was. Was he the one who'd stopped Abraham's hand when he was about to sacrifice his son? Perhaps he'd wrestled with Jacob in that long, sleepless night before he was reunited with Esau, the brother he'd wronged?

At first Sarah hadn't want to bind him, not even in the luxurious square of wedding-dress silk. She looked up and asked Anna why he must be wrapped and put into the box with the rest of the glass. Anna told her of Filomena, the cousin in southern Italy who would cherish and protect the ornaments and take them away to America. It was the only way, Anna told her, that the Christmas Glass might stay safe during the war.

"Like me." Sarah had said, and when Anna asked her what she meant, the child answered, "Coming to be here with you is the only way I can stay safe." And while Anna said nothing, Sarah carefully wrapped her angel.

For five years, Sarah and four other Jewish children lived under Anna's wing; she was an angel of sorts to them, protecting them, making sure they were fed and housed and taught. Impossible as it now seemed, Anna managed to give them what passed for a normal life in the maelstrom of northern Italy between 1940 and 1945.

Anna never raised her voice or acted as though anything was amiss, even when she was scrambling for food and clothes or pleading with her patrons to intercede for her with the Italian or German officials.

No one, certainly not the children, had known at the time what it cost her. During those last two years, Sarah never saw Anna sleep, and she sat down to eat less and less often with the children. Sarah had a memory of her gliding from room to room, in and out of the house, always in motion like a shadow without a body. She grew thin and haggard, but nothing else about her changed.

Even during the worst of those days, Anna and Filomena wrote to each other; sometimes it took months for their letters to pass back and forth between northern and southern Italy. Anna read parts of each letter to Sarah. Anna never revealed that Sarah was Jewish or that she sheltered other Jewish children; she couldn't take such a risk. Instead she wrote of the extraordinary orphan girl who had won her heart, the child Anna had never had a chance to have with Giorgio. By bringing Sarah and Filomena together, Anna planted the seed of a friendship that lasted half a century.

When the war ended and she knew her children would be safe, Anna's will to fight the exhaustion and the consumption that was eating away at her faltered. In April 1946 she put Sarah on a train for the first leg of a journey that would eventually reunite the unwilling girl with her grandparents, who'd survived the war in London and then settled in Brooklyn. Anna pressed a scrap of paper into Sarah's hand at the railway station, and said, "This is Filomena's address in Connecticut. She has only just arrived. Write to her so she knows where you are. She expects to hear from you."

Anna clasped Sarah to her for a long moment, and the girl felt every bone in Anna's now frail body. With a surprising strength, Anna released herself from the girl's arms and pushed her onto the train. When it started moving, Sarah stood at the window watching the small, bent figure diminish. And then the girl did something she hadn't done since her mother died: She wept.

§

Five and half decades later Sarah's eyes again glazed with tears at the memory as she made Sammy's lunch. She'd outlived the only two people she'd really loved: Anna and Ben. Oh, that wasn't really fair. There were Sammy and Jacob and Sharon and Adam, because she did love them. But the truth was that no one had loved her the way Anna and Ben had loved her, and she'd loved no one else so completely.

It had taken Sarah three years to write to Filomena from New York. By then she'd left her grandmother's house—the reunion had been no better than either had expected—and was living with two other girls in an apartment in Brooklyn. They all worked at Macy's in Manhattan, Sarah in the shoe department. When she finally mustered the courage to write to Filomena, she expected no reply.

But within days, she received a letter with a Connecticut postmark. The address was written in a labored, formal script with a fountain pen. Sarah's hands trembled when she opened it.

Dear Anna's Sarah, Where have you been?

The words released a flood of tears that she hadn't known were waiting for freedom. The arguments, the cold silences that had marred her life in her grandmother's house were washed away. Someone cared about her.

Sarah still had that first letter. The rest of it was much like Filomena's letters and phone calls and visits over the years: a combination of worried love and stern commands, the latter always in service of the former—at least in Filomena's mind.

Hearing Sammy's key in the lock, Sarah called, "I'm in the kitchen," and he walked in trailing wet sand and grinning. Sometimes he took her breath away, this young man who was so much like his grandfather with his wide smile and casual ways. And just as she would have to Ben, she groused, "Pay attention! You're messing up the whole place!"

Sammy laughed and asked, "What's for lunch? I'm stuck with airplane food tonight."

She slid him the plate with cabbage slaw and a heaping sandwich of leftover brisket on his favorite whole-grain bread. He attacked it as if he hadn't inhaled three bowls of granola and two bananas just five hours ago. Through a mouthful of meat and bread, he asked, "Not hungry, Bubbe?"

She never was these days. Food hadn't meant much to her since Ben died. She hadn't the will to cook much; the memories of the elaborate dinners they'd made together always got in the way. She ate mostly takeout, cooking only for family or the occasional potluck supper in the building.

Lately she'd been on a sherbet kick, or *sorbet* as sherbet was called these days to justify charging four dollars for a pint. She'd been surviving mostly on watermelon sherbet and cereal before Hanukkah, and looked forward to resuming the regimen.

"Not really," she answered Sammy. She poured herself a glass of iced tea as she told him of Filomena's invitation and the precarious situation that had provoked it. Sammy knew all about Filomena; of all Sarah's family, he paid the most attention over the years. He was fascinated with the whole story, right back to Anna.

Wiping his mouth on the napkin she'd pointedly handed him before he started eating, he smiled. "So, Anna's Sarah, what're you going to do?"

"Well, that's just it, isn't it? What do you think?" she asked.

"Oh no!" he laughed. "I'm not making that call! It might be fun, though. Like your own personal opera."

"*Mmm.* Just what I need."

"I thought you liked the opera," he said.

"I do like the opera, but as a spectator, not a performer," she answered.

"I don't know, Bubbe," he said, regarding her with serious eyes above his smile, "maybe it's time to go onstage again."

She narrowed her eyes and they stared at each other. *Such a brave, beautiful boy,* she thought, and then said, "And when did you become so wise?"

"It's in the genes."

He rinsed his dish and fork and loaded them into the dishwasher. As he showered and packed, she called Guillermo, her favorite cabdriver. Over the years they'd become friends, and Sarah always felt a little uncomfortable calling for him to drive, as though summoning him into service, which, in fact, she was. But when Ben died and she needed someone to help with the arrangements, to help her cope, to drive her around when she was so far gone that she could barely tell him where she needed to go, she'd just called him, and then he was there at the hospital and he knew what to do. He never asked for payment, and it was only weeks later that she thought to offer it. He'd refused with a look that warned her not to ask again.

Since then she always paid him for trips to the airport and other appointments when he was "on duty," but when he called her to say he was going grocery shopping at Whole Foods or to the Aventura Mall, she often went along. He seemed satisfied with the arrangement, and she enjoyed his company. A native of Cuba who'd fled the country when Castro took power, he had a sly, cynical sense of humor and often made her laugh.

Sarah usually rode to the airport with her family when they left, partly to make up for her guilt at being half-pleased to see them go, and partly because it seemed uncaring to take leave of someone at her door when they still had continents to cross. When she'd called Guillermo two days ago to bring Jacob, Sharon, and Adam to the airport, Jacob had said, "Mother, the airport cab service is probably much more efficient."

She ignored him, and when he blew out an exasperated sigh, she asked silently, "Ben, how did we ever raise such a dour, unpleasant child?" She sat in front next to Guillermo on the way to the airport that day and watched his reactions from the corner of her eye, trying not to laugh. Still irritated by her refusal to heed his advice, Jacob ignored the driver, letting Guillermo put all their luggage into the trunk without lifting a finger to help. On the way, Jacob added insult to injury by remarking from the backseat, "I still can't figure out why you live in this city, Mother. It's so ugly. Why you live here when you could live in your own country is beyond me."

"I'm in my own country, Jacob," she responded. "Israel is your country, not mine. I met your father here, not in Israel."

"Where you met Dad has nothing to do with it," he answered as she watched Guillermo raise his bushy gray eyebrows. "Israel is where you belong. Tel Aviv is so alive. Here, you can't even see a beach unless you own property on it. And these miserable strip malls everywhere you look. How can you stand it?"

"It helps that there aren't terrorists blowing themselves up at Wal-Mart," she responded dryly, and Guillermo choked on the laugh he tried to make into a cough.

"Bubbe, that's not fair," protested Adam, defending his father, who had turned red and was staring daggers into the back of Guillermo's head.

"Maybe it's not, Adam, maybe it's not," she replied, tired of the whole subject.

Sarah spent the rest of the ride looking out the window. Jacob was right: Fort Lauderdale *was* an ugly city by most measures. High rises and development wherever you looked, making it impossible to see or easily reach the beaches; roads and highways lined by car-rental dealers, tourist traps, medical centers and hospitals, and flat, colorless shopping centers; enough delis, food stores, and restaurants to feed a small country. Hardly any trees except for the ubiquitous palms. Ben used to say, "South Florida is death's waiting room; the Cubans are waiting for Castro to die, and the rest of us are just waiting to die ourselves." And then he'd laugh, not just an ironic chuckle, but a burst of laughter as though living in death's waiting room was the best joke in the world.

That was the thing about Ben, the thing she missed in Jacob: He'd been comical even when he was serious. She remembered the day he walked into Macy's almost half a century ago. She was bent down, stocking the lower shoe racks, when two large feet in highly polished men's dress shoes planted themselves a yard from her face. Unaccustomed to seeing men in the ladies' shoe department, she'd glanced up, a bit peeved at his sudden proximity. Between twenty-five and thirty, she guessed, a tall man, pencil-thin then. *His eyes are dancing!* she thought when she looked up at him.

She had no chance to ask if she could help him before he said, "I want to hire you."

She studied him. He seemed too well-dressed to be a lunatic, but maybe that was why his eyes danced: He was a crazy man. He took her silence for a bargaining tactic and said, "I'll double your salary and pay you commissions."

He is *crazy,* she thought.

"I've had my own shoe store in Brooklyn for a year now," he explained. "Top-of the-line men's, women's, and children's shoes. I do a good business; I'll do better when I get a good salesgirl, a sales manager, really. Someone I can trust. Someone good-looking." He peered closely at her, waiting for an answer. When he got none, he added hopefully, "Someone quiet."

She'd smiled at that, and it was the beginning. By the time they'd sold the business seven years ago to move to Fort Lauderdale, they had twenty-seven stores in New York and Connecticut, and the corporation that bought them out was planning a national expansion.

And Ben had made her laugh every day.

At the airport, she abruptly embraced Jacob long and hard. He was stiff at first, but then, just as he had when he was a dismayingly earnest little boy, he softened in her arms and held her. There was a sweet and familiar sadness in it; something Sharon and Adam couldn't really understand. Sarah wasn't sure she understood it herself, or that Jacob did, but it had always been this way between them. Maybe they were too much alike.

When Guillermo called up on the intercom to say he'd arrived, she and Sammy took the elevator down to meet him. Sammy carried his own bags and after greeting Guillermo, heaved them carelessly into the trunk before Guillermo could even offer to help. Sarah knew by the slight curving of her old friend's lips that he approved. Everyone liked Sammy; he reminded people of Ben.

She sat in the back with Sammy, who made a show of luring Guillermo into the discussion about "Christmas in Connecticut, Italian-style." Guillermo knew Filomena, having ferried her from the airport to Sarah's condo and back when Filomena had insisted on visiting her right after Ben died. Guillermo had been so helpful that Filomena later sent him a piece of the Christmas Glass, the brilliant star with its slash of yellow gold reflecting through the center. By then Sarah had long since received her angel, and she'd been astounded when her friend phoned from Connecticut after the visit to say she was sending the precious star to Guillermo.

"Mena, you only spent two hours with the man!" Sarah exclaimed. "I mean, he's a good man, but you hardly know him at all. What will your children say?"

"Who cares what they say!" Filomena had answered. "Not me. You think they care about me? No. Do they come together and make up their fight about Daniel for my sake? No. That Guillermo, he's a good man. He took good care of an old lady. We talked. He's Cuban, he knows about family, what it should mean. His family's no good either."

Sarah had known better than to argue; besides she knew nothing about Guillermo's family. Leave it to Filomena to ferret out such information in such a short time. But whatever had passed between them, the elegant star had hung from the mirror inside Guillermo's cab every Christmas since. It was there now.

"So, Guillermo," Sammy said, teasing his grandmother, "don't you think Bubbe should fly to Connecticut to be with the Italians for Christmas?"

Sarah made a sweeping motion with her hand in a mock dismissal of Sammy's impudence, but Guillermo glanced at her in the rearview mirror, just above the lustrous star, and she explained about Filomena's request.

"Sounds like she's got herself into another squabble," he observed.

Sammy laughed. "More like World War Three. Now she needs Bubbe to negotiate a détente."

"And Bubbe needs peace and quiet," Sarah retorted. When Guillermo silently inclined his head a little she wasn't sure if he was agreeing with her. She got her answer a little later after they'd seen Sammy off at the airport.

"You should go," Guillermo said as they drove back to the condo.

"I don't recall asking you—or Sammy, for that matter," she replied tartly, though she *had* asked Sammy's opinion.

"You should go. They need you."

"Oh, please. Filomena is forever getting herself into these predicaments. She'll find a way out. She always does. They don't need me."

"Ah. But maybe you need them."

Annoyed, she said, "It never ceases to amaze me how everyone knows what I need. Jacob. Sharon. Adam. Filomena. Sammy. And now you. Has it occurred to you that perhaps I'm the one who knows what I need?" He absorbed her rebuke in genial silence.

When he dropped her off, she apologized. "I'm sorry. All this visiting is making me grouchy. Sometimes I think you're lucky not to have any family."

He smiled slightly, the same bemused curving of his mouth she'd seen when Sammy had thrown his suitcases into the trunk. Still annoyed with herself for the outburst, she asked him if he wanted to share Chinese take-out, but he had another airport fare.

By the time she finished her dinner of sesame noodles and watermelon sherbet, she'd decided to call Filomena and refuse the invitation. "If my own family makes me this cranky, imagine what that family would do to me," she told herself.

Her hand was on the phone when it rang. She saw from the caller ID she'd installed after Ben died that it was Guillermo. *He's probably calling to make sure I'm all right,* she thought gratefully.

"I'll go with you," he announced as soon as she said hello.

"Excuse me?"

"I'll fly to New York with you and put you on the train to Connecticut. I've always wanted to spend Christmas in New York. See if it's as great as they say. Rockefeller Plaza. Lincoln Center. Ice skaters. You know."

"No, I don't know! And what about work? You always say December is your best month for tips. You're just doing this because you think I should go, that I *need* to go."

"Not true. I'm sick of working Christmas. I'll let the New York cabbies drive me around for a change. Be rude and obnoxious to them. See how the other half lives."

Looking for a way out, she said, "We'll never get airline tickets. It's too close to Christmas."

"I've got them. I have a buddy at American Airlines. We leave the morning of the twenty-second."

5

Mark

You should talk your mother into going," Serena told her husband. Mark's wife was usually quiet, but when it came to his mother, she'd become unrelenting. Maybe it was because Serena was so far from her own family in Mexico that his family dominated their lives.

Or maybe she just wants to see my mother squirm a little bit, Mark thought.

Even more likely, Serena wanted to have a Christmas that didn't revolve around his mother and her husband. Mark, Serena, and the kids had already made the eighty-minute trip from Bodega Bay to Sausalito for Thanksgiving, and Mark knew his wife would welcome the chance to spend Christmas here in their little house on the bay, though he was sure she'd feel differently if she knew about his own plans. Whatever the reason, Serena was convinced that his mother should go to Connecticut for Christmas with his Aunt Catharine and his grandmother Filomena. What's more, Serena felt that he should help make that happen.

"If she doesn't make the reservations soon, they'll never get a seat on a plane," Serena had insisted an hour before, following him out the door as he got Bobby and Laurie, their two oldest kids, into the truck for their after-school horse-riding lessons. "It's the twelfth of December already."

As if he didn't know. As if Maria wasn't calling him every day to "discuss the options." It hadn't been a week since his grandmother had dropped this bomb on Aunt Catharine and his mother—on all of them, really—and already everyone was frantic.

For Mark, the hardest part was being stuck between his mother and his wife, never mind his aunt and his grandmother. Serena and his mother just couldn't seem to hit it off, and he wasn't sure why. Not that he liked to spend a lot of time thinking about it; it was much easier watching his kids, Laurie with her arms fastened around Bobby's waist as they rode together on their favorite pony at their neighbor's ranch. Bobby was a quiet kid, not big on smiling, but when he did, sitting high in the child-sized saddle, the boy reminded Mark so much of his father, it almost hurt.

Much as he liked his mother's husband, it seemed to Mark that she had been calmer when his father was alive; maybe not happier but definitely calmer. Their crazy family back in Connecticut didn't help at all. And now it was spilling over onto him and Serena, just what he needed.

Part of Mark's problem was that Serena wouldn't talk about whatever it was that bothered her about his mother, and Maria didn't want to talk about anything else. Every time he spoke with Maria, whether in his weekly calls to Sausalito or in his much rarer visits, she brought it up. Why didn't Serena like her? What had she done wrong? What had she said wrong? What could she do to fix it? Her questions were incessant, and Mark didn't have any answers because Serena would never discuss it.

Until three weeks ago.

§

He'd broached the subject with Serena on the Tuesday before Thanksgiving. She was in an uncharacteristically foul mood, and it had taken him two days to figure out that it had to do with spending Thanksgiving in Sausalito.

"What's your problem with my mother?" he asked, truly perplexed. "She's nice to you. She likes you. She loves the kids. She and Daniel help out whenever we need it."

She ignored him at first, continuing to mix the crab filling for the appetizer she planned to bring on Thursday. He'd gotten a good deal on Dungeness crab from one of the other fishermen, knowing how much she and the kids loved to eat it boiled and cracked right from the shell, with lemon, pepper, and butter, but now she was "wasting" it, as Bobby had said disgustedly; Serena, as always, was determined to impress her mother-in-law.

When she didn't answer him, he made the serious mistake of bringing the appetizer into it. "This is a perfect example," he said, pointing to the bowl where she was beating cream cheese and spices into the sumptuous claw meat. "I got those crab claws for you and the kids for a treat, and you're making it into some fancy dish just because my mother asked you to bring an appetizer for Thanksgiving. What about cheese and crackers, for Pete's sake?"

She stopped mashing the contents of the bowl together long enough to give him a withering look. "What about cheese and crackers?" she echoed, as if he'd lost his mind. "I'll tell you what about cheese and crackers. Do you even remember what your mother served for Thanksgiving last year, Mark? Of course not. Well, let me remind you. Roast duck with lingonberry sauce and quinoa stuffing with shallots, dried cherries, and slivered almonds. And the year before that, it was venison steaks with a port wine reduction. And the year before that, grilled ostrich breast fresh from an ostrich farm near Mendocino with a mint-and-roasted-cracked-wheat stuffing. Things I could hardly *pronounce*, much less imagine cooking and serving."

When Mark just looked at her blankly, she shook her head in frustration and turned back to the counter, where she began dropping spoonfuls of the mixture into the delicate crepes she'd already prepared. When Mark finally responded to her recital of his mother's Thanksgiving menus with "So?" she whipped around and faced him again.

"So? *So?* I can't even imagine what she's planning for this year, but I'm not going to show up with cheese and crackers. That's probably just what she expects me to bring. That, or tortilla chips and salsa, more like it."

"Oh, come on, Serena. That's not fair." Mark replied, only to be met with stony silence. "And besides, she orders most of the food already made from that shop David and Sandy run."

"It doesn't matter whether she cooks it or buys it! What matters is that it's ridiculous rich people's food that she knows we would never have ourselves. What matters is that she never stops to think that maybe our kids would like normal food because that's what they're used to. What matters is that she's never once asked us what *we* might like. What matters is that she thinks I don't give my family elegant food like she does. What matters is that I'm going to show her that I can cook fancy as good as she and her snobby friends who go all the way to China for a perfect baby when there are enough Hispanic babies right in this country."

Mark stepped back. This sudden vehemence knocked the wind out of him. But then, how often did he think about what she felt, what she wanted, how much she missed her family in Mexico? Evidently, not enough. He'd let himself believe that he'd created a little haven for her here, that the world outside Bodega Bay and their little house and his fishing boat, *The Serena*, couldn't intrude. He'd taken her usual silence as happiness, as acceptance of the gift he thought he'd given her. Suddenly, he didn't know what to think—or say.

She turned away from him and went back to work on the crepes. Resisting the urge to flee the kitchen, he sat down heavily at the table and waited as she finished spreading the filling and folding the crepes, covered the plate and put it in the refrigerator. She gave a final stir to the roasted red pepper sauce she would drizzle on the crepes just before they left for Sausalito and then put the sauce in the refrigerator as well.

She stood, her hands gripping the counter, her back still toward him. Finally, in a voice drained of anger, she said, "You don't understand, do you, that your mother never thought I was good enough for you."

Mark was absolutely certain she was wrong, and he was equally certain that he had no way to convince her. If she'd felt this way for ten years, what could he possibly say to change her conviction now? It felt like his whole world was slipping away. Knowing he needed to say something, anything, he took a shaky breath, but she flung out her right hand, fingers rigidly splayed, to cut him off. Her shoulders shook a little, and he realized that he'd never seen her cry, not even when the kids were born. He felt a combination of dread and helplessness that made tears start in his own eyes.

"I *know* your mother feels that way," Serena continued. Her hand hadn't moved and he knew better than to interrupt. "What I *don't* know is if you agree with her."

Mark almost laughed out loud from the relief. This, at least, he could fix. Released from his paralysis, he was at her side, holding her close.

"Listen to me," he said. "You have to listen to me because I think you've lost your mind. You can think what you want about my mother, I don't really care. But to think that about me? Serena, you're everything to me.

"Don't you remember how I was when I first came out here? When we first met? I was like a zombie. My father had just died, and I couldn't take it. I left my mother in Connecticut—abandoned her, really—I was that messed up, that miserable. If God hadn't brought me here, to you, what do you think would have happened to me? I could barely see the hand in front of my face. I couldn't keep a regular job. If it hadn't been for the golf course development, I wouldn't have had any work. When I wasn't stoned, I was asleep.

"Until I saw you. Do you remember that day? When Pastor Luke introduced us? You always said he felt sorry for you, so he wanted to make sure you'd have a good husband. Serena, you know the truth? The truth is that he introduced us to save *my* life, not yours. He knew that unless I had someone to love me, I was lost."

Luke owned a construction company. He had seen Mark working on his crew, showing up high or hung over, barely able to carry his own weight. He couldn't talk to Mark about God, about Jesus, because Mark just wasn't ready to listen. Every time Luke tried, he walked away. *Who did he think he was,* Mark asked himself, *my father?* He had just lost his father, and no one was going to take his place. So Luke did the next best thing: He introduced Mark to Serena.

"And that day when I saw you, from that second, I started to heal. You healed me. Don't you know that? How can you not know that? It doesn't matter whether my mother likes you or doesn't, what matters is that I love you. I can't imagine trying to live without you."

They were both crying by the time he'd finished. He'd pulled her over to the chair and onto his lap, where they sat, arms wrapped around each other, until thirteen-month-old Melissa woke up from her nap demanding attention. The other two kids had gotten off the school bus, and suddenly the kitchen was alive with activity and the chance to talk had passed.

It was typical of their life. With three kids, the fishing business, and the embroidery Serena took in, Mark wasn't sure whether they never talked because they were both basically quiet or because they never had time. He realized as he released his wife that they couldn't afford—their marriage couldn't afford—the complacent silences they'd grown accustomed to. He didn't even want to consider how long Serena had been worried about whether he loved and valued her. Just the thought of it made him wince as if someone had struck him.

Later that night, after the kids had finally eaten and gone to bed, when Mark and Serena were collapsed on their own bed in front of the blank television, too tired to even turn it on and find something to watch, he told her, "I've always told myself that we're completely happy, both of us. That our families don't matter, because we've made our own family. But that's a fantasy. I spent months after my dad died not talking, holding everything inside. I should know by now that it doesn't work. We've got to make more time to talk, to be together. Maybe we should go out more, get a babysitter once in a while. Have a fancy, expensive, romantic dinner at the Inn at the Tides."

She gave him a weary smile and rolled her eyes, as if gauging the likelihood that they would ever have an expensive, romantic dinner staring into one another's eyes and talking in low voices at the elegant Inn at the Tides. "Sure," she said, going along with his fantasy, "and after our dinner, maybe we will have a room at the inn, one with a high ceiling and fireplace and croissants for breakfast."

Even exhausted with the day's work and high emotion, she looked beautiful lying there in the soft old shirt of his that she slept in, her dark hair curling over the pillow, her darker eyes laughing at him. No longer so tired, he gazed at her for a moment and then grinned and went to close their door. "Or maybe we can just pretend we're already there."

Two days later on Thanksgiving his mother studied the Dungeness crab crepes with the roasted pepper sauce drizzled carefully over them and exclaimed with wide eyes, "Oh Serena, what a good idea—enchilada appetizers!"

Serena looked at him with a wan smile, and somewhere between piercing love for her and annoyance with his poor, clueless mother, he ground out between clenched teeth, "Crepes, Ma, they're crepes with Dungeness crab and roasted pepper puree."

Upset at his tone, embarrassed by her gaffe, his mother had snapped nervously at him. "When did you get to be such a gourmet?"

Daniel, as usual, defused the moment. "I *love* Dungeness crab! And how brilliant to use the meat in crepes! Should we heat them up, Serena, or have them at room temperature?" A discussion ensued about the possibilities, punctuated by five-year-old Laurie leaping onto a chair and nearly yanking down the elaborate floral arrangement Maria had placed on a side table, and things got back to normal.

§

Now, as Mark lifted his two kids off the pony and buckled them into the truck for a trip to Sebastopol, where Bobby and Laurie hoped to find a Christmas present for their mother, he was actually grateful for Serena's before-Thanksgiving explosion. They seemed more aware of each other; there were more quick caresses, more exchanged glances, more laughter. Mark knew they would have to avoid falling back into their old habits. They couldn't keep things from each other anymore.

Except for one thing. Mark had done a lot of thinking over the past couple of weeks about what his wife had given up to be with him and how lonely she must be so far from her family. She'd been back to see them only twice, once with Bobby and again with Laurie. Mark hadn't gone either time.

His reasons were sensible, naturally: With a growing family, they needed all the income they could earn, so he needed to stay in Bodega Bay and fish. And, of course, when she took Laurie, his excuse was that someone had to stay with Bobby. But the truth was, and they both knew it, he was uncomfortable at the thought of being trapped in a place where he didn't know the language—he'd made no effort to learn it from Serena—and where he was unsure of how he'd be received. After all, he'd taken her away from them; she'd been in Bodega Bay visiting a cousin at the time and had planned to go back to her home in a small town southwest of Tecate before she met him.

Serena would always say that her family was pleased she'd found a good man, a hard worker, someone with whom she'd have children who would be born citizens of the United States. But they hadn't come to the wedding—the cost was their excuse, as it was his for not visiting them—and he felt the day had been less than perfect for her because the only representative from her family was Lucie, the cousin she'd come to visit. He glimpsed a small sadness in her expression as she looked at his assembled family. They might be nuts, but they were there.

Yet, over the ten years of their marriage, Mark had done little to remedy the situation. Both times he took her to SFO and put her on the plane for Mexico, she turned back on the way to the gate, holding Bobby and then Laurie close in her arms, and looked back at him. No tears. No words. No wave. Just a long, yearning look. He forced the image out of his mind; by the time he returned two weeks later to pick her up, neither of them made any reference to it.

But her words before Thanksgiving had brought those images rushing back to him. He'd allowed her sadness and disappointment to simmer, and it had to stop. He wanted to do more than just tell her; talk, even between two people who said so little, was still cheap.

So he'd planned a surprise that would assure her that things were going to change. He would take her and the kids home to Mexico, and not in May, when Serena had planned to go with Melissa, but on December 23, two days before Christmas. That way, she'd finally get to show him and the kids the *posadas* she'd described every Christmas since Bobby was born. He'd heard her telling Bobby, who never tired of hearing the story, about the *posadas* this morning at breakfast. Even Laurie sat still long enough to listen, and Melissa, miraculously, stopped fussing when she heard a new note in her mother's voice.

"Where I am from in Mexico," she'd begun, causing Mark to stop just outside the kitchen where she was giving the kids breakfast, "Christmas does not start at Thanksgiving, and surely not on Halloween like it does here. No! Where I am from, Christmas is all about the Baby Jesus, and it begins several days before Christmas Eve, the night when the Baby was born to us. Children do not open all their presents like greedy little foxes on Christmas morning and then forget them by New Year's Day. Or worse, break them!"

Mark smiled at this warning to Laurie, who had broken a brand-new Christmas doll by hurling it at a greedy seagull that was feasting on sunflower seeds Laurie had scattered for "only the baby birds." As Laurie squirmed in her chair, Serena relented and continued.

"Where I am from, we have the *posadas* from the middle of December until Christmas Eve. The *posadas* are our Christmas festivals. A different family is chosen for each night, and their home is decorated and lighted with many candles. Then, at night the people all gather for a parade. Often it is little children like you who lead the parade." Laurie leapt from her chair and marched around the table waving her hand in the air as if holding a baton and making what she considered marching noises. Serena waited patiently for her to sit back down before going on.

"The children carry small statues: Jesus' mother Mary, sitting on a donkey, Joseph leading the donkey, and an angel in front. Sometimes the figures are in a wagon that the children pull along. Many people join along the way."

"Where is the Baby Jesus?" Bobby asked anxiously.

Wiping up the applesauce Melissa had spit on the table, Serena responded, "The Baby Jesus is still inside Mary. He has not yet been born, just as He had not been born all those years ago in Bethlehem when Mary and Joseph went from place to place in that crowded city looking for shelter."

"Like the Nativity play at church," said Bobby, who was one of the three wise men this year, a step up from playing a cow last year.

"Yes, except the *posadas* are all outside at night and more like a parade," said Serena, putting her hand firmly on Laurie's arm at the word parade. Grimacing, Laurie dug resolutely into her oatmeal. "And the people follow the children and the statues of Mary, Joseph, the donkey, and the angel as they go from house to house. At each house, they sing a song asking for shelter. And at each house, the people inside pretend they are like those who turned away Mary and Joseph in Bethlehem, and they sing a song back, saying they are asleep and have no room. So the parade continues on to the next house, where the same thing happens."

"Why don't the people let Mary and Joseph and the donkey and the angel come in?" Bobby asked.

"Remember that they are acting like in the Nativity play," Serena reminded him. "They are imitating what the people in Bethlehem did when they would not help Mary and Joseph."

"But why didn't the people in Bethlehem help? If they didn't have any room, why didn't they give them some food?" Bobby asked.

"Because they were pigs and wanted all the food themselves," Laurie answered matter-of-factly, as if surprised her older brother hadn't figured this out, and then proceeded to make oinking noises to emphasize her point.

"Enough," said Serena, giving her daughter the only look that ever succeeded in quelling her as Mark, still in the shadows of the hall by the kitchen, choked on his laughter. Serena turned to Bobby. "The people in Bethlehem didn't know that Mary's baby would be Jesus. So no one helped them.

"That's why when the people act out the *posada*, the parade ends up at a house where the people carrying the statues will be welcomed, just as Joseph and Mary were finally welcomed at the stable in Bethlehem."

"Get to the party," Laurie demanded.

Serena complied. "Once they have reached the right house, the people carrying the statues bring them inside and place them on an altar that is decorated with many flowers and candles. They all kneel down to pray and sing. Then comes the party with lots of good food, music, and the best part, the piñata.

"The piñata is usually shaped like an animal or bird and covered in bright paper. It is filled with candy and small toys and treats and even sometimes coins and jewelry. Adults hold the piñata in the air, dangling from a rope, or they hang it from the ceiling. All the children are blindfolded and given sticks to try to hit the piñata and break it so that all the candy and treats and toys fall to the floor. In some houses the youngest child is the one who is allowed to break the piñata."

"That's me!" crowed Laurie.

"No," Bobby corrected her. "Melissa is the youngest."

"She's just a baby," Laurie said disdainfully, glancing at Melissa, whose charcoal eyes—Serena's eyes—grew round at the sound of her name. "She doesn't count."

Serena ignored the exchange. "No matter who breaks the piñata, everyone gets to grab the treats that fall from it. There is a different posada—and a different piñata—every night for more than a week before Christmas, and then on Christmas Eve, the night Jesus was born, the statues of Mary, Joseph, the donkey, and the angel are taken to church. In church at midnight, a figure of the Baby Jesus is brought in and put in the manger by Mary and Joseph. After church there are bells and firecrackers and a big meal, because by then it is Christmas Day!"

Though Mark had heard portions of the story many times, this morning was the first time he'd really listened; he made his plan to take Serena and the kids to Mexico for Christmas, and he'd actually be seeing a *posada* in just over a week. He heard the yearning in his wife's voice. Could this trip make up for all she'd been missing, all she'd given up to be with him?

At least it's a start, he told himself in the Sebastopol department store as he tried to dissuade Laurie from the deodorant she'd selected for her mother's Christmas present. "This is the kind she likes!" Laurie protested when he told her to put it back.

"Yes, but it's not a real present, is it?" he said, trying to explain. "Mommy already has this at home."

"But it's perfume!" Laurie insisted, wrapping her fingers tightly around the jumbo can of Secret Fresh Scent for Women.

"No, honey, it's *not* perfume. It's deodorant, and it's not really a present, not for Christmas."

Laurie was not persuaded. "Daddy!" she cried, growing more agitated, "Mommy says it makes her smell nice, so it *is* perfume, and it fits good in her Christmas stocking."

Bobby came up to them at that point and gave his father a sympathetic look before telling his sister, "It doesn't really matter what you get Mom, because my gift is so good she won't even notice yours."

Laurie's eyes widened. "What? What are you getting Mommy?" she demanded. "Let me see!"

Mark watched Laurie put the can of deodorant back on the shelf and follow her brother away from the toiletries. Bobby led them through the maze of aisles to a pretty selection of glass music boxes. "I'm getting her one of these," Bobby told his sister, pointing to the display. When he wound up one that had a cheerful Santa on top and played "Santa Claus is Coming to Town," Laurie's face grew still with wonder. Mark realized that she'd never heard a music box before, and he found himself smiling at her expression.

But Bobby was all business. When Laurie abruptly broke out of her trance to grasp him by the arm and cry, "Me too! I want to give one to Mommy too!" he shook his head. "You already picked out your gift," he said firmly, "You can give her that smelly old deodorant, and I'll give her a music box."

Outrage flooded Laurie's face with color. "No way!" she wailed, and Mark thought Bobby might have overdone it, that the solution would be worse than the problem. But Bobby had spent a lot more time with Laurie than Mark had; his son knew how to handle his sister.

"Well, maybe . . ." he said slowly, as if considering carefully. Laurie tugged his sleeve violently and searched his face, asking, "What? *what?*"

Bobby studied her for a few seconds, pretending to be unsure whether to include her in his plan. Finally, when Laurie was all but jumping up and down in the aisle, he said, "Maybe if we put our money together, we can get the nicest music box and give it to Mom from both of us."

Mark watched the idea dawn on his daughter, the rapid calculations, like clouds across the sun, flitting over her face. She looked at the selection of music boxes. "Which is the nicest?"

Bobby stepped aside to reveal the music box he'd been hiding from his sister. Set on four gilded legs, the glass box itself was snowy white, and atop it were the figures of Mary and Joseph gazing down in rapture at the Baby Jesus. Each figure had a gold-colored halo around its head. Mary's robe was a brilliant blue; Joseph's was a modest brown, and he held a staff in his hand; Jesus was swaddled in purple and white, smiling in delight at them. When Bobby turned the key on the bottom of the tableau, gentle strains of "O Little Town of Bethlehem" floated into the air.

Never taking her eyes from the figures, Laurie whispered, "It's a *posada*! For Mommy. Her own *posada*!"

Bobby and Laurie pooled their allowance money, and when they came up just short, Mark offered to make up the extra under one condition: "I'm only going to help if you put Melissa's name on the card too," he told Laurie sternly.

Frowning, she tried to resist, but then her eyes returned to the figures. "Okay," she said, and then, as if no storm had come even close to breaking, gave him the brilliant smile that he knew would get her out of (and probably into, but he didn't want to think about that) many scrapes in the future, and threw her arms around him.

As they headed home, Mark let his thoughts return to the Mexico trip. Money was always tight, and once he'd decided on this surprise for Serena, he had to figure out how to pay for it. The only savings they had were from Serena's embroidery work and the construction moonlighting he'd done for Pastor Luke. They'd put it aside for some work they wanted to do on their own house.

Though it was situated in a great spot just off the water on Bay Flat Road, the house was really no more than a cottage. They'd used what little money Mark's father had left him for the down payment, and they'd been working to keep up with the mortgage ever since. Meanwhile, housing prices in the village had skyrocketed since the golf course development he'd worked on had opened, and while they were certainly cash poor, they were also relatively house rich. From the all-important "water view" perspective, their property was one of the best in the village. They'd be even more house rich after he and Serena finished expanding—something they needed to do anyway, because the cottage was never intended for a family of five.

Yet now he was ready to withdraw a significant portion of the "cottage cash," as they called it, to pay for a ten-day trip to Mexico. He planned to meet with the travel agent tomorrow, check in hand. He felt a little uncomfortable about not asking Serena, but he didn't want to ruin the surprise. Besides, he was afraid that, if given the choice, she'd sacrifice her family in Mexico for her family here in Bodega Bay. And Mark had just begun to realize that she'd already been doing that for far too long.

§

Bobby and Laurie had placed the elegantly wrapped present for their mother under the tree and they were just sitting down to supper when Mark's cell phone rang. He looked at it to see who was calling and then exchanged a weary glance with Serena. His mother had been calling obsessively about his grandmother's ultimatum—as if *he* had any answers!

Serena tilted her head and indicated that he should take the call; they'd start on the meatloaf and mashed potatoes without him.

He went into the living room, where Serena and Bobby had put up the tree after Thanksgiving. As Mark put the phone to his ear, he caught sight of his family's piece of the Christmas Glass: a delicate glass ball, shot through with green and silver, a match for the red-and-gold piece that his cousin Evie had. Gazing at it, he sighed, "Hey, Mom."

"I've got a solution." Maria started right in, no "Hello," no "How are you?", no nothing.

"Glad to hear it," Mark said. Maybe this would be the last conversation he'd have to have over this manufactured trauma.

"We'll all go."

"Go where?" She couldn't mean what it sounded like she meant—could she?

"Mark, pay attention! We'll all go to Connecticut for Christmas. Daniel, me, you, Serena, and the kids. It'll be like a family reunion. Plus, Nana will be overwhelmed with all her family around her, and she won't be able to push Catharine and me into a confrontation. I even called Catharine, and she thinks it might work. Isn't it perfect?"

Perfect? No, it wasn't perfect, it was the most ridiculous, selfish idea he'd ever heard. And only a member of his family could come have come up with it. He waited, listening to the chatter coming from the kitchen to remind himself that his family was in the next room. When he spoke, it was in a low tone.

"No," was all he said.

There was a long silent moment, and then his mother began, "Mark . . ." her tone a familiar mixture of disappointment and annoyance that she'd used to puncture his resistance as a child. Well, he wasn't a child anymore.

"No, Mother." He spoke evenly. "No, it's not perfect. And no, it's not going to happen."

This time she didn't hesitate. "How can you be so selfish? You know how much I need you. Besides, your grandmother hasn't seen you in years; she's never even met your children. You haven't seen any of your family."

"I see my family every day," he snapped. "I see the family that matters to me!"

He heard her sharp intake of breath and instantly regretted his words. But he couldn't take them back. Not with Christmas in Mexico depending on winning this one.

Maria's voice was cool. "Would you care to share the plans you have for *your* family this Christmas? Apparently they're so important that you're willing to hurt all the others who love you."

Mark wouldn't get into a contest with his mother over which family was more important. "We'll be together. Those are my plans. And not in Connecticut."

"Fine. Good night." She hung up before he could say anything else.

He'd have to figure out a way to make up for it. After they came back from Mexico. He put the phone in his pocket and went back into dinner. He smiled weakly at Serena and said, "Same old thing." She pressed her lips together in sympathy and went back to arranging Laurie's dinner. Lately she wouldn't eat if any of the different foods on the plate were touching.

After they'd finally gotten the kids to sleep, his phone rang again. Mark looked at the number: Evie. He started to turn the phone off and then hesitated. It was after 2:00 AM in Connecticut. Something had to be wrong.

"What happened?" he barked into the receiver.

"Nice way to answer the phone," Evie replied. "Nothing's happened. Does something have to happen for me to call my cousin?"

"For you to call him at two-thirty in the morning, yeah, I'd say something had to happen," Mark answered, irritated that he'd been tricked into a conversation he'd had no intention of having. "Come on, Evie. What are you calling about? As if I don't know."

"Okay, yes, I'm calling to ask you to come for Christmas. Just for a few days, Mark. Come on."

"Look, you and I both know that this is just something Nana's cooked up to get attention, and I'm not going along with it. It's ridiculous. I bet Tom's not exactly thrilled."

"Tom's not exactly going to be here for Christmas, so what he exactly feels doesn't much matter," Eve answered shortly.

"Sorry, I didn't know. He's going out on patrol?"

"Yes, and I don't want to talk about it. Except to say that it would be a lot easier for me, too, if you were here, Mark. You and Serena and the kids. It'd be a lot less lonely."

It'll really be lonely if you sacrifice your husband to our black hole of a family, he thought but didn't say. Instead he said, "I already told Mom no. But I'm guessing you know that."

"Yeah, well, she did call me. If it's about the money, she and Daniel would be thrilled to buy your tickets. And with Tom gone, I've got plenty of room here for you to stay."

Suddenly Mark was furious. What had started as one of the happiest days of his life with the plan for Christmas in Mexico was ending like this. Too tired to control himself, he said, "I'm a little sick of everyone assuming we're living hand-to-mouth out here. Just because I'm fishing and just because we have three kids doesn't mean we're paupers! In fact, in case anyone's at all interested in *my* family and what *we're* doing, I'm surprising Serena with a trip to Mexico for Christmas. Believe it or not, we can actually afford it. So we can be with people who are sane for Christmas. For a change."

Evie and he, both only children, had been close; they'd managed to say just about everything there was to say to one another over the years. Neither ever held back, even when they knew the truth would hurt. But now the silence was so charged, Mark worried that he'd hurt yet another of the few relationships that mattered to him.

After a while, she said softly, "Why didn't you tell your mother?"

"Because I don't want it to be about whose family is more important. There's no winning that battle. Serena hardly ever sees her family, and I need to spend time with her while she does see them. With our kids."

"I understand that." Evie said. The quiet stretched on so long that he thought she might have disconnected. "But, Mark, there's something you should know before you decide. I think Nana is dying."

6

Pastor Luke

She's not dying. She's too mean to die."

Serena stared straight ahead, but Luke saw the panic in her eyes that told the real story. Everything she'd told him was probably true: that she wanted to spend Christmas at her own home, that it was already December 14 and she didn't have time to get ready for the trip, that she shouldn't have to spend Christmas with Mark's whole family when she seldom saw her own, that she certainly couldn't afford the kind of presents "those women" would expect. All that was true and Luke knew it, but the real reason she didn't want to spend Christmas in Connecticut was in her eyes.

She was afraid.

And for good reason, given the terrifying combination of Maria, Catharine, and Filomena. That was enough, Luke reflected, to terrify anyone, never mind a young mother who did fine in her own world but lacked confidence in moving through the wider one. That wider one being Mark's very Italian, very vocal, very tense—and from Serena's perspective—very critical family. Luke remembered them from Mark and Serena's wedding ten years before, apparently the last event that the twin sisters had attended together, and while the women were entertaining and charming to an outsider, they would be no easy challenge for the only female in-law, the wife of the "beloved boy."

Serena gazed resolutely out the window. They were sitting in the chapel, high above Bodega Bay, but Luke had the feeling she wasn't even seeing the sweeping view of the bay, the harbor, and Bodega Head. She was seeing the ruination of the peaceful Bodega Bay Christmas she'd been planning for weeks.

Mark had already been to see Luke, so he knew the whole story; more than Serena knew, in fact, because Mark had described his plan to surprise Serena with a trip to Mexico. But when Evie had shared her suspicion that their grandmother was dying, Mark had felt the whole wonderful surprise slipping through his fingers. By the time he'd come to see Luke yesterday, he was resigned to abandoning the trip. Mark had already told Serena about Evie's fears, but he'd not told his wife about his own plan. Serena, Luke had not been surprised to learn, had agreed they should go to Connecticut. Mark had used the money intended for Mexico to buy the tickets; they were scheduled to leave on the twenty-second. If Mark had his way, Serena would never know about the extraordinary effort he'd gone to in the hope of pleasing her.

And now she was sitting here, angry and resentful, waiting for Luke to come up with something helpful. Sometimes he really hated his job.

He began with the practical. "Serena, you know I talked to Mark yesterday. If you feel this strongly, why did you agree to go?"

"*Why?*" she echoed as if he'd lost his grip on reason. "Because how will Mark feel if that mean old woman actually does die next year? He'll blame me. He'll never forget that he didn't see his Nana for her last Christmas on earth because of me. And you know the rest of them—especially his mother—will be blaming me, too. Every chance they get, they'll remind him. And every time they do, he'll feel the guilt and he'll know it was because of me. Every holiday. Every birthday. Especially every Christmas. No. I can't live with that. We have to go."

"But you don't want to." Luke made it a statement. He didn't dare suggest she was exaggerating about Mark's family; indeed, he wasn't sure she was.

"Would you, Pastor Luke?" she asked, glaring directly at him. "Would you want to spend your Christmas, a day you'd spent a month planning and hoping for, with those women? With that family? In *Connecticut*?" She made the state sound like a disease, and Luke knew that for her, it probably seemed like one.

"Everyone says, 'Oh, Nana hasn't seen her grandchildren. Oh, this is terrible. It should not be so. You must come so that she can see them before she dies.' Well, what about my parents? They are grandparents, too. Have they seen Melissa? No. Have they ever seen their son-in-law? No. But does anyone think that is terrible? That it should not be so? No. No one cares about *my* family."

Unspoken were the words, *No one cares about me.* But Luke heard them just the same, and wished yet again that Mark had taken his advice and told Serena about Christmas in Mexico. Even if they'd decided—together—not to go, at least then they could have shared their disappointment. At least then she would have felt how much he loved her and wished to please her. As it was, they were shouldering burdens of disappointment and anger that they might carry together but that, separately, might crush them—and their marriage.

But Mark hadn't listened to him. "How can I tell her?" he'd said plaintively. "What good would it do? She'd just be more disappointed than ever and angrier at my family. It would look like I was choosing mine over hers. Why make it more difficult? Besides, if I tell her, it'll look like I'm trying to be a hero, when it's my family that's ruining it for everyone. The least I can do is be a man about this."

"So you *do* think Filomena is dying?" Luke had asked Mark

"No, I don't thing she's dying!" Mark had exploded, "I mean come on, Luke, ask yourself, do you really think God wants that kind of aggravation?"

"Okay, then if you don't think she's dying, why go back? Why not just stick with your surprise and go to Mexico?"

"Yeah, and then what if she does die soon? That's a one-way ticket to Guilt City."

That was the crux of it, Luke thought now, trying to figure out how to counsel the agitated young woman sitting next to him. *Guilt.* The one thing all families seemed to have in common, and this one had it in abundance. Whether Filomena was dying or not, from what Luke knew about the family, she wielded guilt as a weapon, and though Mark appeared to have escaped, the shadow of the sword was falling on him now. And on Serena.

Luke decided to try the truth with Serena. "I really don't know what to tell you. I don't know enough about the Connecticut family. But I do know you. I know how you've conducted yourself for ten years in a country that's not your own, far from your family. I know what a wonderful mother you are; I'd venture to say a better mother than any of those you'll meet in Connecticut. That's what will get you through this, Serena: who you are, what you have with Mark. And who they are, and what they *don't* have."

For the first time since she'd arrived an hour before, Serena's eyes filled with tears. "Oh great," joked Luke, "that's the best I can do for you—make you cry."

Serena gave him a watery smile as she took the tissue he offered. "No, no. You've made me feel better. You always do."

Moving to safer ground, he asked, "How do the kids feel about the trip?"

"Ha! You know kids," she said. "They forgot all the plans they had for Christmas at home when they heard about the plane trip. Bobby seems a little worried, but I think it's because he feels the stress in me and Mark. Laurie's so excited she's completely forgotten her plan to trap Santa by putting glue on the floor of the fireplace."

Luke laughed. He loved Laurie. She and Bobby came regularly to his Wednesday evening AWANA club, and she did something amusing just about every week. Lately she'd been refusing to recite "Forgive us our trespasses as we forgive those who trespass against us" in the Lord's Prayer. When he'd asked her why, she said, "'Cause if someone bugs me, I don't want to forgive 'em." Repressing a smile, he'd tried to explain the importance of forgiveness.

"But don't you want God to forgive you when you do something to bug Him?"

"Yup. And He does."

"Well, if God forgives you, shouldn't you forgive other people?"

She was appalled by the question. *Are you cracked?* her expression asked him. And he had to admit it wasn't the most logical concept, especially to a precocious child who blithely assumed that God loved her, and who knew very well that God's talent for forgiveness could not be compared to hers . . . or anyone's.

"But, Pastor Luke," she'd declared, tiny hands on nonexistent hips, "I'm not God."

Luke had puzzled over the exchange for days and still hadn't come up with a good retort.

Laurie's confidence in herself was something he rarely saw, especially in the children of immigrants, who frequently absorbed their parents' fear of being outsiders. Luke knew that Laurie's self-assurance was due to Serena, and he wondered if she knew what an extraordinary mother she was. He told Serena, "I expect Laurie will hold her own in Connecticut."

"She's probably the only one," Serena answered, and he felt a stab of pity when she added, half to herself, "I just wish we could be with my family. Even if not on Christmas. Melissa looks just like my mother."

Luke cleared his throat. He couldn't tell her what Mark had told him in confidence; he just couldn't. Instead he urged, "Why don't you plan a trip home, then? All five of you? Even if you have to save for it."

"No, Pastor," she interrupted with a sadness so deep that it shook him. "Mark would never go. And now we can't afford it, anyway. We had to use our house money for the tickets to Connecticut."

§

As he watched Serena walk down the village hill toward Pelican Plaza, he was overcome with dismay. Why wouldn't Mark tell her? If only she knew what he'd planned, it would make the next few weeks so much easier for her, for the two of them. Leaving the church, he noticed the sparkling glass ornament that hung in the colored-pane window at the entrance. The wise man, clad in a magnificent purple and gold robe, seemed to stare back at him in mild disdain.

"Well, what would you have done then, you old know-it-all," Luke asked the glass figure that Filomena had given him when he married Mark and Serena ten years ago. "The Christmas Glass," she'd said, handing him a plain sturdy box as if there was nothing else to say. When he'd thanked her with what must have been a slightly perplexed look on his face, she added, as if sharing the secret of the kingdom, "A piece of us."

"Poor Serena," he told the wise man and went out to his truck and called his wife.

"How did it go?" Elinor asked.

He'd told her about Mark's visit yesterday and Serena's today; Elinor was much better at figuring out solutions than he was. Truth was, she'd be a better counselor, if only she had the patience. Elinor believed that if everyone did exactly what she told them to, the world would be nearly perfect. The annoying thing about that was she tended to be right.

"Not too well," he answered. "That family drives me around the bend. If only they'd be honest with each other, most of their problems would evaporate—if the old lady were honest with her daughters; if the daughters were honest with each other and found the gumption to stand up to the old lady; if Mark were honest with Serena. I think little Laurie is the only one who knows how to speak the truth. Can you imagine what it would mean to Serena to know Mark had planned the Mexico trip? Instead, her resentment and disappointment are slowly building into a wall, while his feelings of helplessness are turning back into what they were after his father died."

"That's what's really bothering you, isn't it?" Elinor said. "The fact that you brought them together and now you're afraid you'll have to watch them break apart."

He paused. Elinor might not be gentle, but she did hit the target. "I just wish I could do something," he said.

"Call the old lady. Call her and tell her what havoc she's causing in her family. You know she'll remember you."

"I can't call her, Elinor. You know that. And what do you propose I say to her anyway? Maybe something like, 'Excuse me, ma'am, but allow me to tell you how to run your family. Oh, and by the way, are you dying or not?' My job is to listen and counsel, not interfere."

"Well someone ought to—interfere, that is. Someone should have interfered with this family years ago. If you're afraid of the old lady, just go ahead and tell Serena about Mark's plan for Christmas in Mexico."

"That would be even worse! Mark asked me *not* to tell Serena. And, just for the record, I'm not afraid of Filomena. Pastoral counseling requires at least some degree of confidentiality."

"What, you're Catholic now? You do know, don't you, that this is counseling and not confession?" she shot back, and he felt the smile start on his face.

"You know, my beloved helpmate and life partner, sometimes I think you don't appreciate how much wisdom and restraint I have to exercise in my role as a spiritual guide to those in need of direction." He imagined her smirk.

"Right," she said, yawning audibly. "Been talking to your wise man again, have you? Well, if you're done conferring with Balthazar, or whichever one he is, could you pick up some sourdough bread at Pelican Plaza?"

"At your service, my dearest. Anything else?"

"Um, how about a couple of turkey sandwiches and a pint of that wild-rice-and-cranberry thing Marina does on weekends? That way I won't have to bother cooking tonight."

"A situation to be fervently desired by all."

"Very amusing," she said dryly. "And don't forget to ask Marina to put avocado on my sandwich. And whole wheat—I want whole wheat bread."

"As if I haven't been ordering this sandwich for you for decades," he said.

"Well, decades may be an exaggeration, especially since you get it wrong almost as often as you get it right," she said. But the laughter was gone when she added, "Luke, I do think you should consider jumping in on this one. Mark and Serena could be headed for real problems. And the only person who cares more about them than you is me."

He hung up, knowing she was right. Elinor had taken Serena under her wing when the nineteen-year-old first arrived to spend six months with her cousin Lucie. After discovering Serena's skill at embroidery, Elinor's word-of-mouth referrals—and as Luke well knew, there was no word-of-mouth like Elinor's—won Serena several customers. When Luke married Mark and Serena, Elinor had been Serena's only attendant besides Lucie, a role that had given her a front-row view of Mark's family. That night Elinor told Luke, "I don't think twenty-five-hundred miles is going to be enough space between those women and Serena."

Now her prediction was proving true. But how would he "jump in," as Elinor put it? What could he do, given his constraints as a counselor and the thousands of miles between him and Mark's family? Should he do anything? He couldn't help wondering what would have happened if he hadn't played matchmaker between the shy, pretty woman and Mark. Granted, Serena had probably saved Mark's life, but how much of her own had she given up in the process?

After stopping at Pelican Plaza—when he started to order the two sandwiches, Marina handed him a sack, saying, "She already called. Afraid you'd forget the avocado again."—he found the truck heading toward Bay Flat Road instead of home. This happened to him once in a while, the truck driving its own way. He liked to think it was God taking over the wheel, but he guessed it was probably just God directing him to drive himself toward a little solitude.

It was just past four, but already the sun was near the horizon. These December days were so short. He'd read somewhere that God chose to send His Son at the time of year when the world was darkest so as to cheer and encourage all His children. Well, they were all in need of some cheer right about now.

Bay Flat Road circled the harbor, which glowed in the soft light as if trying to seduce the sun into staying just a little longer. It was right around half-tide, and the water from the Pacific was flowing in through the narrow mouth of the harbor. Visitors, especially the hikers and the nature types, were always amazed at how swiftly the harbor expanded from sand flats with a deep channel dug to let boats in and out to a brimming basin. In all tides the bay and harbor were home to a multitude of creatures, from the tiny organisms that attracted the passionate interest of the environmentalists at the Bodega Marine Laboratory to the pelicans and sea lions that needed do little more than open their mouths to dine in the fish-filled waters.

Luke drove slowly around the long, curving road, taking it all in. Someone—a lunatic, Elinor would say—was out windsurfing, though the water temperature would have been unbearable if he (or she) hadn't been wearing a black wetsuit. The wind wasn't up today, but Luke had seen the brave souls—which is how he thought of them, despite Elinor—skimming along the surface of the bay at heart-stopping speed, clinging to their colorful water kites for dear life. It always looked thrilling to Luke, as if those brave souls, with nothing but a brilliantly colored sail and a narrow board between them and the water, were aquatic angels, riding the waves and the wind.

Elinor had long since informed him that she would call out the Coast Guard if he even looked twice at "one of those ridiculous contraptions." When he'd protested that he had the God-given right to take up whatever sport or hobby he desired, she'd just snorted and said, "When pigs fly." That had pretty much been the end of the discussion. But he'd always wondered what it would be like, whether the freezing water and not much warmer air would take his breath away and make him feel even closer to God.

Just being here made him feel closer to God. He'd lived near the bay for almost forty years now, and he was still captive to its beauty. As someone who relied on construction to make a living, he should have been pushing for more development, but he'd been secretly delighted when five old ladies who lived up the highway in Jenner on a prime parcel near the Russian River had managed to hold off a major developer. They'd stalled the project for three years until the guy finally gave up. Each time he'd proposed a new plan, the Five Widows, as they'd come to be known, had successfully opposed it.

Not that Luke didn't understand the developer's perspective. His own small construction business had done very well from the golf course development he could see now across the bay, the large homes looking like dollhouses dotting the two hills at the town's entrance. It had been a boon to the locals as well, and the developer had been willing to work with Planning and Zoning to keep the site from becoming too intrusive. Of course, the deer, coyote, and other wild creatures that had been displaced might have argued the meaning of "intrusive," but they couldn't vote.

With a sprinkling of houses and cottages high up on the ridge to his right, he passed the marina with its diesel tanks, fish processing facilities, and hundreds of boats on his left. Much of the economy relied on fishing. Many of the restaurants that lined the bay were supplied by the commercial fishermen who kept their boats here and in the smaller marina just off the entrance to Bay Flat. He could see Mark's boat, *The Serena*, seven boats in from the shore.

Just past the marina, Luke drove slowly through the small RV park, deserted this time of year, past the boat launch and spigots where small-time fishermen washed down their boats, their catches, or just their feet if the tide was low and the mud was flowing. The blackened grills where the RVs usually parked looked desolate in the dimming light, a melancholy reminder of how fleeting the seasons are and how fast life passes.

He passed the entrance to the Marine Biology Laboratory. A group of brown pelicans floated in the harbor on his left, each with that blank nonchalant look in its eyes, as if it wasn't about to plunge its massive beak into the water and gulp down some poor fish before the fish had a clue what was happening. Three turkey vultures circled close over something Luke couldn't see below the banked road. He spotted the Coast Guard cutter chugging quietly through the channel, the only boat out this afternoon.

Taking a sharp right at the end of the road, he headed up an incline that eventually wound over to Bodega Head. He'd been coming here for years whenever he needed to think, or just get over a mood. It was one of the first places he had found thirty-eight years ago when he followed some girl to Sebastopol, convinced he was in love. Fortunately for him, she wasn't convinced, but he'd been so taken with the wrenching beauty of the Sonoma coast that he couldn't bring himself to return to Ann Arbor. He hired on as a ranch hand up past Jenner for a season. When he met Elinor, it was all over. He hadn't known what love was until then. Today, he couldn't even remember the name of that first girl, but he thanked God for her every day.

He parked in the gravel lot that looked over the Pacific. People had seen whales from this high spot, but he'd never been so lucky. Once he and Elinor had been hiking up here with the kids and they'd almost walked into a huge old skunk. Happily, the Lord had mercy, and the old guy had rumbled away. Luke had spotted birds he couldn't even name without his Audubon guide. He'd see a whale eventually. Elinor had lived here all her life and she'd never seen one either. He wanted them to see it together. No hurry.

But he did feel in a hurry about Mark and Serena. Elinor had sensed it too. Probably Serena had been talking to her and she was keeping her own code of confidentiality. If only Mark and Serena could have what he and Elinor had.

"How can I give that to them, Lord?" he asked out loud, now that he'd reached the place where he most often talked to God. He stepped out of the truck into the roar of the waves and wind.

He didn't expect God to answer him in some basso voice from the sky. It wasn't that he didn't believe the folks who claimed God spoke directly to them, or even admire them occasionally, but that wasn't the relationship he had with God.

Luke felt God with him all the time, felt His presence, was comforted by Him. But Luke wasn't Moses or Abraham; he didn't hear God's voice telling him what he should or should not do. But when he came to God like this, when he was alone in this unspoiled place, he could quiet himself enough to feel God. That was really the only answer he expected. That was prayer. The rest he'd have to figure out for himself.

He knew he couldn't give Mark and Serena what he and Elinor had: the deep—and sometimes painful—honesty, the laughter, the simple trust. Even the ability to fight it out when they had to. He desperately wanted to give all that to the younger couple, but he knew they had to find their own way. It was just that they seemed to be straying farther and farther from it. And he didn't know what to do—he didn't know what he could do—to help. If they wouldn't talk to each other, how much could talking to him really accomplish?

Three-quarters of an hour passed before he climbed back into the truck, his hands so cold he could barely maneuver the key into the ignition. Darkness had come and the night was clear, stars snapping in the cold sky. The moon was still a crescent and would set shortly. He drove back slowly, checking in his headlights for coyotes and deer as he went. The night sights on Bay Flat Road were as exhilarating as the day view, but in a different way, all shadow and flickering light. Night did that in the harbor.

Mark and Serena's house was near the entrance of the road at the edge of the harbor, just behind the trailer park. He slowed down as he approached the cottage, brightly lit from the inside. He could just see their Christmas tree, with its tiny colored lights, in the window. Luke stopped, pulling into the lot where equestrians brought their horses in trailers so they could ride onto the beach. Feeling a little strange, as if he were spying on them, he cut his headlights.

Just then a light went on over the porch and Mark came out of the house, carrying a plastic sack out to the street. He heaved the bag into the green container at the edge of the gravel driveway, but instead of returning to the house he stood there, a silhouette in the distant porch light. For what seemed a long time, Mark stood, his face raised to the brilliant night sky. Then he bowed his head.

There was a movement in the window by the Christmas tree, and Luke glimpsed Serena, her arms folded in front of her, looking out, watching her husband. The space between the two motionless figures, though only a few yards, seemed immense. *An abyss,* Luke thought.

A moment later, Laurie came flying out the door. Mark's head shot up and he turned to his daughter, lifting her in the air and twirling her through the darkness. Luke could hear her shriek of delight. When he looked back at the window, Serena had vanished.

Ten minutes later, Luke walked into his kitchen, kissed the top of Elinor's head, which was bent distractedly over a table covered with Christmas cards and a much-scribbled-on list of addresses so old it looked like parchment, and headed to the phone in the hallway. He punched three numbers and waited for the operator to ask, "City and State, please?"

"Mystic, Connecticut," he said, and thought he saw Elinor smile as she checked another name off the list.

7

Michael

Catharine was appalled that her mother had invited a stranger to her Stonington Mills apartment, and she'd told Filomena as much several times. Catharine had hoped Olivia would agree with her and prevent the man from coming, but she'd flatly refused to help.

"Cath, I can't just forbid someone from visiting your mother," she said, sounding as if Catharine had asked her to slaughter a pig in the courtyard. "I'm the administrator of a residence for seniors, not the Gestapo. Do you think maybe you're overreacting to this? I mean, your mother is really excited about this visit. The man's a family friend, isn't he?"

Not that I know of, Catharine had thought. How could Olivia, of all people, not get this? Catharine lifted the phone again to dial her mother.

"Mother, you don't even know this man," she said as soon as Filomena picked up the phone. "Just because his father worked for you a million years

153

ago and you saw him a few times as a little boy doesn't give him the right to come barging into our lives a few days before Christmas like this. It's December fifteenth already, and given the demands you've made on all of us, I've got a few things to do, you know."

"So do them," Filomena replied implacably, "I don't need you here. I didn't invite you to meet Michael. You're the one who insisted on butting in."

"You make it sound like it's something I *want* to do," Catharine replied, "when you know full well that I don't have any choice. I'm not about to pretend it's perfectly okay for you let some stranger into your home. I mean, really, listen to you: calling him 'Michael' like he's some long-lost family friend."

"Michael *is* a family friend. When we first moved to New London, his father helped fix up our house—a house that was good enough for you until you decided to move up to Mystic. And just because you don't care about family or family friends doesn't mean I can forget them."

It was all Catharine could do not to explode. Filomena would never let her forget that she and Gregory had refused to move back into her childhood home when Filomena had finally agreed to move to Stonington Mills. Her mother had really expected that "one of my own" would always live in the house, and at the time, "one of my own" had meant Catharine. After Gregory placed the house with a Realtor, Filomena hadn't spoken to them for four months. When she finally started speaking again, Gregory's response had been, "Not long enough." Catharine had just about made herself sick over the whole thing.

She struggled to control herself before answering her mother. As it was, her voice was loud enough to make Gregory stick his head into the kitchen where she was pacing back and forth, twisting the phone cord around her hand. "Mother. You don't even know this man. He doesn't live here and hasn't lived here for, what? Over forty years? He's driving three hours from Ogunquit, and what's so important that he's driving down here in the middle of December from Maine? Who knows what he really wants?"

"Michael told me what he wants. He found a piece of the Christmas Glass among his father's things, and he remembered Frank talking about us and the ornaments. He wanted to know the story of how his father got the piece. It's the icicle. You remember, with the silver and gold streaks in the glass? Besides, he's a retired banker, not some criminal."

Catharine counted to ten, grinding her teeth, a practice her dentist had told her just last month was going to cost her. But Filomena wasn't finished. "You probably don't even remember. Well, traditions are important to some people."

Catharine wanted to scream. Instead she asked, "Okay, then, how *did* the icicle come into his possession? All I remember was a big scene that year when you realized it was missing. Had Dad given it to this man's father, this Frank?"

"Of course not. Your father wouldn't do such a thing without asking me."

"Well, who gave it to him then?"

"No one gave it to him. He stole it."

§

Michael kept thinking he should pack a bag. It was ridiculous, but every time he'd been to Connecticut in the past—the very long-ago past—he'd packed at least an overnight bag, although forty-eight hours was about as long as he and his father could stand being in the same place. But Michael only needed to pack one small, delicate item for the trip he'd make to Connecticut tomorrow morning. It wouldn't require an overnight stay. It probably wouldn't require more than an hour, and he still wasn't sure why he was going.

You're making a six-hour round trip for a visit that is likely to take under an hour—and for something that could be handled on the phone in five minutes, he told himself. *Why?*

He wouldn't really know until tomorrow, until after he'd met with the old woman. He'd last seen her almost fifty years before when he was just a child, a dark-haired woman who'd spoken to him in broken English and to his father in perfect Italian. After Frank died fifteen years ago from a combination of too much booze and too many cigarettes, Michael had no need to use what little Italian he'd retained for his father's sake. He'd gotten Filomena's number from information and then taken a week to work up the courage to call. She still had her accent. The old ones would never give that up.

Old ones, he laughed at himself, closing the book he'd been trying to distract himself with. *I should talk. When I knew her, Filomena couldn't have been much more than thirty-five and I thought she was ancient. Almost the same age*

as my father! And now she's in her eighties, and I'm pushing sixty, and I'm still
calling her an "old one." What does that make me?

Michael was accustomed to talking to himself. Since retiring three years
ago from the Boston-based hedge fund where he'd made an obscene amount
of money, his silent conversations with himself had become more frequent.
Have to watch that, he told himself, bundling into his anorak and pulling on
a wool hat and gloves against the damp Ogunquit night. He locked the door
behind him; he'd closed his bed-and-breakfast for the season a week ago
and didn't need to leave the door unlocked for guests returning late.

Ogunquit, as usual for this time of year, was deserted, unless you counted
the handful of year-round residents, and by 10:30 on a frigid Sunday night
in December, all of them were safely ensconced in their houses or winter-
ized cottages. Michael had the streets to himself. It was a perfect night
for a true lover of New England, ice cold and crystal clear. The stars were
brilliant with the moon already set. There was no fog for a change; it had
become too cold for Ogunquit's typical misty shroud, and Michael could
see all along Main Street with its shuttered shops and restaurants. In six or
seven months, you wouldn't be able to move on this street, the crowd would
be so thick; people pouring out of the Village Inn after drinks or dinner,
window-shopping for the sales that really weren't, eating ice-cream cones
or fudge out of small, white paper bags, or just standing in the middle of
the sidewalk trying to decide where to go next.

But now the small seaside village had been abandoned by its fickle lovers and was unlikely to see many visitors until at least Easter. That suited Michael just fine. When he'd first left the financial world, he wanted to get so far away from everyone that he actually thought about places like Tibet or Essaouira in Morocco. He'd even taken a year to visit these and a handful of others, but none of the places that he yearned for in his fantasies of escape had suited him in the end. Maybe he'd never truly believed they would, but he half convinced himself that the reason he never married or committed to a family was so he'd be free to travel all over the world and do exactly as he pleased.

It was easier than acknowledging the possibility that he was a complete failure at anything besides making money.

At the end of his searching year, he'd ended up right back where he started. Or close. In this he could give himself a little credit: Ogunquit was not exactly Boston, and he had at least chosen a place that was far from any financial district and work that had nothing to do with market risk—although it was a start-up of sorts, the rundown inn he'd bought for cash and completely renovated. At first he couldn't imagine who would pay to stay at the place, even redone with elegant little rooms, soothing colors, well (and expensively) tended gardens and grounds, and a welcoming wraparound porch. It wasn't as if he had a lot of close friends—okay, he had no close friends—or business acquaintances just waiting for the chance to do him a good deed by visiting his pretty little money pit in southern Maine. Granted, Ogunquit was a favorite beach town for Canadians and many New Englanders, but there were plenty of hotels, cottages, and B&Bs already in operation and popular long before he'd even heard of the little resort village.

More than ten years ago, while still on the banking treadmill, he'd wanted a place that would be close enough to reach quickly but far enough from Boston to feel he'd escaped. One of his colleagues had been talking about Ogunquit, but, unlike his colleague, when he drove up the coast to Maine, he went alone. It was bad enough to be with people all day long and some-times much of the night if he was working a deal; he certainly didn't intend to share his one haven.

Even now, he couldn't say he'd fallen in love with Ogunquit; he wasn't the type to "fall in love" with places. Or people, evidently. But he came close with the little town on the cliffs overlooking the Atlantic. Still, it had been unlike him to make an impulse buy, which is precisely what he'd done when he saw the dilapidated inn for sale on Route 1, set far back on the property away from the busy road. He still wasn't sure why he'd done it. He'd just finished his second season, when tourists and summer residents flooded the village, and he wasn't yet coming close to making a profit. This last year had been marginally better than the first, but at this rate, he wouldn't be making any real money for another five years.

It didn't really bother him. He found, to his mild astonishment, that he enjoyed the guests, got a kick out of being a host. At first he thought that was the part he'd enjoy the least: meeting people, pretending to care about them. He knew he'd be good at running the place, hiring the help, keeping the books. That part would be no problem. And it hadn't been, but he was surprised by how easy it was to socialize with the guests, complete strangers for the most part—he'd been right about his former colleagues not flocking to the place out of loyalty, much less affection.

He found himself relaxing as he mingled with his guests during breakfast and then again in the early evening when he served wine and soft drinks on the porch. He was almost ridiculously pleased when some of his first-season visitors reserved rooms this past year. He had several satisfying chess games with the ten-year-old son of one of the returning couples. Michael felt no awkwardness with them or the boy, a near-prodigy (at least that's how he explained the kid's humiliating him in five out of seven games).

After decades of chasing the money, hungering for it, seeking all that he thought it would bring him, the fact that he wasn't bothered by losing money was strangely comforting. It gave him hope: hope that he might be wrong about himself, that he wasn't pathetically stunted, unloving, unlovable. Hope that he hadn't turned into a more successful version of his father. Hope that he desperately wanted the old lady to affirm tomorrow.

Michael trudged along the road to Ogunquit's main beach, poorly lit now that there were no paying vacationers to keep street lights and windows bright, but he knew it too well to stumble; his thoughts had driven him out here often enough over the past few weeks. He opened his coat and let the cold assault him, shearing into his bones, as he thought about tomorrow.

He'd been just a boy the year his father had worked on Filomena and Paolo's house on Pequot Avenue in New London. Was it his own recollection of Filomena that made him think she was beautiful, or was it Frank's infatuation with the young mother? Michael didn't know and thought it probably no longer mattered. What he did know at that time was that this was an Italian family like his, but not in any of the important ways.

"Just off the boat," his father would sneer, nothing he'd ever show his customers, because most of them hired him to work on their houses or yards just because he was Italian like them. He was charming enough that they never suspected his disdain. Only his son was treated to those displays, usually after Frank had come home for the night and rapidly consumed a bottle of cheap Chianti. Not that it had to be Chianti. Any wine would do.

Even after years of drinking, Frank always dismissed the idea that he had a problem. "Have I ever missed a day of work? No. So there's no problem. No drunks drink wine. Wine is for food." Except he usually forgot the food part once he got going on the wine. Which meant, of course, that Michael often got no dinner, except what he could scrounge from the icebox's meager contents. Later, as the host of many meals, Michael had drawn more than one suspicious glance from clients in fine restaurants by refusing not only the two-hundred-dollar bottles of wine but also the equally pricey Scotch, imported rum, and anything else that reminded him of Frank. Michael was oblivious to the raised eyebrows. Let them think he was an alcoholic. He'd surely spent his childhood drunk on the fumes.

But around Filomena Frank was always on his best behavior. Yes, she was "just off the boat," but something in the woman had disarmed him. "She's a beaut," Frank would say once he and Michael had gone home for the evening, "and that little Sicilian doesn't deserve her. She wears the pants in that house." Of course, he was referring to Paolo, who was unfailingly decent to Frank and who was not Sicilian. Still, Frank couldn't possibly approve of any man married to a woman who'd caught his attention. Frank generally had no use for women at all, and not much more for men, but Filomena was different.

Michael often wondered if she reminded Frank of Michael's mother, whose name his father never uttered. They had courted and married in Italy, and Frank had come to America alone to work until he could save enough to send for her. She was seventeen, and that was the only way her parents had allowed the marriage. By the time Frank had earned enough to send for her, she was nineteen and he'd soured on America. "Streets paved with gold, they'd tell us in the old country," he'd say to young Michael. "You see any gold in these streets? Huh? You see any gold anywhere in this miserable place?"

But at the time Frank didn't see fit to tell his bride that she'd be moving from her parents' immaculate house near Naples to a filthy, dark tenement in New York. She got off the boat and through immigration, only to find that the *bellissimo* apartment her husband had described to her parents in the letters that finally persuaded them to put her, all three of them weeping, on the boat to America, was a rat-infested dump. She stayed long enough to get pregnant, have her son, and flee back to her parents without him.

All this Michael knew from his father's half-drunk mutterings. Her name, however, never crossed Frank's lips.

Michael couldn't remember much about the house in New London he and his father worked on, or Paolo, or the twin sisters who were older than he was and had little use for a boy running about the place. But Filomena he did remember: thick, mahogany hair, sometimes plaited and worn over her shoulder; warm, dark eyes that saw his longing for a mother behind the smudged faced he'd already learned to keep closed to adults; the voice, always soft with Michael but turning sharp whenever one of her twins would say something mean to "that boy."

§

If there was one woman Frank loved, one woman who didn't draw his usual cynical, snarling comments; one woman to whom he was unfailingly courteous; one woman about whom he never murmured a complaining or disrespectful word, even outside her presence; that woman was Filomena.

Frank always brought Michael along on his jobs in the summer, telling his customers the usual sob story about not having a good woman at home to watch the boy, though if they paid attention they soon realized that

Michael served as his father's unpaid pack mule. The boy worked harder those summers than he ever would again in his life.

For the whole month of August, when Frank was working with Paolo to fix up the old house he and Filomena had bought, the boy came to work with his father. Unlike any of the other jobs Frank dragged him along to, Michael loved it. He dreaded the end of summer, dreaded Labor Day, after which he'd have to go back to school.

Even after school started, whenever Frank worked for Paolo, Michael jumped at the chance to go along. Half the time, Frank didn't bother getting Michael to school anyway; it was easier to take the boy to work. Paolo was kind to the child. Michael could recall several occasions when Paolo had silently taken over some task that Frank had assigned his son. Paolo never said a word to Frank; Italian men didn't interfere between a parent and child.

Filomena, however, had no qualms about chastising Frank for his treatment of his son. And to Michael's amazement, his father seemed to love it.

Seeing Michael, with his skinny arms and legs, struggle with wheelbarrows full of dirt, stone, or brick, Filomena would snap, "Do you call that child a son or a slave?" Every time she said something like that, Michael would hold his breath, waiting for his father's rage to explode. But Frank laughed good-naturedly at Filomena's rebukes. Sometimes he would tease her, saying, "Well, what do you know, with only daughters? It's good for a boy to work."

"It's even better for his *father* to work," she'd shoot back, beckoning Michael to follow her into the house for lunch or a snack. At first, he'd stand frozen to the spot, not sure whether to obey this woman who dared challenge his father. But Frank would always say, "Go then, you heard the lady." Then he'd call after Filomena's retreating back, "Feed him good so that he doesn't eat me out of house and home. I've no wife to cook for him, you know!"

Once they were inside, Michael would hear Filomena mutter, "And no wonder! As if any good woman would stay with you. Eat you out of house and home! The boy looks like he hasn't had a decent meal in years." And then she'd turn suddenly to Michael and ask, "Have you, child? Do you eat well at your father's table?"

Michael always looked away, not wanting to tell her the truth, but not wanting to give up the food she'd prepare for him either. Ah, the food that would come out of that kitchen! Even now, sitting in the chill Ogunquit night at the beach on a metal bench so cold he felt his skin would stick to it, his mouth watered as he remembered her cooking. It was everything he'd yearned for as an always-hungry boy, and more: spaghetti, long before anyone called it pasta, with rich tomato sauce and chunks of pork so tender they shredded at the touch of his fork; homemade pizza cut in thick rectangles, with fresh basil, mozzarella, sausage, and parmesan; dense, chewy bread that was a meal on its own with butter and cheese; minestrone thick with vegetables, potatoes, and macaroni; and on Fridays, flounder, breaded and fried on the stove with a spicy tartar sauce, or eel braised with peppers and onions.

And the desserts! Michael still had a sweet tooth, and he knew its origins were in that half-finished kitchen on Pequot Avenue. Slices of brittle shortbread flavored with anise, the kind that most people thought was invented by Stella D'oro; zabaglione so rich that cardiologists today would ban it; hand-dipped chocolates she told him could only be made on cool, dry days or the chocolate wouldn't "set right"; nougat studded with bits of dried fruit and raisins.

His stomach rumbling at the memory, Michael found himself half-guiltily wondering if she would cook for him tomorrow. It would be worth the ride just to sit with her and eat. But what was wrong with him, expecting an old woman to make his lunch? For all he knew, the poor thing was living on vanilla NutriShakes and Ensure. Besides, if she did cook, he'd probably be too nervous to enjoy the meal.

The last thing she'd made for him was not, to his sorrow, eaten in her kitchen. Michael and his father had worked with Paolo the weekend before Thanksgiving, and on the next Saturday afternoon, Frank came home with a large box and an angry face. He thrust the box at Michael, saying, "No more work over there. The Sicilian says he doesn't need me anymore. She sent this for you."

Michael was torn between joy at the box and disappointment that they weren't needed any longer on Pequot Avenue. He couldn't conceive of life without Filomena and her gentle husband.

Michael studied the box while his father stomped into the sitting room, a bottle in his hand. The box, covered with red foil, was the most festive thing Michael had received in his seven years. He shook it gently, surprised at the rattle from inside. He looked for a note or a tag, but there was nothing. Slowly he untangled the green twine she'd tied in a bow and lifted the lid.

Michael drew a slow breath, his eyes widening. The box was full of every kind of Christmas cookie imaginable. He was overwhelmed by the scents of vanilla, cinnamon, chocolate, nutmeg, anise, lemon and almonds. There were cookies made of cornflakes dyed green to look like Christmas wreaths with cherries for the bow, small balls the size of robin's eggs made of ground almonds and rolled in sugar, large flat discs bursting with chocolate chips, fat rounds of oatmeal dotted with raisins, squares of Rice Krispies and marshmallow layered with chocolate, yellow lemon wafers with golden edges, and two kinds of thick, walnut-studded fudge. Scattered among them were silver-covered Hershey's Kisses and nonpareils with tiny white sprinkles. Michael didn't know how long he'd been standing there before his father grunted from the other room, "Come here. There's another thing."

Something else? Michael couldn't believe it. And then suddenly, he knew what it must be. Filomena and Paolo must want Michael to spend Christmas with them! That must be it. The cookies were just the beginning—a sign of what was to come. They were Filomena's way of letting him know he would always be welcome at her house, especially on Christmas Day. Or maybe she had invited them—Michael knew that Frank would have to come along—for Christmas Eve. She would cook a big, traditional Christmas Eve meal, and then they'd all go to Midnight Mass at Saint Joseph's on Montauk Avenue.

"Did you hear me?" Frank yelled from the sitting room.

Michael put the cover back on the box and placed it gingerly in a cupboard his father seldom used; later he'd have to find a better hiding place. Not that Frank cared about cookies, but it would be just like him to knock over the box in a fit of temper or drunkenness. Michael hurried in to his father.

He could see by the level of wine in the bottle that Frank was already well into his second glass. He drank out of a canning jar, "like in the old country," so the bottle was nearly half gone. But Frank wasn't drinking when Michael came into the room. He was slumped in his brown chair, the worn fabric wine-stained and marked with cigarette burns, but there was something different about him. Frank was staring at something in his large, tobacco-yellowed hand. The look on his father's face made Michael stop in his tracks, his dreams of Christmas on Pequot Avenue dying away like a match that had flamed out.

As Michael watched, Frank's expression changed from disbelieving grief to sour betrayal and finally into a hardened mask of bitter satisfaction. He looked up at Michael, smiled grimly, and held up the object. "See what else we got?"

Michael had never seen anything like it. Still cautious he moved forward, drawn by the extraordinary thing in his father's hand. Glimmering in the weak November sunlight, it made the dingy room look brighter, cleaner, more alive. A long piece of glass—almost a shard, it was so slender and delicate in Frank's big hand—it appeared to have its own crystal light deep within its core. Up close, Michael could see slashes of silver and gold twining within the glass and a small silver crown at the top that held a silver hook. The boy was transfixed, certain he'd never see anything more extraordinary in his life.

"What're you staring at?" Frank growled. "It's just a Christmas ornament. You act like you've never seen one before."

Which was very close to the truth. Frank had done little to celebrate the Christmases since Michael's birth. For Michael, the ornament was exquisite, and it was from her. A diamond could not have been more valuable.

Without taking his eyes off the glass, he breathed, "For me? Is it for me?"

Frank took so long answering that Michael finally tore his eyes away and looked at his father. Frank was watching him with a blank look on his face. There was dark stubble on his cheeks and neck, and his brown eyes were deeply shadowed. Just before he spoke, he looked away.

"Yeah, it's for you. She told me to give it to you. For Christmas."

§

Catharine was halfway out the door when the phone rang. She would have kept going—she wanted to make sure she got to her mother's apartment long before the stranger—but Gregory had already left, and Catharine wasn't one of those people who could ignore the phone.

"Cath?" It was Olivia. But it didn't sound like Olivia; there was an unfamiliar hesitation in her voice. Catharine tried to pull in enough air to speak, but she could only croak, "What happened?"

"Oh no!" Olivia cried. "No, Cath, it's not your mother! I'm sorry! Meme's fine. It's not that at all."

Catharine lowered her shaking body into the chair just as the surge of adrenaline hit, making her heart race and the hairs on her skin tingle. She hadn't had such a feeling since the new neighbor's Doberman had charged her, teeth bared, barking so insanely she'd thought it was the last sound she'd hear in this world. Now she tried to silence the roaring in her ears so she could hear what Olivia was saying.

"It's just that . . . *uh* . . ." Olivia paused again, this time making Catharine more suspicious than worried. Olivia drew a breath, and when she spoke it was with a cool authority. "Your mother has asked that you not come to see her today. She wants to visit this Michael privately."

Catharine laughed. "And what did she say when you told her that she was being ridiculous? Really, I'm sorry she bothered you with this, Olivia. It's not like you don't have enough to do. I'm on my way over there now. I'll let you know what happens afterward."

"Catharine—wait."

In the brief, charged silence that followed, reality hit Catharine just a moment ahead of outrage. "Olivia," she began slowly, "tell me you're not saying that I can't visit my own mother."

"I'm sorry." The cold formality was still there. "Our residents have a right to choose their visitors. At Stonington Mills, we have to respect that. She's an adult, you know."

"No, she's not!" Catharine cried. "And you, of all people, know that! She's a petty, manipulative child living in the body of an adult, and she's always been that way."

"Excuse me, Catharine, but I *don't* know that. Not at all. My responsibility is to your mother in this situation."

"Really?" Catharine said. "And does this responsibility extend to letting her entertain some stranger—some no-name, no-face possible predator who just phones up out of nowhere and demands to see her?"

"First, you and I both know that's not the situation," Olivia began patiently, as if speaking to one of her dementia residents. "Your mother knows this man. She wants to see him. And there is nothing to indicate that he's any danger to her at all, much less a predator or a scam artist."

"Oh, and you know that because . . . ?" Catharine left it open, satisfied that Olivia would have to retreat. She didn't.

"I know it because I checked him out."

"You *what?*"

"I looked him up on the Internet. He's the owner of a bed-and-breakfast in Ogunquit, and he used to be a well-regarded hedge-fund manager—one of the few who left the profession by choice and with quite a bit of money, it seems. So there's nothing Meme has that this man could want."

"Then what *does* he want?" Catharine fumed. "Have you bothered asking yourself that?"

"That is none of my business," Olivia said so primly that Catharine didn't bother stifling a groan. "However, I've asked Meme if I could spend a few minutes with them when he first arrives so I can get a sense of the man. And so that you can be reassured."

"And she agreed?" Catharine asked warily, half hoping her mother had refused. Then, at least, Catharine could avoid the humiliation of having her own mother choose Olivia over her.

"She agreed."

There was another long pause while Catharine tried to come up with an objection Olivia would listen to. All she could manage was, "I thought she wanted privacy."

"She does, and I intend to give it to her as soon as I've satisfied myself about the man," Olivia answered, her tone softening. "Look, Cath, I realize Meme's pulling your chain, but she does want to see this man, and she's worried you'll make him feel uncomfortable."

Catharine had no reply to that; it had been her intention to make him uncomfortable. And to the statement that Filomena was pulling her chain, there was no response except "What else is new?"

Sensing surrender, Olivia added, "I promise I'll call you as soon as I've met him, okay?"

"I'm not sure what option I have," Catharine said frostily, "because I don't want to be carted off your property by a security guard."

Olivia chortled. "At least not until I can raise a small fortune by selling tickets."

§

Unable to sleep even after his long, cold walk on the beach, Michael had carefully wrapped the icicle ornament in tissue paper, placed it in its small oak box, and left Ogunquit well before dawn, thinking that at least he'd miss the rush hour traffic around Boston.

And here he sat, stuck in the rush hour traffic. In Boston, it seemed, it was always rush hour. He'd hated that about the city when he worked here. People said Los Angeles was the worst place in the country for drivers, but Michael believed that anyone who claimed that hadn't driven in Boston.

For once, though, he didn't mind the wait. The sun was just coming up, the wan December light competing with thousands of headlights and street lamps, and he wasn't expected at Filomena's apartment until ten. He'd planned to kill an hour or two driving around Mystic, maybe checking out the Mystic Market, an upscale deli one of his guests at the B&B always raved about. He was always on the lookout for interesting snacks or delicacies, though his newfound interest in food and hospitality continued to amuse him. What would his cutthroat former colleagues think of him now, searching out the best extra-virgin olive oil for his guests to dip their sourdough chunks into during the afternoon social hour?

He tried not to rehearse what he wanted to say to the old woman. It wouldn't make sense, no matter how often he practiced it. The truth was that he couldn't entirely explain it himself, this urgent need to see her. It had all started over the Thanksgiving holiday when he'd put up a Christmas tree for his guests. Michael had never put up a tree before. All he'd ever had was the icicle, and he'd displayed it carefully wherever he was. From that first year, when he kept it on the stool that was both his night table and his only chair, to his last year in the Boston penthouse, where it was laid on a piece of midnight blue velvet draped over the glass-and-chrome coffee table in his living room, he brought it out every Thanksgiving. It was just about the only thing Michael had taken from his father's house when he left for good at eighteen.

This year he'd topped the Ogunquit tree with the icicle, carefully tying the hook to the sturdy top branch. It was the only ornament Michael had contributed to the tree; he had George, the interior designer who'd done the rest of the place two years earlier, choose the ornaments and place them oh-so-perfectly on the six-foot blue spruce he'd set up in the parlor.

When Michael had called, George asked him, "What theme would you like?"

Michael had looked at the phone as if an alien were on the other end. "Theme?"

"For the tree," George said, using his tolerant voice, one Michael had grown accustomed to during the inn's renovation.

"Well, *uh*, festive?"

"*O-KAY!*" George said. "Festive! Yes! Good! We can do festive. But I was thinking more in terms of a color scheme or general, well, story line."

Michael was completely flummoxed. After a while, George said, "You know, like a blue-and-silver tree, or an all-Santa tree, or a snowy tree hung with snowflakes."

Finally Michael knew what to say. "Icicles. The theme should be icicles."

George had done a terrific job, covering the tree in hundreds of tiny white lights and small, glittering silver bows, before filling in the branches with thin white-and-silver glass icicles of all sizes and finishing with a judicious blizzard of silver tinsel. At first Michael had feared that the many small ornaments would diminish the beauty of his long, slender icicle, but in the end the whole tree seemed to be an elegant stage for the sleek form at the top—Filomena's gift.

And that's when the whole thing started. One of the Thanksgiving week-end guests—the father of the prodigy who'd whipped Michael at chess—took special note of the elegant piece at the top of the tree. First asking Michael if he minded, the man dragged a chair over to the tree and stood on it to get a closer look at the icicle.

"That's a spectacular ornament you have there," he said, putting the chair back. "I'm a bit of a collector, and I've never seen one of those old German-blown pieces in such excellent condition. Where're the rest of them?"

Michael felt a small jab between his ribs. "The rest of them?" he repeated with a polite smile.

"You know, the other eleven," the man said.

"That's the only one," Michael answered.

"Really?" said the man with an appraising look. "I'm surprised. That particular style was produced in sets of a dozen in the mid-nineteenth century. They were usually given as wedding gifts or when a child was born. Families who had little else would go without food to keep the set together. And when they were sold, it was usually only to collectors who were willing to buy all twelve. It was considered a travesty to separate the pieces. If the other eleven are as perfect as that one, I can't imagine the owner parting with any of them."

The man gave Michael a speculative look. "Where did you pick it up?"

"In Naples," Michael lied automatically. He'd never been to Naples. The last place in the world he wanted to see was the place of his father's birth.

"Well, you're fortunate to have it," said his guest. "Any chance you'd sell it?"

"None," Michael answered sharply, and then, recovering, he smiled his hedge-fund smile and poured the man a glass of Merlot. "Sentimental value, you know."

Stuck in the Boston traffic, Michael went over the whole scene in his mind yet again. He should have known. Even as a lonely seven-year-old, he should have known. No one, especially not Filomena, would have put the magnificent ornament into the hands of his brute of a father. Frank had stolen it. He must have taken it in revenge for Paolo's dismissing him. Or had his father taken it even before then? Had Paolo fired him because he suspected Frank had stolen from the family?

Had Michael always known the truth deep down and just forced it out of his mind? Had he been so desperate as a boy to hold onto something beautiful, something from the one family that had shown him such kindness?

Michael had no illusions about his father. Frank was an angry, bitter man who blamed the world for all his misfortunes, including the ones he'd brought on himself. But a thief? Michael had never let himself make that leap.

When Michael left home to move to Boston and try to earn his way through college, Frank had laughed derisively.

"Think you're too good for me, huh? College! You'll never make it," he'd said. "Just remember, the apple never falls far from the tree. You'll never be any better than me."

And that was at the heart of Michael's anguish. He'd been so driven to be unlike his father that he worried he'd become just a different version of Frank in the process. All the money he'd made, all the people who'd lost money while he looked the other way, people who'd played the same game but not quite as well, not quite as ruthlessly, and lost everything—was he a thief? Like Frank?

He thought he'd put so much distance between himself and his father, but maybe he'd never left that crummy apartment after all.

Michael had told himself he was going to Stonington to face the music on his father's behalf and restore his treasured ornament to the woman who had the other eleven, the eleven he'd never known about. He told himself he'd apologize, leave the ornament with her and walk away. But what he really wanted was for the woman he'd imagined as a mother to tell him what she couldn't possibly know: that he wasn't like his father.

§

As if Michael wasn't nervous enough, the woman who'd introduced herself as the executive director of Stonington Mills was watching him with eyes that could read souls. She'd answered Filomena's door and now the three of them sat in awkward silence in a small, immaculate, slightly outdated living room. Actually, he was the one who felt awkward; Filomena appeared perfectly comfortable. Michael had noted with absurd pleasure that she was still a beautiful woman.

The other woman was stunning. Though not more than five and a half feet tall, she was strikingly elegant; her dark skin was flawless, and her expression, though somewhat severe at the moment, seemed to conceal laughter. Michael had the impression that she possessed a highly developed sense of the ridiculous and that she might very well believe their presence in this room fell into that category. Her hair was long, pulled back from her face and tied in the back with a bright scarf from which a multitude of tiny braids cascaded down her back. Her eyes were the most disconcerting thing about her; large and wide-set, they seemed to drink in everything about him.

Coffee had been ready when he arrived, and they'd been making small talk for a few minutes when Filomena looked pointedly at the other woman. "I'm sorry to surprise you with Olivia, Michael. She's here to spy for my daughter."

Olivia raised her eyebrows and gracefully stood. "Not true, Meme, and you know it. I'll leave you to your visit now," she said, nodding slightly to Michael as she left.

Filomena went into the kitchen, returning with a tray of Christmas cookies. Michael stared. Every kind of cookie that had been in the box that long-ago Christmas was on the tray. He knew because he'd eaten every one of them himself, even after they'd grown stale. He blinked, unwilling to meet her eyes with the tears in his.

Finally she said, "Ah, so you remember." She smiled; all of the annoyance she'd displayed at Olivia's presence was gone, replaced by a kindness so simple and sincere that Michael felt he'd been transported back fifty years. Everything in him went slack, and he relaxed gratefully in the high-backed chair.

"Michael, how have you been? Tell me about yourself."

And he did—everything. He told her things he hadn't told anyone else, not even himself: about the break with his father; about how hard it had been to work his way through college; about his at first slow and then steady rise at his firm; about the increasingly powerful company he'd kept and how it never seemed to satisfy him; about how none of it—the money, the power, the people—was ever enough; and about the day he learned that an investor with the firm, who'd come to them on the strength of Michael's reputation, had killed himself when he lost millions. Michael was the only one from the firm to go to the man's funeral; he resigned that afternoon. Before leaving Boston, he set up an anonymous fund for the widow and her daughter.

When he finally stopped speaking, Filomena asked, "And there has been no one, no wife, no children, to share all this with you? This burden you carry?"

He stared at her. "You knew my father. You knew about my mother. How can you ask? With my background, can you imagine what I might have done to a wife? To kids?"

"You think you are your father's son." She made it a statement, and even while he was nodding, she shook her head. "You are not your father's son. You never were. Frank may have been the father of your body, but he is not your father in your heart."

"How can you know that? Look at what I've done. A man is dead because of me."

"The man died by his own hand. We should pray for him. He could not live with the decisions he'd made. Just like your father could not live with his decisions and is dead by his own hand; it only took him longer to do it with liquor and cigarettes. Neither died because of you. And you must understand this: Children cannot truly know their parents. Believe me,

I know. Many things in Frank's life worked against him, and he was not strong enough to keep hold of his faith, his joy. And so he became bitter, and that bitterness hurt you. But he was not a bad man."

"But he was! Do you know what he did?" Michael opened the oak box and drew the icicle out of its many layers of tissue. "This is what he did. He stole this from you all those years ago and gave it to me. He told me you sent it for me with the cookies. The one thing I thought he did out of caring for me, the one thing that made him human. But no; he stole it and he lied."

She looked at the icicle, brilliant even in the dimly lit room, and then calmly turned her gaze to Michael.

"He did not steal it. I gave it to him. For you. With the cookies. He might have sold it, never shown it to you at all, but he didn't. He did as I asked."

Michael searched her face for the lie but couldn't find it. He knew the signs; he'd made millions on knowing the signs. She was serene, untroubled. Gradually, he felt something warm open up in him, something light, hopeful, completely unfamiliar. She must have seen it because she gave him that luminous smile again.

"Michael. Have a cookie."

8

Olivia

livia was so tired of trying to cope with her own family's problems that dealing with Meme's family was almost a welcome diversion—almost. She'd hung up the phone yesterday after reporting on "the stranger" to a still-irate Catharine, thinking, *I probably should've warned her that Filomena will surely invite him to their family Christmas.*

Filomena's family dramas were practically comic relief compared to what Olivia was going through. Not that she'd let anyone know about it; it wasn't anyone's business, but it surely would be nice to have someone to share the burden. That's what she missed about not going home for Christmas this year: the chance to be with her friends and especially her father; people who would understand, people she could talk to. December was seventeen days old, and with each day that passed, she missed her home in Accra more profoundly.

Right before Thanksgiving, when she'd finally capitulated to her niece's and nephew's pleas that they not be forced to spend Christmas in Ghana this year, Olivia had never thought it would be this hard. Nor had she anticipated her sister and brother-in-law's outraged—and, eventually outrageous—response to the news that she and their children wouldn't be joining them for the holidays.

The last call had come from her sister minutes ago, right here in the office. Pamela never called her at home on family matters; she didn't want to risk her children's being there and weighing in. Pamela knew that it was her children—not Olivia—who wanted to stay in America this year. Olivia was also certain Pamela had called her at work to make it clear that she didn't think much of Olivia's career. The lack of respect was galling. Olivia had achieved greater success than any of her siblings, and yet they felt free to treat her as though she was still little Livy, the scrawny seventeen-year-old she'd been when she left Accra thirty-three years ago. Though she was older than her two sisters and her brother, they'd acted as though she was their personal servant back then, and things hadn't changed much since.

Her sister hadn't even bothered saying hello when Olivia picked up the phone. "Is it the money?" Pamela shrilled. "Because if it is the money, we will pay. At least we will pay for our children. You, we cannot pay for. Though why we should have to pay for any of you—when you earn so much at your big important job—I don't know."

Olivia held the phone a little away from her ear as Pamela's squawking filled the room. Olivia could give back as good as she got, and that was another reason Pamela always called her at the office: Pamela knew she couldn't, wouldn't, raise her voice at work. Olivia hadn't bothered to respond. She knew Pamela was just getting started. They'd had this conversation, or some version of it, five times since Thanksgiving when Olivia had called to tell her sister that she and the children would be staying in America for Christmas.

"Really, Sister, you should be ashamed," Pamela complained. "You steal our children away and now you keep them there. It is like you have kidnapped them! And do not remind me how I heard it from their own voices that they want to stay in Connecticut for Christmas. You have brainwashed them, kidnapped their minds as well!"

Grace, fourteen, and Charlie, sixteen, had both told their parents, in no uncertain terms—another thing Pamela blamed her for was the children's "disrespectful" talk—that they didn't want to leave their friends in New London for the holidays. This would be their third Christmas with Olivia and they'd dutifully returned home the past two years. This year, they just didn't want to go.

"And what am I to tell everyone, eh? What am I to tell our church when the children are not here for the Christmas and New Year's services? You know how important the New Year Sunday service is! You know! Everyone will be there. You know what people will say if they are not here: that they are now American, no longer African; that they think they are too good for Accra, for their family. I will be so embarrassed. What do I tell Pastor?"

Still, Olivia did not speak. There was no point in reminding Pamela that the large Christmas donation Olivia had sent Pastor for his church school would more than satisfy his pressing need to see Grace and Charlie—or Olivia, for that matter.

"And don't think I am sending presents. No! I am not sending presents! You can buy them all their presents! Their *American* presents!"

Olivia had already passed this dire threat on to Charlie and Grace, who had said, "Our present will be to stay here." Olivia knew they'd rehearsed this, and that they didn't mean it. They knew she'd make certain they would have some presents Christmas morning. So did Pamela.

"Are you listening, Livy? Do you hear me? You are ripping our family apart. You are too much the big career lady to come home. That is fine. That is your choice. But do you have to steal our children, too?"

Finally Pamela paused to take a breath, and Olivia said quietly, "Sister, I am hanging up now." Pamela's screech was cut off when Olivia gently put down the phone.

She sighed. She was too exhausted to be angry. That would come once she'd had enough sleep. Outside her office window, fluffy snowflakes were blowing over the harbor. Although it was not yet three o'clock, the sky was slate-colored, and it looked like dusk had already come. The wind off Long Island Sound whipped the waves, and everything, including Olivia's mood, was gray and turbulent.

She could have said so many things to her sister. She could have reminded Pamela how she and her husband Andrew had begged Olivia to sponsor the children in America, paying for their trip, their schooling, everything. Initially Olivia had refused, parroting the same arguments Pamela now flung at her. America would change the children, Olivia had warned. The schools were much more permissive. Charlie and Grace would lose touch with their culture. Church would not be so central to their lives. They would become more materialistic, more acquisitive. And anyway, she didn't have time to raise children, to watch over them and protect them, to help them adapt to the fast-paced, disconcerting world of a small American city. She'd been forty-six at the time and had just been appointed executive director of Stonington Mills. It was past time for her to be a mother.

But Pamela and Andrew had rejected all her arguments. They called Olivia selfish, saying that she'd always put herself and her career first. They reminded her that she'd not been able to keep a husband because of her single-mindedness, and for that very reason she wouldn't give her niece and nephew the opportunities that America offered. How could she deny the children this?

Then, after insulting and battering her for days on end, they'd resorted to flattery. "Oh, Sister," Pamela wheedled, "you have always been the strong one. Yes, always! Everyone here is so proud of you. Oh yes! All through Accra, they still talk, you know: how smart Livy is, how much she's achieved, her big job in America, how proud we must be of our big sister. And the old ones? The aunties? They go on and on about you, how you took over when our mother died, how you worked and went to school and cared for us. You raised the three of us! And now *you* are an Auntie! Surely you will do the same for my children."

The truth was that at the time, Grace and Charlie hardly knew her. When she'd finally given in and they arrived, they were strangers to her, and she to them. It had only been over the four years before they came that she'd been able to visit Accra regularly, once a year for the holidays. Before that, she'd been too busy, first working and then pursuing her career, never daring to set a foot wrong, never wanting to ask for time off or take it even when she was in a position to do so. On her visits, she spent more time with old friends and teachers than with her siblings, whose demands on her seemed to increase with every phone call and visit home.

And with her father. She always spent as much time as she could with Daddy. He never made demands of her. He'd gone into a deep depression when her mother died so very young, one from which he'd never fully recovered. He had been principal of Accra's largest elementary school, and his colleagues could do just so much when he refused to return to work. Both the teachers and the students loved him, but after a while all they could do was mourn the bright, brilliant man they'd lost.

Olivia had never mourned him. She'd simply taken care of him—and her three siblings. She'd had help from both her aunties, her father's sisters, who were sharply ashamed of their brother's breakdown. After haranguing him for months, while he lay in bed with his arm stretched over the empty space where his wife had slept as if he were still holding on to her, his sisters simply gave up on him. He didn't care. He'd taken to turning his face to the wall whenever they entered the room.

Olivia never resented her father's depression, his "weakness," as his sisters called it, shaking their heads in disgust. She was old enough when her mother Celia died to understand, at least on some level, the love between her parents. It was as if each had certain parts that the other didn't. Together they had been complete; neither would be whole without the other.

During that first year after her mother died, only Olivia could bear to spend time with Daddy. His other children were at first afraid and then resentful. They couldn't bring themselves to blame their mother for dying, so they blamed their father for abandoning them. It was fourteen-year-old Olivia who cooked what used to be his favorite dish, plantains, and then coaxed the food into him. She didn't try to get him to talk or force him back to work; she tried to get him to stay alive.

And she succeeded. After a little more than a year, her father had taken a job as a janitor in the school where he'd been principal. The administration paid him twice what a janitor would earn, for which Olivia alone was grateful—her father didn't seem to care how much he was paid. Still, it was less than half of what he'd earned as principal, and so Olivia took in washing from her better-off neighbors. She pretended not to hear them cluck about how Celia would turn in her grave at the family's degradation. Olivia knew that her mother wouldn't turn in her grave; she would marvel that her husband, bereft of spine and brain, could work at all.

The students were gentle with him when he returned and didn't greet them laughing every morning in a suit and tie or swing the little ones up into the air. But children somehow understand such things, and they'd speak softly to him and bring him small gifts. A shiny rock. A piece of green sea glass from Accra's shore. A small bamboo carving of a bird. These he kept in his room at home as if they were the greatest treasures he'd ever received.

In the fourth year after her mother's death, Olivia's father arranged for an old college friend in Connecticut to become Olivia's American sponsor. The man and his wife took Olivia into their home in Hartford's West End and enrolled her at St. Joseph's College.

No one in Accra could figure out how her father had managed such a feat. Everyone was astounded at what this silent half-man had done. But not Olivia; she knew what had happened. Her father had remembered something important—he still had a heart.

In the years between her mother's death and her father's setting her free, Olivia had become the spine and the brain of the family. Within a year, her sisters and brother—and, for that matter, her aunts, uncles, and cousins—had come to depend on her as they'd depended on her mother. She'd become as efficient, hardworking, and as brusque sometimes as Celia had been. How else to get everything done? How else to hold everything together?

If either of her grandmothers had been alive, the full burden of raising the children, helping her father, and keeping the house together wouldn't have fallen on Olivia. But she had never known her grandmother, just as her own children—if she'd had any—would never have known Celia.

That was another reason her family treated her so poorly: She had no children. *As if I'd had time,* Olivia reflected, watching the snow drift down over the harbor and making a mental note to check on whether the maintenance staff had started salting and shoveling the paths.

Children—the single most important objective of every real woman, according to her family. Her mother had managed to have four. But Olivia had never wanted to have children. She was happy to let everyone assume that she'd simply been too busy—first getting her LPN accreditation, then working, then getting her RN, then working, then getting her MBA, then working—to have children. The truth was that by the time she left Accra after four years of caring for her demanding siblings, she'd had enough of children for a lifetime. She let her family believe that she'd lost her fiancé to her ambition, that he'd thrown her over for, according to her sisters and her aunties, "a traditional woman."

"You are losing a good man, an *African* man, because you are too much the 'career lady,'" Pamela had scolded. The fact that James was from Sierra Leone—"a neighbor!" one auntie had squealed—was all anyone in her family needed to know.

Pamela had been relentless. "How many good West African men do you think you will meet, Sister? With your studies, and your job, and your nose in a book always? Do you think they will line up outside your dingy little apartment—all these good West African men—and say, 'Oh please, Miss Olivia, let us vie for your favors. It is our objective in life to follow you around as you pursue your precious career. We will be happy to stay home with our children, to do without cooking and a clean house, to take care of your every need while you ignore us.' Are you waiting for those men, Sister? Because let me tell you, if you are, your whole life will be consumed in waiting."

God forbid they ever learn the truth: that she and James had loved each other deeply right up until the moment they parted in sorrow. But it hadn't been Olivia's ambition that drove them apart; they'd disagreed only on one thing: whether to have children.

Though he'd been in America for longer than Olivia and, by all appearances, was as progressive as any well-educated American man, James had quietly retained the Sierra Leonean values his parents had instilled in him. He could accept a wife with a career; indeed, he'd been proud of her education and her work. He could accept a wife who knew as much as he did about the world and could hold her own in any discussion. What he couldn't accept was the idea that they would never have children; that his name, his line, would not continue; that they would never be, as he put it with puzzled dismay, "a family."

Yet Olivia was adamant. She believed that as soon as an African woman—any woman—had children, all those other things would fall by the wayside. Having raised her mother's children, she would not have another woman raise hers, and so all the things that she'd soared above and beyond would fall to her again: the endless cooking and cleaning; the day-by-day, minute-by-minute, care of children and the constant worry over their health, their behavior. Her work, all that she'd studied and strived for, would be postponed, maybe for decades. Her independence would evaporate. James promised repeatedly that he would share equally in the responsibilities, but Olivia knew it would never be so. Not with an African man. Probably not with any man.

She remembered one discussion, not their final discussion, but it might as well have been. He'd just gone through his usual plea: He didn't want a traditional marriage or family; he'd be an equal partner once the children came.

Determined to make him see the truth, she said, "What does that mean, 'equal partner'?"

He looked at her blankly, and she pressed on. "Does it mean that you will ask your employer for leave to care for the child so that I can go back to work? Does it mean that you will stay home as often as I do when the children are sick and can't go to school? Will you change as many diapers as I will change? Will you cook as many meals as I will cook? Will you clean half the house every week?"

His eyes had grown rounder with every question, and he couldn't hide his first response: disbelief that she would ask such things of him. He finally realized what she already knew: He was the man, and the man did not do those things. Not in Africa, and from what Olivia had seen in the twenty years since that discussion, not often in America. By then, they'd been together for nearly two years; Olivia was almost thirty and James thirty-one, and they feared facing the still disconcerting world of America without each other. So they tried to stay together. But the parting had already begun that day, and after seven painful months, James took a job in Washington as much to get away from Olivia as to advance his career.

Pamela and the rest of her family had never let her forget it. Why, *why*, had she even told them about James in the first place? Why hadn't she hidden the engagement as she'd hidden so many things once she'd come to America? It would have been so easy. But, no, she was too proud of herself, too anxious to make sure everyone in Accra knew of her success, knew that she was an American woman who could "have it all."

Her father never mentioned James, mourning silently as he knew Olivia mourned. But her sister never missed a chance to remind Olivia of what she'd lost. So when Pamela first learned that Grace and Charlie wanted to stay in Connecticut for Christmas, she resorted to the most damaging weapon she had. After ranting first at Olivia and then at her children (who rolled their eyes as their mother raved on, so much like American teenagers that Olivia was relieved Pamela couldn't see them), she demanded to speak to Olivia again.

"I know why you are doing this, Sister," Pamela said. "Oh yes, I know. It is because you lost your chance to have children, to have a husband. Have I told you that we hear of James all the time these days?"

Olivia inhaled sharply and Pamela, hearing it, pounced. "Oh yes, Livy, he is quite the big man now here in Accra. Minister of Education! Imagine! We see him often in the paper with his pretty wife and children. They are all excellent children. Ghanaian children."

Pain stabbed Olivia; Pamela had been saving this news for a special occasion. Olivia managed to end the conversation calmly, but not before Pamela delivered her parting shot: "You should change your mind, Sister, and bring our children home for Christmas and the New Year. It will break our Daddy's heart not to have his oldest grandchildren with him."

Again and again in the calls that had come from Accra since that day, the same threat had been made: "Think what it will do to our Daddy!" The irony was that Olivia knew that her Daddy would not miss Grace and Charlie all that much. His other grandchildren would be quite enough excitement for him, not to mention his nieces and nephews and their children. Olivia knew very well whom her father would miss so deeply. It was her face that he longed to hold gently in his two hands, her voice that he wanted to hear. Her father would be seventy-seven in February, and this would be the first Christmas in eight years that she wouldn't be with him.

What seemed most unfair to Olivia was that the only reason she wasn't making the trip was that Grace and Charlie wanted an American Christmas. In this, Pamela had hit the mark: Her children were now more American than African. What had she expected? Had she really thought that the children wouldn't be influenced by the culture, the wealth, the freedom from tradition? That they would return happily to Accra year after year and after college obediently go back to marry Ghanaians and raise African children?

Olivia wanted to see her father and how her sisters and brother were treating him. She worried that they largely ignored him, that they didn't treat him with the respect a father deserved. She always used these annual Christmas trips to lavish attention on him, to fill his rooms with Christmas presents, to be sure that he had all he needed.

Olivia stared darkly at the phone for a moment and then decided to get out of her office. She could check on the maintenance staff and the snow and then leave. She had errands to run anyway. Then, at least when Pamela called back—and Olivia knew she *would* call back, if for no other reason than to berate Olivia for hanging up on her—she wouldn't be there.

She'd just finished closing her briefcase when her office door flew open and Evie burst in, her eyes a little wild, her mouth opening in preparation for whatever crisis had brought her here. Olivia sighed softly; she wouldn't be leaving early after all. Something in her face caught Evie up short. Her mouth snapped shut, and she stared uncertainly at Olivia.

"I know you were raised well enough to grasp the concept of knocking on a closed door," Olivia said. "I know you were."

Evie flipped one hand into the air dismissively as if to say, "Oh, is that all that's bothering you?" The determination flooded back into her face, and, squaring her shoulders, she fixed her eyes on Olivia.

"I have to know. Is my Nana dying?"

Olivia gazed out the window where the snow was now hardly visible in the heavy dusk. Headlights from the truck plowing the parking lot swept the courtyard outside her office, revealing a moving beam of whirling flakes and suddenly illuminating the Christmas Glass hanging in her office window. The wise man's green-and-gold robe flashed in the headlights, and Olivia wished that she could know what he knew.

"Evelyn. Close the door and sit down."

§

An hour later Olivia was sitting in Filomena's ancient rocking chair, sipping hot chocolate and trying to resist a second anise cookie. Her smart red winter coat was thrown over another chair and her briefcase abandoned on the rug by the door. She'd already kicked her shoes off and put her feet up on a warm hassock, and she decided not to reprimand her old friend for keeping the thermostat set so high. For once Olivia wouldn't worry about the cost of fuel and Stonington Mills' end-of-year balance sheet. After all, she doubted any of her trustees were chilly on this snowy night.

It had not always been this way with the two women, this sense of trust and comfort. Twelve years ago when Olivia had first walked into Filomena's home to work as a live-in nurse while Filomena recovered from a hip replacement, things between them were anything but comfortable. Of course, that had had a lot to do with Filomena's daughters. Maria hadn't yet moved to

California then, and she and Catharine paced the house, circling each other like two lion cubs who would tear each other to shreds if they were not so terrified of their roaring mother.

Filomena had been furious with them, first because they'd already begun shredding the fabric that had made them twins, and second—and most important from Olivia's perspective—because neither had volunteered to care for their mother during the long convalescence. For a house full of normally voluble women, the silence screamed. Catharine wouldn't speak to Maria, who had already set her heart on Daniel; Maria wouldn't speak to Catharine because Catharine wouldn't speak to her; and Filomena would speak to no one—including, at that point, Olivia. That first day, Olivia had thought she should quit on the spot.

But she couldn't. The job perfectly matched her needs at the time. She had four months before she would begin her MBA at the University of Connecticut, and she needed the money and a place to stay. Though she'd planned to work out the time in her nursing job at New London's Lawrence & Memorial Hospital, when a friend had told her the sisters were looking for a live-in nurse to care for their mother, Olivia had applied. Her lease on the small apartment just down Pequot Avenue from Filomena's house was about to end, and she liked the idea of putting the rent money toward her degree. So she was interviewed by both Catharine and Maria—separately, of course—and negotiated room and board as part of her fee for the four months Filomena would require help. In the end, she stayed another two years, living with Filomena while she pursued her degree.

But on that first day, there was nothing but silence, and Olivia had never experienced a silence so charged with anger and betrayal. Gradually Filomena warmed up to her, and Olivia learned about the problem between the twins. Olivia joined Filomena's oldest friend Sarah as the only people who knew how deeply Filomena doubted herself.

Olivia gazed at her old friend, relaxing on the sofa in a way she never would if her daughters were present—they always saw the ramrod straight spine, the head perched high on the neck—and smiled.

"Why do you have that look?" Filomena asked suspiciously.

"I was just thinking how much the same all families are. Not in looks or race or religion, but in how we act, how we treat each other, how we love—and how much damage we do in spite of the love."

The older woman sighed. "You think I've made a mistake trying to force Catharine and Maria to come here for Christmas."

"I don't know," Olivia answered. "I think you've set more in motion than you intended. They're all coming, right? Last I heard, Maria would not come without Daniel, and Mark and Serena have somehow been convinced to come and stay with Evie, with their kids all packed into that apartment because Tom will be out on patrol. Do you have any idea of what might happen when they all get here?"

Slowly shaking her head with what only Olivia would recognize as trepidation, Filomena said, "There's more. I got so nervous, I begged Sarah to come. And then, yesterday . . ."

"Yesterday, you invited that poor man Michael," Olivia finished for her, laughing.

Filomena tried to look regretful, but Olivia knew it was a ruse. Nervous she might well be, but Filomena liked nothing better than having her way, even if it meant chaos. Now she asked Olivia, "What about you and the children? You shouldn't spend Christmas alone, you know."

Shaking her head, Olivia raised her eyebrows in mock outrage, and Filomena responded with what Olivia had come to think of as her signature look. She shrugged elaborately, flipping her hands into the air as if to say, "What can I do? I can't help the way I am."

"You and my sister ought to get together. Two brilliant manipulators," Olivia said wryly, and then told Filomena about Pamela's latest phone call.

Filomena observed her silently for a time and then said, "But it's your father you're really worried about."

"He is all alone there."

"He has your sisters and brother, their children, your aunts." Filomena pointed out.

"Yes, but what is he to them?" Olivia answered swiftly, the words crowding themselves. "A useless old man, who might as well have died thirty-five years ago as far as they're concerned. Nathaniel and Victoria hardly even remember him, how he used to be, and Pamela is too full of her own problems to care. And their children? All they know of him is what their parents think."

"Then go home."

Olivia looked miserable. "I can't just go home now. It's too late. There are no flights in time for Christmas. Do you know what we West Africans call Air Ghana? *Air Perhaps!*

"It's too late for Christmas, but not for his birthday," Filomena said shrewdly. "Valentine's Day, isn't that what you told me? Don't your niece and nephew have a school vacation around that time?"

Olivia gazed at her, wondering how after all these years this old woman could still surprise her. Against all odds, Olivia believed Filomena was actually growing sharper as she got older. While other older widows in Olivia's care were lucky to be able to recognize family members, Filomena was scheming not only to bring her own family together but Olivia's as well.

And the fact was that she'd come up with a perfect solution: Olivia could be with her father in less than two months, and the knowledge of that alone would get them both through Christmas. Olivia couldn't keep the spark of excitement out of her eyes.

"So," she said, deciding to change the subject and see what it produced, "Evie was in to see me today, just before I came over here. She wanted to know if you are dying."

Filomena's eyes flamed and then narrowed. "And?" she barked, sitting up a little straighter. "What did you tell her?"

Olivia let her wait a moment. "I told her that we're all dying."

§

Shortly before midnight, after the lights in Charlie's and Grace's rooms had gone out, Olivia climbed up to the third floor of her house. She'd loved everything about the house from the moment she moved in a little over eight years ago. Everything in it was hers, either carried here from her past or more recently acquired with care and patience. Everything, from the rose-color paint of the tiny first-floor guest bathroom to the sleek office where she now stood, had been carefully selected and saved for. This was her favorite room. It was so private, the only room on the narrow third floor, its sliding glass door opening onto a small porch. She stepped out into the freezing night.

She was high enough to have a sweeping view of Long Island Sound, the waves beating a steady pulse on the shore. The snow had stopped shortly after ten, and the skies had cleared so rapidly it seemed miraculous. It was too late for any of the ferries, lit up like floating Christmas trees, to pass, and her sense of solitude was complete. With the moon already behind her, she could see a multitude of brilliant stars in the southeastern sky.

"My God and Father," she whispered, thinking of what she was about to do. "I leave everything in Your kind care."

Then she went in and picked up the phone. It would be around dawn in Accra, but her father would be awake. Like her, he didn't sleep well or often. She dialed and then listened to the series of clicks. Finally, he picked up the phone.

"Yes? This is Oliver here."

She could just see him, sitting on the bed, his bare feet flat on the floor, holding the phone expectantly, carefully, to his ear, an exotic instrument he didn't often use, fumbling with his heavy, black-framed glasses as though he needed them to hear.

"Daddy. It's me!"

"Daughter!"

And with that brimming exclamation, all the pleasure and surprise and joy he poured into that one word, Olivia's tears finally started to flow.

"Daddy, I want to come home. For your birthday."

There was a long pause, but Olivia knew they hadn't lost the connection. She waited.

"*Daughter!*"

9

Louis

Most people would think it was ridiculous, trying to get counseling over the phone. But Evie didn't care. Louis, or Padre Lou, as she and Tom and other Navy families called the Key West minister, understood what she was going through. No one here in Connecticut really knew her anymore, and they certainly didn't know Tom and Jack, not the way Padre Lou did. No one knew their secrets, the challenges to their life together.

When Evie had wanted to go to counseling in Key West, Tom immediately rejected the possibility of a naval base counselor. He even refused to see the chaplain. It was only when Evie suggested Padre Lou, whom they'd occasionally heard preach at his storefront church on White Street, that Tom reluctantly agreed. They visited Lou intermittently for over a year,

Evie more often than Tom, but he helped them both. There was something accessible about the easygoing Haitian minister, who'd probably been through more himself than everyone in her family put together, no matter how much they magnified their woes and worries.

She'd thought about waiting to call Padre Lou until Tom boarded his sub in two days for the six-month patrol. But if she waited, Tom would leave with this chasm between them. He would leave with the memory of her anger and sarcasm, her pain and disappointment. He would leave wondering, just as she was, how their relationship would survive—not just for six months, but forever.

Evie wouldn't wait. She couldn't risk it. She prayed that Lou would come up with something, anything, that would make this leave-taking better, easier, more loving. She knew, at least, that he would listen. All she had to do was call.

§

He shouldn't even be here, standing outside his office. Wednesdays were Louis's day off. Theoretically, that is; it never quite seemed to turn out that way. "What do you expect when you give everyone and his brother your cell-phone number?" chided Marguerite, his secretary/assistant and world-class scold, as often as he gave her the chance. "Do you expect peace and quiet? Do you expect them to leave you alone to your meditation and your Bible studies?"

Ah, what would he do without Marguerite? The truth was—and they both knew it—he couldn't get along without her. He was too disorganized, too inattentive to his own welfare, too "unwise in the ways of the world," as she frequently reminded him; too alone.

And how would she cope without him? Probably very well, thank you. When he bought the vacant three-story building on White Street eight years ago, she'd been the previous owner's property manager. She agreed to stay on at his request, reluctantly at first, when he told her of his plans to convert the first two floors into a small church and headquarters for his ministry while he would live in the tiny studio on the third floor. She'd given him a long, dubious look, finally asking in the Jamaican accent that reminded him of molasses, "Church for who?"

"For everyone," he'd replied without thinking. And that was exactly what he wanted to do. He wanted to run an open-hearted ministry that would welcome everyone—from the homeless, who came to Key West for the warmth, odd jobs and restaurant dumpsters filled with food, to the natives, who called themselves Conchs, to the tourists and wealthy "snowbirds," to the residents of Key West's Bahama Village, who came from everywhere in the Caribbean to work in the restaurants, boutiques, and homes of the wealthier islanders. He also wanted to serve the Navy families. His adoptive father had been Navy, and Louis knew enough about that insular world to realize a lot of base-dwellers—particularly the spouses and children—needed help.

He'd told all of this to Marguerite on a May afternoon more than eight years ago, standing on this very sidewalk, his words drenched with enthusiasm. Her skepticism only grew. "What you gonna call this 'open-hearted' church, then, Preacher? The Love Boat?" she asked, her eyes widening in challenge.

He laughed. "Maybe I will! Is that your recommendation, ma'am?"

"Don't you call me *ma'am*! I'm no older than you—maybe a bit younger by the looks of you," she snapped back, the first of countless reprimands, but before he could swallow his fresh laughter fast enough to apologize, she gestured at the run-down building with its peeling paint and broken curb and said, "Well, from what you say, you should probably call this elegant church of yours The Church of Good News, Hope, and Tolerance for All Souls."

"Perfect!" he exclaimed sincerely, startling her into a look of surprise and causing her to shake her head over such a naive, lost cause. Right then and there, she might have high-tailed it for safer ground—after all, she had a reputation as one of the best managers on the island and had clients who could pay much more than Louis—if it hadn't started to rain. And not just rain, but rain like it rains only in the tropics. Sheets of warm, driving water poured down as if a giant faucet had just been turned on full blast directly overhead.

Marguerite ducked into the building, muttering darkly, but when she turned to continue haranguing him, he was still outside. Louis loved the rain. He'd loved it as a child in Jeremie in the mountainous northwest of Haiti where he'd been born; he'd loved it in Miami, where he'd spent the best part of his childhood being shuttled back and forth to hospitals by Isabella, his adoptive mother; and he loved it in Key West, where he now stood, his arms and face raised to the sky like he was taking a shower with all his clothes on. It was something he'd first done nearly forty years ago as a small boy in Haiti, his mother laughing at him and shaking her head. "Ti Louis, child, you don't know enough to come out of that rain!"

Suddenly he felt himself being yanked inside the storefront where he faced a sputtering Marguerite. Louis was a slight man in body though not in spirit, and Marguerite managed to appear statuesque at about five and a half feet as she glowered at him.

"What's your problem, Preacher? Haven't you enough sense to come in out of the rain? You want to catch your death of cold? Pneumonia, maybe?"

He started to protest that the rain and the temperature were much too warm for him to catch a chill, but she kept talking over him. "People see you out there like that, dancing in the pouring rain, and the only souls you'll get in this fool church are the loony birds. They'll think one of their very own has come home to roost."

She paused until he dared open his mouth and then overrode him again, "And I think they'd be right!"

He didn't even try to reply. But he couldn't keep the grin out of his eyes, and she folded her arms and gave him a lengthy appraising look. In that long moment, a good part of Louis's future was sealed, and his ministry was ensured success.

Marguerite sighed and shook her head. "You're nothing but a child yourself, aren't you? You may be a good preacher—you look to be crazy enough
to do anything from a pulpit—but you're like a babe when it comes to the
real world. You know what it is to balance a checkbook, live on a budget?
No, I didn't think so. Well, you can't do this without me, so let's get to it."

And from that moment on, Marguerite had been his right-hand woman.
It was she who ran The Church of Good News, Hope, and Tolerance for All
Souls, immediately shortening the name to The Church of Good News, telling him that if it took longer to say the name than to attend a service, no
one would ever show up. There would have been no church without her,
because she was not far wrong about Louis and his lack of worldly wisdom.
He'd inherited what, to him at least, was a fortune from his adoptive parents and used some of it to buy the building in which they stood dripping
from the downpour. Of course, the Realtor, lawyers, insurers, and absentee
landlord he'd bought it from were thrilled with Louis. He paid full price,
asking no questions. It wasn't that he couldn't be clever—it was that he
chose not to be, and in this choice, Marguerite was the perfect enabler.

Because if Louis had been a dream-come-true for those he did business
with, Marguerite was their worst nightmare. She couldn't do anything to
get back his original investment, but she guarded what he had left like a
tigress. She dismissed the contractors he'd talked to about working on the
building, and when he timidly observed that he had a "gentleman's agreement" with them, she said coolly, "Lucky for you I'm not a gentleman."

She told him that there were good workers in Bahama Village who could do the job for a third of the amount and in half the time. "Preacher, that crew you hired was gonna rip you off, and what's more, as soon as they got a better offer, they'd have left your job half-done and moved on. You got to use your head when you deal with people. And because your head is in the clouds with the angels, we're using *my* head. Thank the Lord."

For eight years, Louis had gratefully kept his head in the clouds with the angels. While Marguerite took care of the administrative side of his ministry, he held services, preached, counseled, baptized, prayed, guided people into rehab services, visited the sick, and comforted the poor souls on the island prison in the middle of the bay. While she labored in his office, kept his accounts, reigned over his schedule, and even tidied up, his reputation as a powerful and Godly minister had grown. And just as he'd dreamed, those he ministered to ranged from a wealthy Canadian couple who rented a suite at the Hilton for six months every year to Jerry, a homeless man who got around on his bicycle and made money collecting bottles. He also had a considerable following among the Navy enlisted men and women, many of whom didn't want to expose their problems to officers, even if they were counselors or chaplains.

One day, about a year after he and Marguerite had first met, Louis strode out of his office to where she sat at her desk, staring at a computer screen full of calculations, and asked her anxiously, as if something terrible had just occurred to him, "Marguerite, do I pay you enough?"

She looked up briefly, noted his uncharacteristically furrowed brow, raised a corner of her mouth in what counted for a smile, and then rolled her eyes and went back to her work. He'd taken this as a yes.

§

Now he took the stack of messages she'd just handed him, while she complained once more that he'd never get any time to himself if he kept showing up on his one day off. He grinned at her, nodding in agreement, and retired to his office, leaving the door ajar. He liked to know she was there, and the open door made it easier for her to chastise him.

Louis knew that a good number of people expected that he and Marguerite would marry. One man in his congregation had been bold enough to insinuate that they were as good as married anyway, and Louis might as well "get some sweet with the vinegar" Marguerite dished out. The man had subsided into a shamefaced silence at Louis' wordless glare. Eventually he'd stopped coming to church at all, and Louis had prayed for forgiveness at his pleasure in the man's absence.

Louis knew he and Marguerite would never marry. She was his taskmaster, his protector, his confidante, his best friend, his only real critic, but she would never be his wife. The simple truth, as Louis knew it, was that Marguerite was a beautiful, sensual woman, and beautiful, sensual women just didn't see him as husband material.

Indeed, he'd come to be at peace with the fact that women in general didn't see him as husband material. He was happy to settle for whatever it was that he and Marguerite had; it was so much more than he could have hoped for.

At forty-four, Louis was hardly even conscious any more of his appearance, but he'd spent enough time at it as a youngster and, if he were being truthful, a young man feeling excruciatingly aware of how he looked. *At least it's gotten better,* he thought with a smile on the rare occasions when he still slipped, briefly, into self-pity.

He'd been born with a cleft palate, which was too nice and polite a phrase, he'd always thought, for the mess that was his first face. It had looked like someone had taken puzzle pieces and forced them together, jamming pieces into places where they didn't belong. The bones in his right leg hadn't been formed properly either, though that problem didn't become evident until he was a toddler.

His mother, Julia, was seventeen when he was born and had already lost one infant. She was determined to keep Louis alive. She named him immediately, ignoring the murmurs of others in the village who believed the child would die before he could earn his name. Pierre, his father, a charcoal maker who barely acknowledged his mother, had no interest in a son who wouldn't grow up to help him work in the charcoal pits.

Julia would not be dissuaded. A fiery girl, she refused to speak to anyone who wouldn't call her baby by name, and the words she had for those who turned away from him were not words Padre Lou would repeat. Because he could not fit his deformed mouth to her breast, she collected the milk in a small bowl and put it, drop by drop, into the hole in his twisted little face. She held him constantly, carrying him with her wherever she went. She refused to work any longer with Pierre, saying that the baby needed her.

But Julia didn't leave it at that. She told Pierre that he must support her and the baby until she could find a better job. Not that there was any prospect of finding a better job in Jeremie; Pierre was lucky to have the miserable job he had, and he told Julia that she had to keep working in the pits if she wanted to feed herself and the boy.

People around Jeremie still gossip about what Julia did to make him contribute enough to keep her and the child alive. Louis, knowing his mother, always believed that she'd threatened to wait until Pierre was drunk and than make him look worse than the son he scorned; if there was one thing Pierre was proud of, it was his handsome face. Whatever she said to Pierre, he gave her a portion of his meager pay until he fled to Port-au-Prince one night shortly after Louis's fifth birthday.

By then, Julia was something of a legend in Jeremie. Not only had she kept her son alive against all odds and forced Pierre to support her; she'd also demanded that Louis be treated like any other child. She was fiercely protective of him, and even after his leg showed itself to be a match to his poor face, she insisted that he be included in anything the other village children were doing.

Louis only realized much later, as a young man, that it was not so much her aggressive defense of him that made others accept him as her deep and visible love for him. The people of Jeremie came to care about Louis because they could not despise a child so wholly loved by his mother. Whatever beauty, intelligence, and sweetness Julia saw in him, she made others see it in the mirror of her eyes. And so when Louis himself looked into those shining eyes, he saw not a small monster with a misshapen face and leg, but a beloved son.

Yet Julia, whose faith in Louis was surpassed only by her faith in God, was not naive. She knew that her son would need more than a few coins from his father and the affection of impoverished neighbors to survive. She prayed constantly for Louis. She didn't pray that he would wake up one morning with a perfect face or leg. or even for an end to his pain. What she prayed for every day from the day of his birth was that God would take her little son into His loving hands. And one day, a year after Pierre deserted them, He did.

Louis was nearly seven when the missionaries came from the Diocese of Miami, a place most people in Jeremie could hardly imagine, much less hope to see. What they knew of it came in letters from the few villagers who had made it to a place called Little Haiti. The people of Jeremie had no idea whether Little Haiti was a village, a country, or an island. They only knew from the letters, dictated to a priest in Little Haiti and read to them by their own priest, that it was in Miami, and that the Haitians who ended up there had food every day, found work that had nothing to do with charcoal, and lived in houses. It sounded like paradise to most people in Jeremie; for Julia, it was an idea of a very particular paradise.

Julia imagined that Miami was the answer for her son. She believed that once there, he would receive medical care to straighten his leg and repair his face.

She wouldn't be around forever to protect him; she'd had to return to charcoal-making after Pierre left them. At the end of the day, she was often covered with soot. And she coughed. Barely twenty-five and frequently weakened by hunger, at times she couldn't even catch her breath.

When Julia heard that church people from Miami would be spending a week in Jeremie, she knew God had provided her this opportunity. So when they showed up, she didn't hang back shyly, awed at their sleek bodies, white skin, and fresh new clothes. She observed the group long enough to note their mannerisms and then pushed forward, smiling widely and putting her hand out to be shaken as she'd seen them do. Doubting they would understand her Creole, she smiled and bowed and gestured and kept her words to a minimum. She went down the line of people, shaking hands and nodding until she finally came to a man and woman who met her gaze and held it.

Julia paused uncertainly. The others had shaken her hand and then looked away. But this woman's face was such a mixture of compassion and curiosity that Julia forgot herself and began pouring out her story in a stream of Creole. By the time she realized her mistake and abruptly stopped talking, she saw understanding in the woman's eyes. In French, the woman introduced herself as Isabella and her husband as Jim. She asked Julia to continue.

For a moment, Julia was speechless at such a blessing. But only for a moment. She told the woman all about Louis, what a wonderful, clever boy he was. She ignored the grumbling of the villagers behind her, who knew what she was leaving out, and the uncomfortable glances of the other Miami visitors. The Miami priest, the only black man in the mission group, was supposed to be their translator, but he remained quiet while Julia talked.

When Julia finally stopped, Isabella asked, "Where is your son?"

And this was the moment that Julia had been both dreading and yearning for. She searched Isabella's face again, and again saw only interest and concern. Would that be enough? Was she simply being kind? Was there enough kindness in her to see Louis without turning away? Would she see his beauty?

Seeing the anxiety in Julia's face, Isabella whispered, "Don't worry. Show me."

§

For as long as she lived, Julia claimed that at that moment she had seen Louis' next mother, the angel she'd been waiting for, in Isabella. And Julia didn't just tell her son that she *thought* Isabella was an angel, or that Isabella *looked* like an angel. No, she insisted that Isabella *was* an angel, that she knew the first time she looked into Isabella's face that she was an angel sent from God. Louis never figured out whether his mother really believed it, or whether she had said it at first to ingratiate herself with Isabella and Jim and later simply stuck with her story.

Either way, Louis remembered, staring out his office window at the usual slow commerce of White Street, Isabella did indeed become their angel. But there were two sides to the story, and by the time Louis was a young man, he'd long since realized that Julia had been just what Isabella was looking for as well. They had used each other (in the best possible way, Louis reassured himself frequently) and both had gotten what they wanted—sort of.

Isabella and Jim had come on the trip not so much to gauge the poverty of Jeremie, but to lift the burden of the region by the weight of one small body—Louis's, as it turned out. They wanted a child.

Jim was forty-eight, Isabella, forty-four, and in many ways they had the perfect romance. They'd met at the end of World War II when Jim was stationed in France and Isabella worked at a cafe, having been forced to suspend her studies by the war. She returned to America with Jim when his tour was over. Isabella was beautiful—*yes*, Louis smiled to himself, *like an angel*—and she used to tell Louis, "I married your father because he was the only soldier who didn't try to pick me up!" Jim, still the quiet stoic he must have been in that village near Nice, would smile at this and raise one eyebrow in one of the expressions Louis had come to love. His adoptive father communicated volumes, from discipline to love, by how he arranged his features, and this half-amused, half-quizzical look was carefully reserved for his wife and son. Perhaps that's why Louis had loved it so much. Jim used to give him the same look when he carried Louis back and forth from hospital to clinic to doctors' offices. Louis would reach one thin hand up to Jim's comically quirked eyebrow as if to catch the look.

Jim and Isabella had books filled with photos. Once they brought Louis back to Key West, he spent hours with the photo albums, mesmerized by the pictures that Isabella had to assure him again and again were of actual people and events. Through this photographic history, he learned about the couple who became his parents, and Isabella explained every single picture to him.

Had Julia imagined, when she was dreaming of a perfect future for Louis, what that future would cost her? Louis had come to believe that his mother had known exactly what she was doing and was absolutely willing to pay the price. She'd known when she signed the papers allowing the extensive surgery that Jim and Isabella would pay for, and she'd known when she later signed the adoption forms. She'd known she would lose him. She knew it from the moment she met Isabella's steady gaze.

At least that's what Louis told himself when he began to realize what his mother had given up; he had to do something to dissipate the sorrow and guilt that came with understanding.

Julia had helped him judge himself innocent. On the trips Jim arranged for him to be with his mother, Julia was always spirited and full of praise for Jim and Isabella.

"Do you call her *Maman*?" Julia would demand. "You must, Louis, for she is your *Maman* now, the one who will help you and make you well and send you into the world a man! She has waited many years to be called *Maman*; she came to find you because she could have no baby of her own. You are more important to her than her life, as you are to me, but she needs to know this. I already know."

But did she? Louis couldn't help but wonder. Had she been able to dismiss his childish prattle and teenage praise for his Key West parents and all they'd given him? Or was she pierced with a new arrow every time he talked of a new bike, guitar lessons, the used car Jim bought him when he graduated from high school?

Isabella and Jim had offered to move Julia to Little Haiti in Miami and help her find work. The offer had probably made them feel a little less guilty for accepting Julia's gift, "all she had to live on," as Louis knew Jesus had said of the poor widow who put her last cent in the alms box.

By refusing the offer Julia surprised everyone, not least her fellow villagers who thought of Little Haiti as a first step on the path to heaven. She stayed in Haiti, accepting a small sum of money each month from Jim, more than enough to give her a relatively carefree life in Jeremie. Through the Diocese of Miami, Jim also paid for a small cement dwelling where she could live out the tropical storms that regularly destroyed the shacks people in Jeremie called homes.

She lived for another twenty years, certainly longer than she would have lived with the burden of her severely disabled son weighing her down, but not nearly as long as that son, made well, wanted her to live. Insisting that Jeremie was her home, she refused all his efforts to move her to Key West or Miami.

Louis' good nature was tried by Julia's refusal. Once, he actually lost his patience with her, snapping, "You do this to spite me! You know I want you near and you refuse," and before he knew what had happened, for the first time in his life, she'd slapped him.

He was stunned; his ears rang with her stinging blow. Before he could respond, she was speaking rapidly in Creole, and she wasn't, as he imagined she surely would, apologizing.

"How dare you! How dare you say such a thing to me! That I would do anything—*anything!*—to spite you? You spoiled, selfish, unthinking boy! I would give my life for you—I have!" She had to stop to catch her breath. After a few moments she said more calmly, "Think what you are asking, Louis. What you have asked constantly now for almost ten years. Oh, you have broken my heart with asking! And what do you ask?

"That I force Isabella to share you with me."

"That I say to this woman who has given you life in a way I couldn't, 'Now, I push you aside. Now that you are an old woman who has given all you could give, I push you aside. I want back what is mine.' That is what you want me to do? Never forget what they've done for us, Louis. They gave you a new life, and then, as if that were not enough, they helped keep me alive to see it. And I will not throw that in her face."

Remembering that conversation almost twenty years later, Louis's face still stung, now from shame instead of Julia's slap. He'd been so self-centered, probably because he was the apple of three pairs of eyes, and those of the two women shined particularly brightly. The most difficult challenge he'd faced was losing them both—all three of his parents—in the same year. Julia died of swiftly moving lung cancer more than nine years ago, and seven months later, Isabella and Jim were run down in Miami by a driver who'd fallen asleep at the wheel. Louis had been contacted by a lawyer who wanted him to sue, but he had no interest. The poor man was suffering enough—Louis knew, because he'd spent time with him—and money would not bring his parents back. Any of them.

Money didn't interest him much anyway, even after his Key West parents died and he inherited plenty of it. He was a counselor at the time, with quite a reputation on the naval base, but after losing both mothers and the father who'd taught him how to be a decent man, Louis took a leave of absence. He grieved, deeply, in private. For the first time in his life, he was truly alone.

He hid at a mission hospital in Jeremie run by the Haitian Health Foundation, which gave him plenty of space and asked no questions. For months he could barely function, ignoring calls from those he'd counseled. When he finally recovered enough to return to Key West and buy the White Street property, Marguerite entered his life, and his fluttering spirit began to heal.

The Navy hadn't been the problem with Evie and Tom, he remembered, looking at the message Marguerite had reluctantly handed over. He hadn't heard from the troubled couple since they moved to Connecticut earlier in the year. He had counseled them off and on for almost two years. Their little boy, Jack, had been a true delight, but even Louis, ever optimistic, had not been sure the parents would make it. Louis disliked the saying "Opposites attract" because, though it may well be true, it wasn't always a good thing when acted on.

That seemed to be the case with Evie and Tom, who could not have been more different. How could two people so unalike ever truly understand what the other was feeling? Faith and patience could sometimes see a relationship like that through, but Evie had no patience, and Tom, no discernible faith. Still, the feelings they had for each other went well beyond the physical attraction he'd first thought of as the only glue that held them together. Louis had hoped the Connecticut move and the sacrifice Tom had made in transferring to submarines would improve things. Apparently it hadn't.

Poking his head out his office door, he told Marguerite, "I'm calling Evie now. It's almost four, and I could be awhile, so feel free to close up and head home."

She gave him a slow, questioning look that suddenly made him uncomfortable. Whether it was the fact that she was silent for more than a few seconds or the disconcerting frankness of her gaze, he found himself clearing his throat and retreating into his office. Before he could disappear she said, "I'll wait. We have something to discuss."

"We do?" he squeaked, but she'd returned to her work and didn't look up.

He quietly closed the office door and rested his back against it for a few moments, surprised at how quickly his breath came. She was leaving. He just knew it. The moment he'd been dreading for eight years had come, and he was utterly undone at the prospect.

He'd had a feeling. Though she never told him, her sister mentioned at church a month or so ago that Marguerite was "keeping company with someone." He'd just smiled and nodded as if he already knew, but a small, cold fist clenched inside him. And then, last Sunday, her mother had told him that he "wouldn't be the only eligible bachelor" at her Christmas dinner table. He'd laughed knowingly while his spirit flinched at the thought of sharing Christmas Day with a stranger who might very well ruin his life.

That's what she's going to tell me, Louis thought, limping heavily to his desk and dropping into the expensive chair Marguerite had insisted on purchasing for him because it was "ergonomically correct." *She's going to warn me that not only is her man coming for Christmas dinner, but they'll also be making a big announcement at the family table. One week from today.* And, of course, she'd have to leave the ministry. Leave him. How would he smile and laugh through that?

For some time he stared at the translucent blue-and-green starfish Evie's grandmother Filomena had sent him right after he'd baptized Jack. Marguerite had hung it on his desk lamp where it would catch the light. He took comfort from its unique shape and its seeming fragility. "We're not so different, sea creature," he said softly and then reached for the phone and peered at the pink message slip Marguerite had given him. He dialed, waited, and then said, "Evie, it's Louis. How can I help?"

§

Almost ninety minutes later, he hung up the phone. He hoped Marguerite had given up and gone home, but he could hear her banging around in the front room. At any other time he'd be dreading the tongue-lashing he'd get for talking so long at the church's expense. Now he wished that was all he was in for.

Marguerite rapped on his door. "Come in," he called, trying to recover the hope he'd forced into his voice when talking to Evie.

She walked purposefully into the office and stared at him. The expression on her face was like nothing he'd ever seen there before. And then she did something that really terrified him: In a soft, careful voice, she asked, "May I sit down?"

10

Guillermo

Hey, *hombre*, where can I get some good Mexican food around here? I'm talking real Mexican, none of that *mole* stuff; I mean, come on, who wants chocolate sauce on their chicken? I'm thinking tacos, burritos and best of all, some good, strong *cerveza*."

Guillermo sighed. He'd learned years ago when he started driving a cab that there was no point, and certainly no advantage, in correcting loud, ignorant Americans. Especially not those he picked up at Miami International Airport, fresh off the plane, like this guy. Most of them couldn't care less that he was Cuban, not Mexican; that he despised being called *hombre* by anyone, much less a beer-bellied fool who shouldn't be wearing such a tight pair of shorts and ridiculous T-shirt (no one who spent two minutes with this guy would need to be reminded by the words on the shirt: It's

All About Me); and that *cerveza* and beer were the same, though guys like this seemed convinced it had special intoxicating properties that American beer didn't possess. Guillermo would have liked to say all that and more, but he couldn't afford to risk losing the big tip this Anglo would probably leave just to prove what a good guy he was. Still, Guillermo couldn't resist occasionally testing his own assumptions, so he said courteously, "Actually, I'm not Mexican. I'm Cuban-American."

The guy gave him a blank look and said, "Oh yeah? Castro, right? The bastard. More power to you for getting outta there. So, where can I get a good burrito?"

Guillermo eyed his fare in the rearview mirror. The last thing this guy needed was a burrito and a beer. His first stop ought to be the Whole Foods Market in Miami for fresh vegetables and sunscreen to keep him from being burned like a roasted pig.

Guillermo knew he might as well resign himself to one more hour of keeping his mouth shut. For the past week he'd been doing little besides delivering the Christmas arrivals to their hotels and, sometimes, to their families. Each day had become more difficult, with spoiled, screaming kids and pale, squinting adults, some headed for a reunion that would likely result in something just short of bloodshed. Not exactly Guillermo's idea of how the Lord would like us to celebrate His birthday.

I used to enjoy Christmas, he grumbled to himself. *Now I spend December ferrying around rude people who have so many expectations and demands that no one could satisfy them.* But it would all end with this guy. It was

December 20, and after he unloaded this poor loudmouth at the Residence Inn near the Aventura Mall, he would turn off his cab light and be finished for a week. Early tomorrow morning, he'd be using the cab to drive himself and Sarah to Miami International so they could swim against the tide of disgruntled arrivals and board a plane to New York. Once there, they would meet Sarah's grandson Sammy—the only one of her family worth her time as far as Guillermo was concerned—for an early lunch, after which they would put Sarah in a limousine bound for Connecticut. Guillermo would be alone in New York. Maybe.

"Not very talkative, are ya?" said the guy in the back of the cab. "Last Spanish driver I had couldn't stop yakking. I thought you guys loved to talk."

It was all Guillermo could do not to stop the cab in the middle of the highway and throw the man out. He actually signaled to pull over to the side, but by the time he'd changed lanes, he realized it would not be a good way to start his next week. He took a deep breath and murmured, "Sorry, sir. I've a lot on my mind."

"Hey, I hear you, man. Christmas and all, right? It's that whole expectation thing. Families, presents, peace on earth. Who needs it? What a headache. Me, I avoid the whole thing. Get on a plane and spend the week on the beach drinking margaritas and catching a few rays."

Guillermo didn't voice the reply that came to mind. *I'm sure your family's grateful.* He glanced in the rearview mirror and immediately felt remorseful. The guy probably knew very well that whatever family or friends he had wherever he'd come from wouldn't miss him. His annual escape to Florida for Christmas was likely more a flight from the sad reality of his life than a vacation. "Good for you, sir; sounds like a good plan," Guillermo answered.

Pleased at such a positive response, the man asked eagerly, "So what's your story, man? Missing your family in Cuba?"

"No, I have no family left there. My daughter's in New York."

And I haven't heard from her in fifteen years, he didn't say.

After he dropped the man off, Clemencia was still on his mind. Was ever a child so unsuited to her name? It was as if she'd rebelled against it; clemency, much less forgiveness, was not in her character, at least when it came to her father. He switched off his cab sign, drove to the Aventura Mall, and parked the car.

He walked to the park across the street from the Residence Inn where he'd dropped off his passenger, strolling along the wide esplanade and wondering how long before the man would have his burrito. Or would he settle for a six pack of *cerveza* and forget the food altogether? Guillermo had spent a few years doing just that, and though it was far in his past, he hadn't forgotten the loneliness and despair. The late afternoon sun was still warm on his skin as he stepped around the ducks that congregated at the park's ponds and canals, boldly blocking the paths of walkers and joggers. For years after his wife had returned to Cuba, he'd been as oblivious to humans as these birds were—and about as self-centered.

Last night, Sarah, who was still anxious about her visit to Filomena and more than a little irritated with him for engineering it, had phoned and, without even saying hello, asked, "Why are we going tomorrow, Guillermo? More to the point, why are you?"

In an odd way, Filomena was the reason he'd pushed for this trip. He'd never told Sarah much about the time he and Filomena had spent together when she visited Sarah after Ben's death. And he was sure Filomena hadn't told her friend how Guillermo had driven her endlessly around this long circle because she'd been too nervous to face Sarah. And because Sarah had told her that Guillermo, a trusted friend who'd been immensely helpful, would meet her at the airport, Filomena had confided in him.

As soon as she sat down in the cab, dressed in a black gabardine dress that must have been unbearable in the Florida heat, she said, "I made a mistake. I can't go."

Guillermo was taken aback at the uncertainty of the regal-looking woman fidgeting and wringing her hands in the back of his cab. "But Sarah is expecting you," he said quietly, and that unleashed a torrent of words that he still remembered.

"I know she is expecting me," Filomena moaned. "Of course she is, and I am to blame for this. Didn't I force myself on her, telling her she needed her friend with her immediately? Didn't I talk over her worries and objections and tell her I was coming regardless until she finally agreed? Of course she is expecting me!

"Now that I am here, now that I have my way, what do I say to her? Did two people ever love each other as much as she and Ben? No! Were there ever two people who laughed more and argued less? No! They were the world to each other. What can I do about such a loss? What comfort can I give her, me with my big mouth so ready to push for my way?"

Guillermo watched her anguished dark eyes in the rearview mirror and finally murmured, "We will drive a little."

By the time they'd covered the distance between Miami International and Fort Lauderdale, she was, if anything, more agitated. Much later he realized that he'd probably seen a side of this woman few others ever had. Whether it was because he was a relative stranger or simply that she took his silent concern for compassion, she'd revealed a vulnerability that went much deeper than her doubts about visiting Sarah.

After they'd circled the green eight times with no end in sight, Guillermo parked near one of the ponds, hoping the sight of the ducks might distract her. She didn't even notice them. It was then that she told him about her family, her twin daughters, their separation. She blamed herself for the rift and insisted she'd do anything to repair the damage. He listened silently. When she finished, he began speaking.

When he finally delivered her to Sarah, Filomena had recovered herself. She'd also become the only person to whom he'd confided his own terrible mistake.

§

Guillermo sighed and headed back to his off-duty cab. Easing himself into the driver's seat, he stared at the piece of Christmas Glass he'd hung from the rearview mirror, a crystal star shot through with gold filaments—"To light your way," Filomena had written in the card that arrived with the ornament a week after she returned to Connecticut. Now he would have to tell Sarah what he told her friend that day five years ago. He owed Sarah that much before they got on the plane tomorrow. Though perhaps after he told her, he'd be getting on alone.

He called from the cab to make sure she was in. Her voice was emotionless when she told him to come up.

She answered the door with her lips pursed, her face pale. Before she could say anything, he spoke. "You asked me last night why we were getting on that plane tomorrow. I've come to tell you."

A small light of curiosity sparkled in her eyes. She gestured for him to enter. Taking a deep breath, he walked in and sat on the couch, while she took the chair opposite him, the chair that had been her husband's favorite. On the glass coffee table between them was a take-out box of sesame noodles and another of vegetable chow mein with two sets of chopsticks, one unopened. She did not offer them to him. She sat back, her arms folded lightly in front of her, and waited.

"I let you believe that I've pushed this trip tomorrow because I think Filomena needs you and, more important, that you need to do something like this to . . . to get out in the world more," he began awkwardly. "And that's all true. But it is not the only truth."

He paused. She raised her eyebrows a little and waited. It was something he liked about Sarah: She was a quiet woman. She'd spent so much of her life waiting.

"Before Castro came into power, my family was doing well. My father and his brothers owned a sugarcane plantation, and it supported all of us. He and my uncles had a good relationship with the American companies that controlled the sugar mills. We were honored and respected. As soon as Castro took over, that was finished. I was seventeen in 1957 when the trouble started. Suddenly, we were the oppressors, elite landowners to be despised. My parents were not like others who waited too long, hoping that Castro would lose power, hoping the United States would depose him, hoping against hope they would wake up tomorrow and find it had all been a nightmare.

"No, my father saw what was happening, and knew that it would only get worse for families like ours: land confiscated, honor destroyed, humiliation, poverty. My father sent my mother and me out of the country in 1958. It was a dangerous journey by boat, but my mother and I survived. My father did not. He and his younger brother died trying to protect our land. Another brother disappeared. No one has heard from him for more than fifty years.

"My mother and I ended up in Miami. What little money we had left after bribing the officials and paying the boatmen to help us escape was soon gone. My father was able to send us nothing. In Miami my mother was not the elegant wife of a successful planter, and I was not the heir to a thriving sugarcane business. We were just 'a couple of spics,' and people called us worse than that. My mother ended up waitressing in a diner, while I worked in the kitchen washing dishes. She was strong; she had to be.

"My mother never remarried, but working together in a growing Cuban neighborhood, we made a life for ourselves. But the memory of the life we'd left behind never left her. She was determined to regain the respect she felt she deserved. She worked her way out of the diner and eventually became the office manager of a clinic. She never retired. Everyone from that clinic, and even a few of the bigwigs from the HMO that took it over in the early nineties, came to her funeral when she died three years ago."

Sarah raised a hand. "Wait. Are you telling me your mother was living while you knew Ben and me and you never introduced us?"

That's the least of it, Guillermo thought to himself. "I'd always meant to tell you about her. But then Ben died, and it didn't seem right just then. As time went by you became good at keeping people at a distance."

Sarah interrupted him. "Don't dare give me such an excuse! Your mother had suffered like me. You knew that. We could have been friends."

"I've never thought of you as wanting friends."

Rather than snap back at him, she was quiet. Eventually she said, "Go on."

"My mother was not pleased with Christina, the girl I fell in love with the first day I saw her in that diner. I married her anyway, and it wasn't until my mother held Clemencia, the newborn granddaughter we'd named for her, that she reconciled herself to our marriage. Perhaps that was the last day any of us were truly happy."

He paused, looking out the window at the night, pierced by so many lights; it was never truly dark in Fort Lauderdale. Sarah unwrapped the second pair of chopsticks and pushed them toward him, gesturing at the food. Then she rose, went into the kitchen, and returned with two glasses of red wine. He hadn't picked up the chopsticks, and he didn't touch the wine. He looked at her briefly, smiled a little, and went on.

"Christina was just a year younger than me, but she had not escaped Cuba like I had. Her family hadn't been wealthy when Castro took power, and so they had not fled. Later they wished they had—so many wished they had. To protect his family, Christina's father became a member of the Communist Party. His wife and daughter, my Christina, were allowed to travel. The day she walked into my diner, she was on a visit to her mother's uncle.

"She was so beautiful, Sarah: black eyes, long black eyelashes, skin like creamed coffee; black curls spilling out from beneath a wide-brimmed straw hat with a white camellia in its band. She wore a white sundress with flat black sandals that had gold ribbons tied up around her ankles. I could barely move, never mind work. That was the only time I've ever come close to being fired from a job!

"I pestered her until she agreed to have a *café con leche* with me, and pestered my mother until she deigned to be cordial to Christina's mother. It was disturbing for my mother: In her day in Cuba, Christina would not have been considered suitable for me. After Castro, it was I who might be considered unsuitable: a poor refugee who'd lost everything, courting the daughter of a Party member. But I was determined: By the end of that month, I had Christina's promise that when she returned the next year, she would come to me again. In the meanwhile, we would write to each other.

"Sarah, I wrote more in those eleven months than I'd ever written before and have written since. Oh, I was eloquent! A poet! By the time she returned, we were secretly engaged, and before that second visit was over, we'd married. I was twenty-two, she was twenty-one; her family was furious, and my mother was far from happy.

"A year later when Christina gave birth to our beautiful Clemencia, both our mothers came around.

"Clemencia truly was a lovely child. But oh, what a temper! She was born squalling, and sometimes it seemed she only stopped long enough to eat and sleep to get the energy to start again. From the first, it was as if she was determined to deny her name; she had no mercy, that girl.

"We were happy, anyway, and on the rare occasions during that first year when she was calm, our little Clemencia was a delight. She charmed my mother, to the point where I think she actually forgot for hours at a time how far she'd fallen in the world. The fact that every time my mother held Clemencia, she was looking at a mirror image of my wife didn't hurt the relationship between the two women. By the time Clemencia was four, Christina and my mother were almost as close as mother and daughter.

"Things were not going well for Christina's parents in Cuba. Castro had grown more powerful and was free to do whatever he wished. My mother-in-law seldom visited, and Christina's father didn't dare come even to see his new granddaughter. Castro and his spies would take anything and make it into a sign of disloyalty, even treason. My mild-mannered father-in-law didn't dare go to see his treasonous son-in-law and exiled daughter.

"When he grew ill, the shadow fell heavily on us. The worse the news, the more Christina chafed. Worry etched lines on her face and dimmed the light in her eyes. Even Clemencia, rambunctious as she was, was afraid to upset her mother.

"I'm afraid I did little to help. In my fear over the changes in my wife—in our little family—I became angry. I ranted about Christina's parents. Why hadn't they gotten out when they still could? My mother did; why hadn't they? Why had they gone along with Castro? And if she tried to defend them, I said they'd gotten what they deserved for betraying Cuba and supporting *El Comandante*.

"My mother tried to warn me. 'You will drive her from you. Speak words of comfort to her or we will lose her.'

"'Drive *her* away?' I roared back. 'She drives herself away from me, from us, with these silences, these tears, these looks of reproach. She treats you as if you were a stranger!'

"The truth was, I was terrified. I could see my wife slipping away from us, and when I saw her so restless, attending only to Clemencia and ignoring the comfort my mother offered, my fear became panic and my helplessness turned the panic to cold fury. I knew I could do nothing to console Christina, nothing to help her family. If I tried to go back to Cuba to see them, I would be thrown into jail and maybe executed. I felt useless, worthless, not a man.

"Just before Clemencia's fifth birthday, Christina asked if she could take the child to visit her parents before, as she said, 'my father dies without ever seeing her.'

"How could she even think about going back there herself, no less with *my* child? Castro was a monster, and she wanted to take *my* child into such an environment? Surely she knew that I could not go with her? After the Bay of Pigs,

Cuba had become even more dangerous. Did she understand that Clemencia was American and not Cuban, the daughter of a dissident, the child of one of Cuba's landowning families? What if they weren't allowed to come back?

"But what was really going through my mind was, 'What if she *won't* come back?'

"Even then, my mother warned me: 'Do not forbid her. You will push her to recklessness.' But every time Christina so much as hinted that she wanted our child to see her grandfather, I erupted.

"Finally, the inevitable happened: When Christina got the news that her father would die within the month, she insisted she must go. 'Go,' I said coldly. 'But not with *my* child.'

"And she went."

Guillermo looked at Sarah. She was leaning forward, expressionless, her hands clasped on her knees, her eyes on his face, her food and wine untouched. "I never believed she would do it," he said. "I never believed she would leave. I never believed she would abandon her child."

"You forced her to leave her child?" There was no judgment in Sarah's voice.

"I was crazy with fury and grief. My pride was shattered. I sent a message to Christina's family: *Don't come back. You are no longer my wife, no longer my child's mother.*

"Later I learned it arrived on the day after her father died. And the joke was on me, because she had no intention of coming back. She had had enough of my machismo, my demands that she be happy with me every moment of every day. By then, no one from either family stood in the way of our divorce. Christina demanded to see Clemencia as part of the agreement, but I made it impossible. I told her that Clemencia was an American citizen, and no American court would give her access to the girl, especially if it meant sending her to Cuba to be with a mother who'd abandoned her—who'd abandoned America! I used my mother, too, telling the lawyers and the judge that my mother, still a young woman at forty-eight, would help raise my daughter. My mother agreed; she did not want to lose Clemencia too. Naturally, the court agreed: Clemencia would stay in her Miami home, not go to some hovel in Cuba.

"I'm sure it broke my wife's heart. I know it nearly broke Clemencia's. She begged constantly for her mama. For every answer we gave, she had another question. The child was relentless. She gave us no rest. And finally, in desperation, we told her that her mother was dead.

"I wanted my life back, I wanted to control my world. And Clemencia would never see her mother again anyway. So what should we have done?

"I know, I see—*now*—that it was wrong. But I was too hurt, too blind, to know what was right. Maybe I didn't care. And yes, maybe I wanted a little revenge. But I suffered for it. When we told Clemencia—for this I needed my mother sitting beside me, for this I had no courage—she howled. For months she cried, grieving for her mother as if she could open heaven to earth with her wails.

"When she wasn't crying, she was interrogating me. Why had God taken Mama? Where was Mama? Why couldn't she see heaven? Was Mama talking to God right now? Would God let Mama come back for a visit? Would God let her go to Mama for a visit?

"Can you imagine my anguish when she asked me that? When the answer was that it was Papa, and not God, who'd refused her mama a visit? Of course, I could not bring myself to tell the truth, to let her know what a monster I'd been, and a liar as well. In the end, when I thought I could bear no more, the crying and the questions simply stopped. On her fifth birthday, Clemencia stopped weeping and questioning. It was as if she'd not only accepted that her mother was gone—dead—but also that she'd forgotten it.

"I should not have accepted this abrupt silence, I know, yet it was such a relief. Still, we should have known that silence after such a grief was not healthy for the child.

"But her silence helped me to forget what I'd done, my selfishness, my pride, at least for a time. I began to wonder if Clemencia had forgotten Christina. After a few years of hearing nothing from my daughter on the subject of her mother, I began to convince myself she had. That first year she slept with a photo of her mother, but as time went on—as Clemencia grew more and more to resemble Christina—the photo stayed on her desk in its silver frame.

"Every week for that first year, Christina wrote to her from Cuba. And every week, I tossed the letter into a box I kept on the top of my closet shelf. After the first year, Christina wrote less frequently, but at least once a month. She sent cards on each of Clemencia's birthdays and every Christmas and Easter. Those went in the box, unopened, like the rest. When Clemencia grew old enough to get the mail, I had the mail delivered to a post office box that only I or my mother visited. And I got a small safe to replace the box on my shelf. I'd gotten an unlisted phone number after the first time Christina tried to call. In those days, it wasn't easy for those living in Cuba to communicate with the US, and I made it impossible.

"Why didn't I just throw the letters out? I never read them, yet somehow I couldn't bring myself to destroy them. Maybe I thought that someday I'd tell Clemencia the truth. Maybe someday, I'd take her to meet her mother. I probably imagined myself the hero of such a day. I don't know.

"Clemencia was almost eighteen when Christina's younger sister showed up at our door one humid Saturday afternoon. The air was heavy with wet heat, and when I opened the door, it hit me like a blast of steam. I recognized Carolina right away. She'd been searching for us for weeks; she'd left Cuba secretly over a month before to find us so she could tell Clemencia that her mother was very ill. She'd hoped to convince Clemencia to go to Cuba and see her mother.

"But I'd gone to great effort to hide us from anyone in Cuba, and by the time Carolina tracked us down, Christina had died. As she stood out there in the heat, her eyes burned through me. Before I could slam the door in her face, she pushed by me and strode into the house, calling Clemencia's name. My daughter came down the stairs from her room where she and my mother had been working on her college applications. With her glasses hanging from a loop around her neck, my mother was close behind her, and I remember how she peered questioningly at Carolina, and then, realizing who she was, closed her eyes in a spasm of despair.

"The rest, as you may say, Sarah, is history. Carolina had suspected I'd lied to Clemencia about her mother, but she'd never imagined I'd told our daughter that her mother was dead. The look she gave me flayed the skin from my bones and stripped away whatever manhood I had left.

"I couldn't even look at Clemencia. I walked up the stairs woodenly, retrieved the safe, and opened it on the table before my daughter. Then I left the house.

"When I came back the next day, bleary and polluted after a night of drinking, my mother was staring vacantly out the window and my daughter was gone. I've never seen her or heard her voice again.

"Eventually Carolina let my mother know that she'd spent a month with Clemencia. Carolina, may God bless her, didn't let my daughter fall into self-pity and paralysis. Nor did she give in to Clemencia's demands that they return to Cuba together so Clemencia could visit her mother's grave. 'Keep your mother in your heart,' Carolina told her. 'It is wiser and safer that way.' Together, the two of them went through the letters and cards in my strong-box—twelve years' worth—and found what amounted to a few thousand dollars that Christina had somehow hidden away and sent to her daughter.

"At the end of their month together, Carolina put my daughter on a plane to New York, where she used her mother's money to go to nursing school. When that money ran out, she got loans and worked part-time jobs so she could finish school. By the time she contacted my mother, seven years had passed and she was an RN living in Brooklyn and working at a clinic.

"It was a short, cold letter: Clemencia told her grandmother that she held her as responsible as me for destroying her childhood by lying to her about her mother. She wrote that we had as good as killed her mother as far as she was concerned, and that as much as she wanted us to be dead to her, she'd recently held her own newborn daughter in her arms. She did not want to see us then and thought she might never want to, but she did want us to know that she was safe, married to a good man ('Not like the one my poor mother married,' she wrote), and with a beautiful baby girl. There was a photo of the infant, named Chrissy. My mother tried to show it to me, but I couldn't look.

"Every year from then on, we received a photo of Chrissy at Christmas, sometimes with a brief note, sometimes not. Writing a thousand words for every one she received, my mother wrote back often, but I never dared. I feared that even hearing from me would end all communication from my daughter. But when my mother died, I had to write and let her know. I couldn't let her think that her grandmother had stopped caring enough to write. Almost immediately, she sent back a plain envelope made of fine, heavy paper. It contained a single white square card that said, 'I am sorry for you. The only person who loved you is gone.'

"I deserved that, I know. But I held my breath two months later when Christmas drew near. I didn't dare hope that I'd receive a picture of my granddaughter. Clemencia's mercy was unlikely to extend far enough to reach me. But it did. I received a photo. And one the year after that. And the year after that. And this year."

Guillermo stared at the floor, not raising his eyes to meet Sarah's. It was so quiet that they could hear the grandfather clock Ben had insisted on buying for the apartment. When it seemed that the ticking would go on forever, Guillermo said, "When I got the photo this year, Chrissy had signed it. That never happened before. I think it's time for me to try . . . to get back what I lost; I know I can't. But maybe to get a look at it."

He smiled weakly. "After all, if that dragon-lady Filomena can try to fix the things she's done, maybe I deserve a chance too."

He heard Sarah rise and her footsteps moving away from him. He looked up quickly now, his fear that he'd lost her friendship naked in his face. She turned at the entrance to the hallway and met his gaze.

"You're disgusted with me," he said softly. "You're not going tomorrow."

She gave him a long, weary look. "Of course we're going tomorrow. You robbed me of the chance to know your mother. You never told me about your wife. I'm not going to let you keep me from knowing your daughter and your granddaughter. Be here at six if you want breakfast before we leave for the airport."

The smile in her eyes did not extend to her lips, but it was enough for him. Shaky with relief, he rose and started for the door.

"And Guillermo?" she said.

He turned, worried she'd changed her mind.

"Bring your Christmas Glass. I have a feeling you're going to need that star."

11

David

I t was Blossom's first real Christmas with them—last year she'd been too new to America and too sick to enjoy it—so David was eager to give their daughter as many chances to celebrate as possible. At twenty-two months the beautiful little Chinese girl he and Sandy had adopted and finally brought home last October was delighted by all the excitement. The tree, which had been up for two weeks now, was an object of particular interest to her. David thought she'd sleep under it if they let her. The lights, silvered tinsel, and ornaments fascinated her as much as the lavishly wrapped presents heaped under it, most of them for her. Sandy had moved the Christmas Glass Nativity from Blossom's bedroom, where it had been since last Christmas, to a small table beside the tree. The baby had not slept one night without it since her godmother Maria had given it to them last year.

Tonight would be the first real Christmas party in their Sausalito condominium. They'd planned to spend Christmas Eve with Maria and Daniel, but when Maria told them about the call from her sister Catharine, both David and Sandy had urged her to go Connecticut. Whether it was their own joy at finally having the child who made them a family or the small spark of hope they saw in Maria's worried eyes, they'd quickly offered to move the Christmas Eve party to tonight, December 21. Early tomorrow morning, David would drive Maria and Daniel to SFO for their flight to Connecticut. Maria's son Mark and his family wouldn't be leaving until the next day.

From there, David thought, plugging in the Christmas tree lights, *it's anyone's guess what will happen.* He'd never met Filomena or Catharine, but from what Daniel and Maria had told him, it sounded like the family was never at peace. "Drama and trauma," as Daniel put it, was evidently the norm. And now Filomena's Christmas ultimatum. David couldn't imagine anything good coming out of such blatant manipulation, but he and Sandy had agreed to encourage Maria to go, "just in case." *Still, what a way to screw up Christmas.*

David couldn't understand it. Why did people do so much damage to those they should cherish the most? Some of the families that came into their shop were appalling. Kids, tired of being dragged through all the stores in Sausalito's center, demanded treats so expensive David wouldn't consider buying them for himself, never mind a three-year-old who wouldn't know the difference between a Godiva chocolate and a Hershey's Kiss.

More often than not, the parents would buy whatever outrageously expensive sweet the screaming child pointed to and then let their little darling unwrap and eat it in the store. Just today a little boy had loudly demanded a Ghirardelli dark chocolate caramel square, showing all the signs of an oncoming tantrum. David had watched the red-faced father, annoyed at being distracted from discussing which of the variety of blue cheeses had the most flavorful "veins," hurriedly buy the chocolate and thrust it at the boy. His tears gone, the child snatched it, broke it apart, and after nibbling on a corner of it, smeared the caramel filling all over the counter glass. The father never said a word. David wasn't sure he even noticed.

That had been merely irritating. Yesterday, David had gone to Mike's Bikes to buy a helmet for Sandy—not the most romantic of Christmas presents, he knew, but at least it would keep her safer among all the mad cyclists ("bike Nazis," Sandy called them). He was standing in the checkout line when he noticed a reed-thin man about thirty years old, with a fashionably short haircut, wearing full biking regalia from the clinging black racing tights to the insignia-covered shirt. It wasn't so much that David noticed the guy as it was the guy making sure that everyone in the store couldn't miss him.

He was loudly debating the merits of two of the most expensive racing bikes in the store, making sure the staff, not to mention everyone else in the place, understood just how impeccably informed he was. David knew most of the young staffers at Mike's Bikes; they were all fairly laid back, but you couldn't find a more knowledgeable group of bike geeks anywhere. These guys loved bikes and everything about them; they didn't require a lecture.

Apparently the man had mistaken their easygoing style for a lack of expertise and had taken it upon himself to display his know-how. He was pontificating on the need for superior training bikes for dedicated racers like him. It had taken David a while to realize that the little boy wandering aimlessly through the store was the loudmouth's son. He looked to be about three or four years old, and David noticed him at first because he seemed to be alone. A bit uneasily David assumed that he must be with one of the many adult shoppers in the store. But then he noticed that whenever the loudmouth's drone became particularly voluble, the little boy would look in the man's direction with a gaze of such adoration that it made David's heart contract. The boy was still young enough to think that his father commanded everyone's respectful attention; he didn't see or understand the eye-rolling and the annoyed smirks.

While David was examining the helmets, he saw the boy sidle over to his father, who was now bending the pretty tri-pierced ear of a slender blond woman in jeans and a UCSF sweatshirt. When the man failed to notice his son standing right beside him, looking up at him with shining eyes, the boy very slowly, with a hesitation that David found excruciating, lifted his thin arm and ever so gently touched his father's leg. Instantly, without taking his eyes off the woman he'd trapped into a one-way conversation, the man lowered his hand and firmly moved the child away, saying, "Not now. Daddy's talking. We don't interrupt."

The boy's look of desolation made David want to do some interrupting of his own. But he'd learned from confronting people like this before that the guy would either dismiss him as a meddling jerk or get angry. Either way, the boy wouldn't be helped. The guy didn't deserve such a beautiful, worshipful child, and though he probably had no idea of the kind of damage he was doing, he certainly wouldn't allow himself to be enlightened by David. When David saw one of the Mike's Bikes guys crouch down and talk quietly to the boy, he returned to his search for Sandy's helmet, suddenly wanting to be finished and out of the store.

Five minutes later he was standing in line with the helmet and a tiny Mike's Bike's T-shirt for Blossom when he felt something softly encircle his knee. David slowly looked down at the boy, who'd wrapped his small arm around David's leg as if it were an anchor and was peering up at David's face. The boy had the largest blue eyes David had ever seen. David gently placed his hand on the boy's head, and they stood looking at each other for a moment. Hearing the father yammering on, by now to yet another female victim, it was everything David could do not to drop his purchases, scoop the boy up, and run. There was a time not so long ago, while they were waiting to hear about Blossom and not sure they would ever get her, that he really might have done it.

He seemed to stare forever into the depths of the boy's eyes before he heard the father's latest target say, "Oh, isn't that your little boy over there? How cute!"

The father frowned. "James, what are you doing? Do you want a timeout? Come here right now!"

The boy didn't move. His arm tightened a little around David's knee, and his sapphire eyes stayed fixed on David's, not wavering, not even blinking. "No problem," David said evenly. "He's not bothering me."

"That's not the point," the man said. "The point is, James, you know better than to misbehave like this. And what did Mommy tell you about talking to strangers?"

"Actually, he hasn't said a word," David said, refusing to be a prop for the man to shame his son. "I think he just wants a little attention."

"James' problem is that he gets too much attention as it is, isn't it, James? Good boys learn that the world doesn't revolve around them."

"Good boys usually learn by example," David snapped.

Glaring at David, the man grabbed his son's hand and strode out of the store. The boy never made a sound. He watched David the whole time, even through the window, peering through the spokes of tires displayed in the showcase.

It wasn't until today, just an hour ago, that he'd felt able to tell Sandy about it. She understood; he knew she would. Was it all the time they'd waited for a baby, or just that they knew each other inside out? She stopped what she was doing and made him stop too, so he could speak without distraction and she could listen with her whole body.

They were closing the shop, counting the money, getting ready to haul a sleepy Blossom out of her store playpen only to carry her up the hill to their small, rented condo on Harrison to deposit her into her crib. When he finished recounting the scene in Mike's Bikes, Sandy said softly, "That poor little kid."

She placed her hand on his upper arm and leaned into him, gently pushing her face into the curve of his neck under his chin where it fit so well. She remained like that, silent, until he gave a long sigh and circled her with his arms. After a while she pulled away, murmuring, "We'd better get out of here before the hordes see us and try to give us more money"—"the hordes" being their private name for the tourists and locals who made the shop successful. Despite the season, they'd agreed to close at five tonight so they could get ready for their pre–Christmas Eve party.

He lifted Blossom into his arms. "Yes, my dear," he told her, "the world does indeed revolve around you, and I intend for it to always be that way." Sandy smiled, and Blossom, half-asleep, drooled on his neck.

Blossom was now curled peacefully in her crib, a few feet from her napping mother in the apartment's single bedroom. Sandy's hand would be resting in Blossom's crib, a habit she'd started from the first night the baby had come home. All their friends protested. They would spoil the girl, she should learn to fall asleep by herself, they should find a bigger apartment.

Frankly, David didn't care whether the sleeping arrangement "spoiled" their daughter. She'd come to them having known nothing but deprivation and loneliness; they were not about to deny her a mother's touch to ease the way into sleep. Besides, most of the naysayers had kids who slept in cribs full of expensive, politically correct stuffed creatures and dolls, or with pacifiers stuck so deeply into their mouths you'd think they were an extra set of lips and tongue. Elaborate murals were painted on their lonely nursery walls and mobiles crafted from designs by renowned pediatricians dangled above their cribs. Blossom had never slept with anything but her mother's hand within reach. David would choose their arrangement over the others any day.

Though soon, he thought, surveying their small domain, *we'll need another apartment.* He knew the building that housed their shop would be for sale next year, and everyone—friends, colleagues, even his accountant—thought it would be a brilliant move for them to buy it. They could keep the store downstairs and move into the two-bedroom, two-bath apartment on the second floor. Oh, and the value of the place was sure to go up: Look at the history of real estate in Sausalito.

Yeah, yeah, yeah, David thought, flinging a red tablecloth over the large table that served as desk, office space and dining surface. Despite the endless assurances, he and Sandy still weren't sure they wanted to buy the building. They weren't at all certain they wanted to work in the same place that they lived. Sandy had nightmares about demanding customers—and there were enough of those in Marin County—expecting them to open the store regardless of the hour or the day. As it was, one wealthy customer who liked to throw last-minute, late-night parties and who knew they lived just a half-mile up the hill, called them regularly at home to ask if one of them could "run down and open the shop so I can purchase a few provisions." David could only imagine what would happen if people knew they lived right upstairs.

"We wouldn't even be able to turn our lights on!" Sandy warned whenever the subject of buying the building came up. It wasn't that they weren't grateful that the store did well; they were, and they were constantly amazed at what people were willing to pay for high-end food and drink. But they didn't want to be at the beck and call, 24/7, of everyone who had an appetite to indulge and the money to do it with.

For David, purchasing the building and moving above the shop was unattractive for more personal reasons: Blossom, for one. In the year since they'd finally gotten the baby, every moment he spent with his wife and daughter away from the shop was precious, extraordinary. Even their routine gave him joy: food shopping with Blossom, first slung in a carrier on his chest and now wanting to sit in the grocery cart; or waking in the morning, when they would take the baby into their bed for a few moments and come to full awareness of the day in the knowledge that they were together as a family. Every morning they said a prayer of thanksgiving for this miracle, and he and Sandy were sure their solemn little daughter understood their moment of praise.

Then they'd plod together out into the room that hung high over the bay. This time of year, it was dark when they woke, and they'd have breakfast looking down on the town below with Christmas lights twinkling in the dawn, still lit from the night before. Every morning it took his breath away. Every morning his daughter pointed down at the tree by the ferry terminal and laughed, her dark eyes sparkling with joy.

David wanted more of that. He didn't want to rush off to open the shop or cater a breakfast or drive into San Francisco or up to Napa to haggle with his suppliers. He didn't want to spend the greater portion of his life away from the greatest part of his life, Sandy and Blossom.

And that brought him to the second reason he didn't want to buy the building: He wasn't convinced he wanted to continue with the store. Sandy felt the same way, but she was concerned about money. He knew she was just being sensible—the store was incredibly lucrative.

"You might as well be printing money in there," complained the woman who ran the art gallery next to the store. *Maybe if she'd try selling something that didn't look like the wall of a slaughterhouse, she'd make a little cash herself,* David thought, putting out platters of brie-stuffed pea pods, Dungeness crab cakes, roast beef with horseradish on sourdough slices, and guacamole with hand-crafted tortilla chips made from organic corn.

"Hand-crafted, organic chips," David muttered to himself. "What a bunch of baloney."

And that was precisely the problem. To David, the emphasis on what he considered ludicrously expensive food and drink was becoming, well, disgusting. It's not that he didn't want to eat well or that he didn't want others to eat well. It was just that it seemed ridiculous to make it the sole focus of life. Sure, he understood the emphasis on local and organic, but what about the people in the rest of the country who didn't live in California? Maybe that was it—his frozen Maine roots were getting to him; but really, how were people in Moosehead and Buffalo, Chicago and Detroit, supposed to eat local and organic? Not to mention that most people couldn't afford to buy the stuff.

He'd almost choked last week when he and Sandy treated Maria and Daniel to the newest wine bar on Caledonia Street. After presenting the ten-page wine list with enough pomp and ceremony for a coronation, the haughty young man behind the marbled bar approved their choice with the comment, "An excellent local selection grown right up the road in Napa. These grapes have never left the ground. Not one plume of airplane fuel, and a negligible carbon footprint." Daniel had started laughing so hard, he had to excuse himself and flee to the men's room.

The bottom line was that David didn't think food and drink should be a religion. And he didn't think that the more you spent on what were no more than expensive groceries, the smarter, better or worthier a person you were. Practically speaking, this was not the best attitude for a guy who ran the most successful high-end comestibles and catering shop in town. Another ten years at the store and he and Sandy would be able to retire. It was the thing Sandy kept returning to whenever they discussed closing the shop. "Just ten more years and then—freedom!" she'd exclaim.

Problem was, David wasn't sure he could last another ten years.

Rubbing the sleep from her eyes, Sandy came into the room to admire his handiwork. The tree was lit, the table set, and the food laid out. "Pretty impressive," she said, hugging him. Then she looked closely at his face. "Uh-oh. What now?"

He smiled weakly. "Same old stuff. Just thinking about what life would be like Without The Shop."

She looked at him, a mixture of empathy and frustration. "Ah yes, the old WTS dilemma. But, David, what would we do? If we sell the business, we won't get enough from it to retire. Maybe buy ourselves a year or two, yes, but what then?"

He grinned sheepishly. "I know, I know. It doesn't make sense. But don't you ever feel that it's ridiculous? With all the problems in the world, we're catering to people whose greatest ambition is to throw as much money down their throats as possible. Meanwhile, people right here in the Bay Area, never mind the rest of the world, are hungry, homeless, addicted, you name it. Doesn't that bother you?"

"Yes, it does bother me. Not as much as it bothers you, obviously, but yes, I do think about it. And we've talked about it. And we've agreed that the thing we can do now is donate to the groups helping families and kids, and that's what we've been doing. Then, when we can afford to retire, we'll give our time as well. Besides, it's not like our customers are monsters or anything—at least not most of them. This was never such a big issue for you until we adopted Blossom."

She was right. Blossom had been the trigger; not just his desire to spend more time with her, but the whole process of adopting her. They'd witnessed the desperation of women—and girls—forced to give up their babies. Not to mention the anguish of couples like them who would go to almost any lengths to have a child. Then there was the poverty in that region of China. What he'd seen of how people were forced to live—what he'd seen in the orphanage—had changed him almost as much as having Blossom.

It wasn't as if he'd been unaware of poverty and suffering before. There were families who were barely surviving, living in public housing in neighboring Marin City and San Rafael, not to mention San Francisco, Oakland, and Richmond; single mothers forced to depend on handouts from churches and food pantries just to pay the already-reduced rent and put a paltry amount of food—decidedly nonorganic—on their tables. David had surely known about all that before, but after Blossom, it was as if his heart had opened and everything he'd been able to screen out had come pouring in like a relentless wave. In every direction he looked around this beautiful bay, people were struggling just to stay alive while he rang up forty-five-dollar bottles of aged balsamic vinegar and chocolate truffles at five dollars apiece.

Something was wrong with the picture, but David wasn't sure how to change it. Was he having some kind of reverse midlife crisis where, instead of wanting to buy a red Corvette, he wanted to get rid of anything suggesting indulgence? Should he have joined the Peace Corps as a kid and gotten it out of his system? Clearly Sandy, though understanding, didn't want to throw away their financial security, especially not now that they had Blossom. Yet he kept thinking about Jesus angrily overturning the tables of the money changers in the temple and driving them away, and he wondered how He would react if He wandered into their store.

Sandy had awakened Blossom and was holding her hand as she toddled into the room, encased in a white jumpsuit with reindeer running all over it, her eyes shining with silent glee at this special Christmas party. David looked at his daughter and his wife.

"There must be something we can do, something to make life a little easier for others," he said softly, almost pleadingly, to Sandy. "Look at what we have."

She drew in a long breath, tilted her head, and turned to answer the door.

§

Maria was a bundle of nerves. It took ten minutes of holding the unflappable Blossom on her lap before she could relax enough to enjoy herself. Blossom, of course, was thrilled with the new stash of presents Daniel hauled into the living room, and insisted on dragging each one under the tree herself. Then she allowed herself to be seated on Maria's lap like a miniature yogi radiating calm. Even after a glass of champagne and ten minutes of Blossom, Maria could talk about little besides the impending confrontation with her mother and sister, not to mention her daughter-in-law.

"It's like walking into a loud, twisted opera where the battles take place between sessions of gorging on obscene amounts of food," she said with a groan. "I'd rather spend a week in an underground fallout shelter."

"You're showing our age, my darling," Daniel said with a smile. "I don't even think they have underground fallout shelters anymore."

"Whatever. And I don't see why you're so calm. You're not exactly my family's favorite person."

"I keep telling you it's all about safety in numbers," Daniel explained.

"With so many people around, it's going to be a virtual free-for-all. Your mother and sister won't be able to concentrate on just you."

"Bet me." Maria replied morosely.

"Can they really be that bad?" wondered Sandy, who'd never met any of Maria's family other than Mark.

"Yes!" cried Maria at the same time that Daniel said, "No."

Maria stared at him mutinously, and he continued, "Look, we knew ten years ago that our being together would upset your sister and therefore your mother. But we loved each other, and we were both free, and we wanted to be together. And then we let it fester. We let it get the best of them and the best of us. Whatever happens over the next week probably should have happened a decade ago. Then it would have been over with. As it is, we've cut ourselves off and allowed them to make us into monsters, and now we get the chance to make it clear that we're not. The problem is not the upcoming confrontation. It's that we waited so long for it to happen. It's past time to clear the air."

Maria gazed out the window over the bay for a moment before saying softly, "I know you're right, but that doesn't make it easier for me."

Sandy started to say something, but David shook his head, and they waited. The silence was heavy until Daniel said, "That's why I'm going to be right there with you. And I'm going prepared to eat our way out of it, if need be. I've been dieting all week."

They all laughed, including Maria, and Blossom turned her luminous grin on her godmother and then slid off her lap, wriggling to the floor and plunking herself down under the tree by her piece of Christmas Glass. "Now that was the best gift I ever gave anyone," said Maria. "I wish it was as easy to make my own grandchildren happy."

"Actually making *them* happy is never really the problem," added Daniel. "It's making their mother happy. But I think you hit on a brilliant present this year. I think she'll be speechless."

"She's always speechless," Maria observed. "I just hope this time it's with pleasure and not that mild scorn she so effectively beams in my direction."

"What did you get her?" David asked.

"I'm writing a book for her," Maria answered a bit shyly. Encouraged by David and Sandy's exclamations of approval, she continued, "Every Christmas she tells the kids the story of the *posadas* that she remembers from her childhood in Mexico. They're kind of an extended Christmas pageant for entire villages or neighborhoods."

"I'm surprised she told you about them," Sandy said. "From what you've said, she seems pretty shy with you."

"Believe me, she didn't tell me about them." Maria responded. "Bobby did. Apparently, the story of the *posadas* is the highlight of December evenings in their Bodega Bay kitchen. Not that Mark ever bothered telling me either. No wonder Serena thinks we're the Ugly Americans. We know so little about her or her culture."

"Yes, and I'm sure she'd be delighted to hear us discussing 'her culture' over Prosecco and stuffed pea pods," Daniel said dryly.

"It's not like I'm saying it *to* her, is it?" Maria retorted. "Anyway, I did some research on *posadas* and got in touch with my publisher. Of course, she's thrilled, counting up the dollars she thinks the book will pull in from the Hispanic market. Obviously, it's too late for this Christmas, but I put together a story with some sketches and had it bound—an original first edition, dedicated to her and the kids, if she even cares."

"She'll care," Daniel declared. "I think she'll care more than you can imagine."

"I'm going to sign it and enclose a note, but I'm still driving myself crazy trying to figure out what to say."

"I think Daniel's right." Sandy said, "I can't imagine a better gift. It probably doesn't even matter what you say in the note. She'll be thrilled. I can't believe you've had the time to get this done."

"She's been working around the clock for over a week, now," Daniel said, gazing at his wife proudly, "and the story's amazing. Really beautiful."

"Once I get the idea, the writing and drawing are the easy parts," Maria explained. "It's the editing I hate."

"Your editors would be crazy to change a word of this story," Daniel said, "Of course, it's not like that's stopped them before."

"Why is it," David began, "that we start out thinking we're doing exactly what we love and end up appalled at what it takes to get it done?"

"Oh boy, here we go," said Sandy, rolling her eyes humorously at her husband. "David is feeling sorry for himself because he has a successful business and a stable future."

David chuckled. "It's true. I admit it."

"Seriously," Daniel said, gazing intently at David, "what's up?"

"Nothing, really," David answered, suddenly feeling foolish. "It's just that sometimes I feel like what I'm doing is kind of pointless. I mean, look around at the world. So many people need help, or just attention, and what am I doing? Running a gourmet store."

"If anyone wants me I'll be putting the baby to bed. I don't want her to get splattered with our angst," Sandy said, lifting Blossom, whose eyes were already half-closed.

"But people depend on the store," Maria said, trying to be helpful.

"Right," David said. "I'm sure they'd be starving without our almond paste, stuffed olives, and organic toffee-chunk macadamia-nut cookies."

"That's not what I meant," Maria said, "It's just that I don't think you're being fair to yourself."

"So you're not going to buy the building?" Daniel asked, getting right to the point.

"That's what brought this all on," acknowledged David. "I'm just not sure I want to spend the next ten years of my life . . . I don't know . . ."

"'Catering to Money County' was how you put it before," said Sandy, returning to the room and flinging her arm affectionately around her husband as she settled on the arm of his chair.

"So what do you want to do?" Daniel asked.

"Something with kids. Maybe in Marin City," David answered without thinking about it.

"Where did that come from?" Sandy looked at him in surprise.

"I don't know. I guess it's been in the back of my mind. Mostly, I think it's about Blossom. I mean, how blessed are we? How blessed were we to get her after all the waiting, after almost giving up a hundred times? I know you feel the same way."

"Of course I do. We've talked about it. But this is the first I've heard about doing something with kids in Marin City. Not that I'm against it, but what are you thinking, specifically?" she asked, her bantering tone gone.

"Unfortunately, that's about as far as I've gotten. My mother used to say, 'Let go and let God,' but I've never been very good at that. Maybe now's a good time for me to start." David smiled, and looking at Daniel and Maria, asked, "Any ideas about what God wants us to do?"

"I can't say I know exactly what He wants us to do, but I do think He has impeccable timing." Daniel gave them his wide-open, face-splitting Scots grin and, turning to his wife, asked, "Do you want to tell them, or should I?"

"Me!" answered Maria. "It'll take my mind off my crazy family. I've been talking to a few other writers in the Bay area and we've been kicking around the idea of starting a small foundation to help kids with a percentage of our royalties. We'd make a challenge-grant request to churches in the area to try to match our funding. It's pretty informal right now, but a few churches have expressed interest. Just to show David for sure that God has a plan, one of our target areas is Marin City."

David leaned forward, almost pulling Sandy off the arm of the chair. "How would it work? I mean, what's the plan for spending the money in Marin City?"

"There are so many options," Maria said. "We'd work with the Housing Authority there and the Saint Vincent de Paul Society because they're already providing food pantries and rent assistance. One possibility is starting a preschool or daycare program and making it exceptional enough to attract kids from the wealthier towns and Marin City. That way we could get some real integration going, sort of like a preschool magnet or charter school. We'd get the Marin City Library involved and the social workers who are dealing with the kids and families most at risk. Also, the sheriff's office, because they're trying to keep the kids out of gangs and in school. It's all still in the planning stages, but we're putting together a volunteer board of directors to help us shape it. Daniel's already volunteered."

"More like I've been drafted," Daniel put in, still grinning, "and I could use some help. How about it?"

David had the presence of mind to turn to his wife, his eyebrows raised, seeking permission, or at least a sign of approval. Sandy thought about expressing her concerns. Where would he find the time? Could they afford to hire someone to help at the store? How would she fit in? After all, David wasn't the only one who got tired of catering to their customers. And because she knew the board members of any nonprofit were expected to donate to the cause, how much would it cost? But looking into her husband's eyes, she closed her mouth, opened her heart, and simply nodded.

He closed his large hand over her small one, and told Maria and Daniel, "I'd love to. When do we start?"

12

Filomena

N ow that the day she'd planned and schemed and waited for had finally come, Filomena could relax—a little. It was late in the afternoon on Christmas Day, and she looked out at the unlikely group of people assembled around her and remembered the moment she'd awakened this morning. It seemed as if days had passed, though it had only been twelve hours. She hadn't slept well—she never did—and had finally started groggily out of a sluggish sleep just before dawn. It was still dark when she slowly, cautiously—*That's all I need, to fall and break something*—knelt by her bed and prayed to the Baby Jesus, Who had made everything possible, that the day would go well.

Had it? In some ways, yes, though not everything had turned out the way she'd expected, or, to be honest, the way she'd wanted. She realized that today was more of a beginning than the wholesale resolution she'd pushed for, but perhaps she'd finally come to understand that she couldn't control everything. And it had only taken her eighty-plus years! She smiled at herself and surveyed the scene.

Now that was one thing she hadn't been able to arrange, and it still irritated her a little: They weren't sitting in her own living room, the room she'd promised to give up if she could just have this one day. But Olivia and Sarah had prevailed once they'd figured out how many people would be attending "this potential catastrophe," as Sarah had put it. They'd demanded that she move the dinner into one of the common rooms in the apartment complex.

"You can't expect sixteen people to spend the day and eat a big meal in this tiny room," Olivia had begun, standing in Filomena's apartment, hands on her hips. "And besides, what were you thinking? *Sixteen* people?! Including four little children who need room to move and play out their excitement on Christmas Day!"

"I didn't realize that it would be sixteen at first," retorted Filomena, ready for battle, "and the whole point was for me to have the meal *here*, the last Christmas meal in my own apartment before you move me to the dying building."

"Oh, please." Olivia said derisively. "The 'dying building.' You'll probably outlive all of us just so you can torment us for the rest of our lives."

Then Sarah, smiling slightly, took over. "Filomena, the real point of all this, as you say, was to have your twins come together. But even you can see it's become much more than that. Your whole family is coming, not to mention the friends and strangers you've invited for protection. And you know that's what you've done. You aren't sure anymore what you've wrought, so you want as many people around you as possible. And there's simply not enough room in this small apartment."

"I invited no strangers," Filomena snapped, deliberately ignoring Sarah's point about why she'd invited so many, which was, of course, absolutely true. "Michael is not a stranger to me. He's an old, old friend from when he was a boy working on our house in New London. And Guillermo is my friend *and* your friend, so how can he be a stranger?"

"You know what I mean," Sarah continued implacably, as Olivia flapped around the room, muttering to herself and waving her arms in the air. "These men are strangers to your family and you've invited them—and me—to be a diversion. Regardless of your motivations, we must have the meal in the common room where there will be more space."

"I will not have my family—my life—laid out in a dirty common room for all to see!" Filomena shouted.

"Dirty?" Olivia matched her volume. "How dare you call that room dirty!? That room is spotless just like every other common space in this facility, and you know it!"

"So you say!" Filomena shot back. "Besides, even if it were clean enough for my family, I do not parade my business for all the old crones and busybodies in this place to see."

After taking a few deep breaths to calm herself, Olivia said, "You know very well that almost all the residents of this building will be out with their families that day. And those who won't be out are not interested in you and yours. This may come as a big surprise to you, but the whole world does not revolve around you. Everyone in the universe does not spend every day thinking, *Hmm, I wonder what that grouchy old Filomena is doing today? I wonder how we can find out every detail about her and her family?* Disappointing as this may be for you, no one cares about your so-called business except for you and the poor people who can't seem to escape your clutches!"

Filomena gave her old friend a sour look. "The room is shabby. Even if it's clean, it is shabby. How can I have my family's Christmas in such a room?"

"And this apartment isn't shabby?" Olivia replied in disbelief. "This complex was built at the same time. Your apartment isn't any newer than that common room. The only difference is the common room has enough space for sixteen people at dinner; your apartment does not."

"I promised everyone I would cook Christmas dinner in my apartment," Filomena said mulishly.

"As if they care," Olivia muttered under her breath.

Sarah decided to intervene. "And you still can cook the meal here. There are enough of us to carry everything down the hall to the larger room. We'll set up a nice table, decorated beautifully for Christmas. Evie has even promised to put up a small tree. There will be room for presents, and everyone can open them there. The room will be lovely, Mena."

"*Humph!* That Evie! She should mind her own business!"

"Wow, there's a thought!" said Olivia sarcastically. "But how likely is that, given her genes?"

Filomena ignored her. "You two! You have double-teamed me!"

Sarah raised her eyebrows and sent an inquiring look to Olivia, who rolled her eyes and explained, "She gets that from watching the UConn girls' basketball team. That team is an obsession around here, especially with the ladies. We almost had a riot the other night when the cable went out before a game. They wanted to call the governor."

"And why not?" Filomena demanded hotly. "Those girls, they're winners. They could beat those boys with their big man Irish coach."

Once again, Sarah brought things back to the matter at hand. "So, we will prepare the common room, yes, Mena?"

"I will think about this common-room Christmas," Filomena had replied with exaggerated dignity.

Sarah hustled Olivia out of the apartment before she could pull rank as the executive director, an option they'd discussed as "a last resort." As it was, they'd won. Nothing else was said, but the two women quietly went about arranging the room. Evie did indeed put up a tree, with Serena's help, and now Filomena turned her gaze to it: a small pine tree set up on a table in front of the window.

It was a miracle she thought she'd never see: a tree sparkling with all the pieces of the Christmas Glass, brought together for the first time in more than fifty years. Evie—"that Evie!"—had done a beautiful job and had kept her efforts a secret from her grandmother. *How did the girl become so sneaky,* Filomena wondered admiringly.

§

On Christmas Eve, in the middle of all Filomena's cooking, Evie had knocked on her door. "Nana," she said, "come look at the room for tomorrow. It's all decorated. And there's a tree."

"No time for that now," Filomena replied. "I'm cooking for tomorrow. You think it's easy to cook for sixteen people? You think it can be done in an hour before everybody shows up?"

"You're the one who wanted—" Evie started, but then took a deep breath and said calmly, "It'll just take a minute. Come on, Nana, I've worked hard on this." Grumbling, Filomena followed her down the hall.

When she entered the room, her breath left her. It was dark and there, on the table, was the little tree, its hundreds of tiny lights illuminating the Christmas Glass. For a moment, Filomena doubted her eyes. But, no; the tree, the ornaments, were real; she went up to it and touched each of the precious pieces.

After a long moment, she turned to Evie. "How . . . ?"

Her granddaughter was smiling widely, her eyes sparkling in the glow of the tree. "Sit down, Nana, and I'll tell you."

§

Evie—and everyone else, it seemed—had planned this miracle.

It had, of course, been easy to get Catharine's blue, green, and silver–streaked fish; Catharine had contributed it willingly when Evie asked.

Maria also responded immediately to her niece's request, carefully wrapping her gold, orange, and red fish and carrying it on the plane with her so it wouldn't be in the checked luggage.

Evie had taken her own exquisite red-and-gold orb from the small tree she'd set up at home, though she told her grandmother that Jack howled when she took it off. "He must have thought I was taking the whole tree down before Christmas!"

Procuring the rest of the ornaments had taken a bit more work. Mark had readily agreed to bring the matching green-and-silver glass ball; Serena, apparently, wasn't terribly fond of the piece.

"That's because my daughter has not made a good job of bringing her into the family," Filomena said, nodding sagely. Evie refrained from comment, knowing that her grandmother had invited Serena to breakfast that morning.

Mark had asked Pastor Luke if they could "borrow" his wise man, and the minister had reluctantly agreed, asking if he could have the piece back after Christmas. "Apparently, he talks to it," Mark told Evie.

"Of course he does!" Filomena said. "I talk to mine too. Mine is Gaspar. His is Melchior. And Olivia has Balthasar."

Evie glanced at her dubiously. "How do you know which is which?"

"Never mind," Filomena waved her hand airily. "I just know these things."

It hadn't occurred to Evie to bring all the pieces together until Maria had called very late the night before she left Sausalito. "I'm bringing my piece and the piece I gave David and Sandy for Blossom," her aunt had said excitedly. "We had a little Christmas get-together earlier tonight, and as Daniel and I were leaving, David gave me the Nativity glass. I'd mentioned that Pastor was letting Mark borrow his wise man for the holiday, and David thought we should have as much of the collection as possible for Christmas Day. Do you think there's any way we could have all twelve? My mother would be beside herself."

Evie began plotting at that moment. The next day she'd called Sarah, who'd quite wisely refused to stay with Filomena and was booked into the Mystic Residence Inn. Evie was going to ask Sarah whether she could have someone in Fort Lauderdale retrieve the angel from her apartment and ship it overnight to Connecticut. Evie couldn't believe it when Sarah told her that not only had she brought her silver-winged angel, but she'd also advised Guillermo to bring his gold-speckled star; he'd left it with Sarah for safekeeping while he searched for his daughter in New York.

"What made you bring your angel?" Evie had asked Sarah curiously.

"It seemed right that your Nana should see it on Christmas," Sarah said promptly. And then after a pause, she added slowly, "And I wanted, finally after all these years, to tell my old friend how I first met this angel."

"So did she tell you?" Evie asked her grandmother.

"She did." Filomena responded quietly.

"And?"

"And, someday, I will tell you." Filomena said smiling, "Now finish telling me how the rest of the Christmas Glass came to be here."

It had been easy to get Olivia's green-and-gold-robed wise man, and to Evie's surprise, Olivia offered to call Michael, the mysterious stranger from Maine, who possessed the silver-and-gold-threaded icicle that had vanished half a century before. Filomena invited Michael to Christmas dinner over Catharine's protests, and Olivia told Evie that he was coming in the night before and would stay at the Stonington Inn.

"How do you know that?" Evie asked Olivia incredulously.

"He called and asked me to have Christmas Eve dinner with him." Olivia replied nonchalantly, as if being invited to dine with a complete stranger on Christmas Eve was an everyday event for her.

"And you said *yes*?!"

"Of course I didn't say yes! Who goes out for dinner on Christmas Eve?" Olivia snapped, and after waiting for the relief on Evie's face, added, "I asked him to have dinner with my niece and nephew and me at my house."

Evie stared at her dumbfounded until Olivia finally asked, "Do you want me to call him and ask him to bring the icicle or not? He's coming early in the morning to help me shop, so we can drop it off around noon."

Evie could manage nothing more than a nod.

"How did he come upon that icicle?" Evie asked her grandmother as they sat arm in arm in front of the small, shimmering tree.

"I know you already asked your mother that question," Filomena answered cagily. "So what did my angry Catharine have to say about it?"

"She wouldn't tell me," Evie admitted.

Her grandmother turned and looked into her eyes. "Is that true? She actually managed to keep her mouth shut?"

"Yes, Nana, occasionally she does manage to do that, you know. But that means *you* have to tell me how he got it."

"Why don't you ask Olivia? I'm sure he's told her."

"You know, I'm not going to tell you about the last ornament," Evie groused. "I'm the one who went to all the trouble, running myself ragged the past two days, and no one tells me anything. It's not fair."

"Fair!" her grandmother snorted. And they both laughed.

The last ornament had actually been an easy one for Evie; she'd arranged for it on the twenty-second, asking Padre Lou in Key West if he could carefully wrap and overnight the glimmering blue-and-green starfish Filomena had sent him two years ago after he'd baptized Tom. He replied that he wouldn't even attempt such a thing but that Marguerite would surely take care of it for him. Evie had laughed, remembering Lou's fierce assistant, and she smiled telling the story to her grandmother. She didn't tell Filomena that Lou had shared something else: Marguerite had asked him to marry her.

"I can't believe it!" Lou told Evie, "I made her repeat it three times. And then I asked her to write it down."

"What did she say to that?" Evie asked, grinning as she imagined Marguerite's response.

"She said she had another man pressuring her to marry him, and because I was too blind to try to keep her, she'd have to keep me!" he said joyfully. And that brought Evie to the twelfth ornament.

Earlier on Christmas Eve afternoon, she'd stolen Filomena's last piece, the handsome, slender wise man with gold sparkling in his crown and scarlet in his robe. While Serena diverted Filomena with a question about a recipe, Evie nabbed the figure from Filomena's nightstand.

"I didn't even miss him," Filomena said wonderingly, half to herself.

"Too busy with your cooking and scheming," Evie said with a laugh.

I've spent so much of my life cooking and scheming, Filomena thought, surveying the boisterous group surrounding her on this Christmas night, sitting over the remains of a dinner that had lasted for hours. *As it should,* Filomena told herself. *Nothing wrong with cooking and scheming if this is my reward.*

Yet everything hadn't turned out perfectly—at least not yet, and maybe never. True, Catharine and Maria weren't glowering at each over the table, but neither were they talking in the secret, quiet voices of sisters. In fact, Filomena wasn't at all pleased about the seating arrangements. She had told her daughters to sit on her right hand, next to each other, so she could keep on eye on them, but instead they'd put their two husbands between them. So Catharine sat next to Filomena, followed by Gregory, Daniel, and then Maria, seated too far from her sister to have any real conversation.

Then there was poor Serena on the other side of the table. *That girl is uneasy so far from her family.* Filomena observed when she invited the girl to Christmas Eve breakfast. *Maria hasn't done a good job there; she should be a better mother-in-law. Not that Catharine had done any better with Tom in the mother-in-law department. Though Tom and Evie aren't yet married—and with a child!* Filomena sighed, causing Catharine to narrow her eyes at her mother. Filomena ignored her.

Still, all things considered, Filomena told herself that she'd done her best, and Jesus had certainly answered her dawn prayer to prevent the day from becoming a disaster. Now, Mark's son Bobby piped up in a shy but determined voice, "What about the Christmas Blessings?" He stared expectantly at his mother as the room grew quiet.

Serena, who would have normally sent a panicked look to Mark, silently pleading with her husband to take over the explanation to his family, now glanced quickly at Filomena. The old woman lifted her chin, and Serena said quietly, "At home every Christmas night after dinner, we each say how we feel most blessed. It is our tradition."

"Serena started it," Mark put in proudly, as if anyone in his family might have imagined *he'd* instituted such a tradition.

"It is a good tradition," Filomena declared. "We shall do it now."

"All of us?" Michael asked, hoping the recitations might be limited to family members.

"Is there anyone here who does not feel blessed with something?" Filomena asked. When no one, including Michael, dared speak up, she said, "Bobby, you reminded us, so you should start."

The boy sat up tall in his chair, looked straight ahead and said, "I'm blessed to have ridden on an airplane, and to have Dad show me the whole country between California and Connecticut." Bobby had indeed been mesmerized by everything about the plane from going through the metal detector at the airport to watching the giant projected map of the US on the wall at the front of the plane where he'd intently studied the trajectory of their progress from SFO to Connecticut. He'd even loved the airline food, delighted with what he called "airplane TV dinners" because his mother wouldn't give them TV dinners at home or even allow the TV to be on while they ate.

"My turn!" Laurie cried, imperiously assuming that she would naturally come after her brother as she always did at home on Christmas night. When she had everyone's attention, she folded her hands primly. "I'm blessed by bossing Jack around. Mommy says I shouldn't do it, but I'm blessed by it."

"Sweetheart," Mark said gently, "do you really think bossing Jack around is your special Christmas blessing?"

"Yes, Daddy!" she said, surprised at how dense her father could be. "Because Melissa's too much of a baby to boss around, but Jack's just right, and he does whatever I tell him." And it was true; Laurie had been delighted to discover that her cousin was independent enough to follow someone who was not his mother but pliable enough to comply with whatever interesting commands she might issue.

The situation had been made even better, from Laurie's perspective, by the fact that Mark and Serena were staying with Evie and Jack. The chaos and high emotion of those few days before Christmas had been the perfect laboratory for Laurie to test her abilities as a leader. In the three days they'd been together, she and Jack had managed to knock over Evie's Christmas tree twice, get lost playing hide-and-seek around the bookcases at Barnes and Noble where Mark had taken them to give Evie and Serena a break, steal Evie's neighbor's Santa Claus doormat—because, as Laurie put it, "we wanted Santa in our own house," and disrupt the Christmas Eve pageant at church by helping Jack climb onto the life-size cow in the manger.

All in all, Jack's willingness to be a follower had indeed been a blessing to Laurie, and Mark decided to let it go, saying, "Well then, it's my turn, I guess. I'm blessed by Nana's wonderful Christmas present."

Everyone murmured agreement and nodded as Mark took Serena's hand in his. Catharine's husband, Gregory, lowered his head to hide a small smile. A week and a half ago when Mark and Serena's pastor had called him from Bodega Bay, he'd been surprised. He'd only met Luke once, ten years ago at Mark and Serena's wedding, and though he'd been impressed with the man's forthrightness and apparent calm in the face of the storm that was the groom's family, they hadn't had much chance to talk.

As soon as Luke had started talking, though, Greg understood. "I want someone in the family to know that Mark is giving up a Christmas trip to Serena's family in Mexico to attend Filomena's command performance. His cousin Evie suggested Filomena was very ill or dying, and Mark doesn't feel he has a choice." Luke worried that the decision could hurt Mark and

Serena's relationship. "I'm not sure I should even be calling. I just felt that someone besides me should know, and you're the only one in the family . . ."

He'd trailed off and Greg finished for him. "Who's sane enough to try to do something about it?" Gregory laughed. "No, no, don't worry. You're not far from the truth. I'm glad you called. Let me see what I can do."

It had been surprisingly easy. He went to see his mother-in-law and explained the situation. Filomena had listened silently. When he was finished she gave him his instructions.

"You will do me a favor, Gregory. Make arrangements for that family to fly from New York the day after Christmas to Serena's family in Mexico. Buy the tickets so that they can return to California afterward. Find them a place to stay for a week near her parents so they are not a burden, and rent rooms for them. Then go to the mall in Waterford and buy a thousand dollars worth of gift certificates so Serena can get whatever they need for the trip. Also, she will want to get presents for her family. And then bring everything to me. I will pay."

Gregory and his mother-in-law exchanged a long look; then she patted him on the arm and motioned for him to go. He'd returned the next day with the tickets, an itinerary, and the Crystal Mall gift certificates. He drank a cup of coffee while she wrapped everything in Christmas paper. He couldn't remember the last time he'd felt so content.

Later, when he'd told Catharine about it, she was speechless. After a while she asked him, "Do you think Evie's right that she's ill?"

"She never said so," he answered, "and I didn't push it. I do know that, in some way, she's trying to undo the damage she's caused. And that alone is pretty amazing."

Now Gregory spoke up, though it was not his turn. "I feel blessed by clean slates and fresh starts." Filomena gave a little smile as Catharine pressed her husband's hand under the table.

"It's your turn, Mommy," Laurie observed officiously, determined to restore the proceedings to their proper order. Serena, still holding Mark's hand, was quiet. Glancing briefly at Maria, she said softly, "I am blessed by my gift from Maria, *Posada Noches*."

The truth was Serena wasn't sure exactly *how* blessed she felt by the book her mother-in-law had written based on the stories Serena told her children each Christmas. She knew that Maria expected her gratitude, and to be fair, Serena did appreciate the effort her mother-in-law had gone to in producing the extraordinary gift. It thrilled Serena that her story—the story of her village, her family, her people—would be told and illustrated by a successful American author. She just wished it had been another author.

Something about all of it—Maria creating the book, selling it to her publisher, and then making a gift of it to Serena—made Serena uncomfortable. She couldn't quite put her finger on it: Was it that Maria had taken the story without asking her, without even telling her? Or was it that she felt Maria was trying to become part of something that wasn't hers—something that belonged to Serena alone and that only she should pass on to her children?

Whatever it was that disturbed Serena, she felt was being petty and so hadn't let on about her feelings, not even to Mark, who was only too glad to find something to praise his mother for. Maria was trying to find a way to Serena's heart, even if she couldn't seem to discover the best path. Knowing this, Serena had accepted the offering of the book with thanks as warm as she could manage, and now she would show her gratitude in front of the whole family. Maria's gift was a start, and for that, Serena did indeed feel blessed.

"Now it's Melissa's turn; she's next to Mom," said Bobby. But Laurie piped up, "Melissa doesn't have blessings. She's too much of a baby. And, she's not sitting *next* to Mommy. She's sitting on Mommy's lap. She doesn't even get her own seat."

Mentally counting the minutes until he could get his children back to Evie's and in bed after this long day, Mark announced, "Melissa *does* get a turn, and I'll help her with it. Melissa feels blessed by naps."

Laurie met this with dignified disdain, "Naps! Only a baby would be blessed by naps." Melissa slumbered on.

Jack was next, seated between Serena and Evie. Evie leaned over and asked softly, "Jack, what do you want to say thank-you for today on Jesus' birthday?"

His eyes lit on his "new" cousin Laurie, whom he found irresistible, trailing her like a small puppy ready for whatever adventure she cooked up. But then, remembering old alliances, he looked over at Olivia, his best friend. Still wearing the wool hat with floppy reindeer antlers he'd found under the tree that morning from his father, Jack closed his eyes and scrunched up his face as he considered his options. Suddenly a look of surprise came over his features, as though he'd realized something amazing. His eyes flew open and he peered up sideways at Evie. "Thank you for Daddy on the sub'rine!"

Evie swallowed the lump that rose in her throat and said, "That's a good one, Jack!" Tom had left for his patrol five days ago, and every night since she'd added a prayer to Jack's night list "for Daddy on the submarine." Apparently he'd been paying attention. Thanks to several counseling sessions over the phone with Padre Lou, Evie had come to know the always inescapable truth: They loved each other, but they just didn't seem to know how to live with each other. How much of that had Jack picked up?

"Now it's my turn," she told Jack, "and I'm going to copy you. I'm going to say thank you for the blessing of Daddy on the submarine."

§

I t would have been more accurate for her to say "I'm blessed by the Internet," because this morning she'd found a long e-mail from Tom waiting for her. The patrol had come into port on Christmas Eve—*where*, he couldn't, of course, tell her—but his Christmas e-mail included much more than the scanty facts she usually got from him. Indeed, she was happily astonished to discover he was quite a writer.

She'd sent him an e-mail the morning after he left, having spent a sleepless night of imaginary conversations in which she started out blaming him for everything and ended in self-recriminations. She wrote out of exhaustion and sorrow, pouring out her heart and her fears in a way that she couldn't have if he were sitting next to her. Following Padre Lou's counsel, she wrote only about herself—what she wanted, what she felt was wrong, and what she felt she was doing wrong in their relationship. She made no accusations; instead, she confessed her fear that returning to Connecticut had been a mistake, that she'd become too deeply involved in her mother's family before they had fully anchored their own. She sent the e-mail without even spell-checking it, knowing that if she read it over, she'd never send it.

He wrote back, admitting his own anxiety about their ability to form a real family out of their love for each other and Jack. He'd been around other submariners long enough now to see the toll their work took on their marriages and families. He didn't want a relationship with Jack like the one he had with his father. And he didn't want a cool, efficient wife like his mother; he wanted Evie.

As she read his message at dawn on Christmas morning, at around the same time her grandmother was praying for a day that wouldn't be a disaster, Evie began to cry in earnest. She found to her surprise that quiet, taciturn Tom had ventured a possible solution. What if he didn't become a career Navy man? What if they spent time figuring out together what they wanted to do and where they wanted to do it? What if Evie could manage to complete her marine biology degree while they were in New England? Then he would have Navy and submarine training and Evie would have her degree. Couldn't they go just about anywhere?

Maybe, Evie had nodded through her tears, *maybe we could.*

§

arah was sitting next to Evie, directly across from Filomena. The two old friends exchanged glances and Filomena said, "What about Anna's Sarah? What is your blessing?"

Sarah looked around at the assembled group. Not one member of her own family was present, and yet she felt more useful, more at home in this room than she'd felt anywhere since Ben had died. From Guillermo, seated next to her after arriving from New York just in time for dinner, to Filomena, who, for all her sound and fury, had made her feel at home from the moment she arrived, Sarah felt like a part of something. Granted, it wasn't something that she'd want to be part of every day—too much drama, too much stress, and too much joy—but it was something she felt grateful for right now.

The angel Anna had given her to wrap more than sixty years ago, the angel Filomena had given her as a gift, glimmered on the little tree. That angel had given her back her voice, kept her alive, and brought her here. When she finally told Filomena the evening she arrived how she'd first come to see and touch the angel, the older woman had not seemed surprised. She merely said, "I must have known it was yours when I chose it for you."

As Sarah gazed at the angel, its wings seemed to stir; in their reflection she could almost see Anna, just as she'd stood on the platform at the train station all those years ago, wasted away by illness and by cares, waving good-bye as the train she'd put Sarah on rolled away.

Sarah's eyes were dim. "Anna's Sarah is thankful for Anna's angel." She patted Guillermo's large, gnarled hand and added, "Now it's your turn, my dear."

Startled, Guillermo shook his head, "No, no. What can I say? I'm just a guest for dinner."

"You are more than that," Filomena said decisively, "as you well know. So you must take your turn at a blessing. Besides, you eat at my table, you do things my way."

"There's an understatement," Catharine muttered and Maria, two seats away, choked back a laugh. Pretending not to hear or notice, Filomena stared imperiously at Guillermo until he shifted heavily in his seat, took a long swallow of the good Turkish coffee, and was silent. Finally, his voice soft and catching, Guillermo said, "As Gregory said: I am blessed by second chances."

§

But would the slim second chance he'd been given be enough? He couldn't know that now. Four days ago, after putting Sarah in the limousine to Stonington, he'd set out to find the return address on his daughter's last note with the picture of Chrissy. He'd never been to Brooklyn and found himself liking the place. It had been dressed for Christmas with everything from elaborate lighted Nativity sets to tastefully illuminated wreaths and garlands to plastic Santas. Brooklyn seemed like a place that had room for everyone. He saw Hasidic Jews, with their long beards and sober faces and black hats, and he saw men in turbans and women with their heads completely veiled. Even in cold December, some were lingering on corners, some hurrying to the task at hand.

Finding Clemencia's address had taken a while. Not that he'd hurried. He was in no rush to knock on her door. Nevertheless, that was what he'd come for, and it was late afternoon when he dragged himself up the steps in front of the three-story brick building that bore her address. He saw from the mailboxes that she lived on the third floor. As he stood hesitating, a black woman about his age in a nurse's uniform came up, key in hand. She was carrying groceries and a large canvas bag. Eyeing him suspiciously, she asked, "Can I help you?"

Without stopping to think, he blurted out, "I am Clemencia's father. From Miami."

The woman's challenging stare turned into an expression of welcome. "So you're Guillermo! She talks about her dad all the time!" she exclaimed, sending a shock through him that he could barely conceal. "Well, come on in. I'm Roberta. I know she's home, because tonight's my night to cook; I live on the second floor and every other night one of us cooks enough for both of us and we share the food. We've been doing it since, you know, the separation. Don't ring the bell; won't she be surprised!"

You have no idea, thought Guillermo, smiling weakly as Roberta surrendered her bags to him and led him up to the second floor. *And how long had Clemencia been separated from her husband? How was she managing? Better without you than with you,* he cautioned himself. *Remember that.*

"Listen," Roberta said conspiratorially when they reached her apartment, "You go on up and knock on the door yourself. She'll think it's me! Oh, I'd love to see her face! But it's only right you see each other alone first. And Chrissy—what a good kid! She'll be so excited. Tell Clem I'll be up in an hour or so with enough food for all of us—and a nice bottle of wine. We're celebrating tonight!"

She shooed him up the stairs, and he waited until he heard her door close. Then, with perhaps a little unearned confidence, he knocked on his daughter's door.

He knew she'd be expecting Roberta when he heard the locks tumble as Clemencia unlatched the door. He almost wanted to warn her, to shout through the door, "Wait! Stop and think if you really want to do this; it's not who you think it is!"

But then she was standing there, the smile of welcome she'd worn for Roberta freezing and then fading. She was still beautiful, but age and worry and even some laughter had etched lines in her face. He saw in her eyes that she was considering closing the door in his face, and he remembered how he had thought to do the same to her aunt Carolina all those years ago when she'd come from Cuba to tell his daughter the truth about her mother. He knew he'd deserve it if Clemencia did slam the door and refasten all the locks, but then, behind his daughter, he caught a glimpse of a dark head bent over a book on a table strewn with books and papers. *Chrissy.* He wanted just a moment, he needed just one moment, and he said with a lopsided, desperate grin, "So Roberta said you talk about me all the time."

Clemencia stared at him, her brow darkening, her eyes slitted. He'd blown it, he could see it in her face. Had she seen the despair in him when he half turned to go? But before he could leave, she sighed dramatically and said, "I have to talk about you. Can't have the neighbors thinking I've got no family, can I?" And she pushed the door open a little more and stepped back so he could come in.

It hasn't been an easy few days, he thought now, staring at his Christmas Glass star topping Evie's pretty little tree. He and Clemencia had talked little about the past; indeed, they'd said little at all. Chrissy and Roberta had done enough talking for all four of them. He'd rented a room with a kitchenette in a nearby hotel so he wouldn't be imposing on them and had spent time getting to know his granddaughter. Just the thought of Chrissy made his heart swell: The idea that someone with his blood in her could be so bright and good gave him hope. Clemencia must have felt something like this because she invited him to Christmas Eve dinner and, when he'd left in the morning, said she'd consider his invitation to come to Miami over Chrissy's February school break. "For the sake of your granddaughter," she added sternly, but it was enough.

§

Jack was clapping his hands, crying, "Livy! Livy's turn!" Olivia smiled radiantly at "her" family, this quirky, frantic family that had come to depend on her in so many ways. Yet, for the first time in memory, they'd managed to bridge their differences and do something magnificent for her in a way she'd never imagined. And so she meant it from her heart when she said, "I am blessed by your marvelous Christmas present."

All of them, from Filomena to Jack, were grinning so widely that she had to laugh out loud. For as long as she could remember, the family had given her cash for Christmas, a gift that had been welcome in the early years, but more recently had been slightly embarrassing. For the past five years, without telling them, she'd donated their Christmas cash to New London's homeless shelter. But this year their gift had a different twist: Knowing of her upcoming trip home, the family had taken up a collection for her to spend on the poor in Accra, the city where she'd grown up and where many still suffered terrible deprivation. They'd given her a jar filled with cash and checks—pennies proudly dropped in by Jack and Melissa, wads of cash stuffed in by Filomena, and sizable checks written by Daniel and Maria and Greg and Catharine.

There was enough for her to buy medicine, food, clothes, and even school supplies for many families; some things she would buy here and ship over, others she would buy there with the cash that merchants all over West Africa still craved. The gift was generous and would make an enormous difference. Not to mention the extra surge of guilty pleasure she'd get telling her sisters and brother how she planned to spend every penny on the poor. It would make her homecoming and reunion with her father even sweeter.

"Thanks to all of you, Christmas will come in February to many poor people in my home," she said. She saw no need to tell them that Michael had given her a check ten times the amount they'd collected. She'd already thanked him.

Everyone turned to him expectantly. He tried to beg off but met even more outrage than Guillermo had in his failed attempt to avoid the blessing circle. Filomena glared at Michael, saying, "You are the oldest friend at this table! Except for Anna's Sarah, you have been in this family longer than even Greg and Daniel. And you say you have no Christmas blessing? I won't hear of such a thing!"

Noting Catharine's dismay at her mother's inviting him to this table, Michael tried to defuse the situation, telling Filomena with what he hoped passed for jocularity. "I've been living alone for so long, I don't know how to count my blessings in public. Let me just listen and learn."

But Filomena was too clever for him. Ignoring her daughters' disapproving glances, she said slyly, "You look like you feel more blessed than anyone here. Do you want to name your blessing, or should we guess?"

Now it was Michael's turn to feel awkward. She was right; he did feel blessed, but he'd always been an intensely private man, and old habits die hard. In the weeks since he'd come to visit Filomena, his life had changed, but he wasn't sure how to put that change into words for these people, or whether he wanted to.

§

The relief Michael felt after his conversation with Filomena released something in him, something he really couldn't describe, but he had an odd sense of freedom from himself. After she reassured him that his father hadn't stolen the glass icicle, he realized that he didn't have to go through the rest of his life strangled by the past. It wasn't that he believed Filomena—Michael had known in his heart for a long time that Frank had stolen the ornament; what had freed him was her determination to convince him that he was not like his father. She'd known him as a boy; the fact that she'd believed in him then and, after all he'd told her about himself, still believed in him now had given him the courage to believe in himself. Enough, at least, to call Olivia the day after he'd met her at Filomena's.

They spoke every day afterward, and when he'd asked Olivia whether she'd see him if he came down a few days before Christmas, she agreed with a promptness that gave him even more confidence. They spent the day before Christmas Eve together, Olivia shopping for her niece and nephew, Michael blissfully following her wherever she led, much as Jack followed Laurie. That night they had dinner at the Lighthouse Inn in New London, where he was staying, just a few blocks from her house near Ocean Beach.

He felt he'd talked more in those twelve hours than he had in his entire life, and he'd been amazed that she wasn't ready to cut him out of her life at the end of the night. Instead, she asked him to Christmas Eve dinner with her and the children.

Olivia's niece and nephew were polite, though slightly perplexed at his presence, and the evening passed without too much tension. Now he was angling for an invitation to go with them in February to Accra so he could meet her father, but he doubted she'd agree to that. No matter; he understood her need to be with her family, especially her father, without the shock of a brand-new man. He could wait.

Michael wasn't about to say all this to the people around the table, though everyone could see he was smitten with Olivia. But he wasn't about to embarrass her, either. Finally, looking directly at Filomena, he said, "I'm blessed by the lessons I learned from my father." The old woman smiled.

§

Daniel was next. He was the odd man out at this gathering, and he knew it. Though he'd been born and bred in New London like many here, he was the one who'd left. He'd made a life on another coast across the country, hurting and angering at least two of the people sitting at the table. Despite all this, Daniel was perhaps the most comfortable person in the room. He'd never set out to hurt anyone; he was confident of his own decency, and though sorry for any pain he'd caused, he believed that Catharine was responsible for her sorrow and Filomena for her fury. Daniel was one of the few people in the room who was aware of what he was responsible for—and what he wasn't. And he also believed that God worked everything out for the good of those who believe in Him.

Which is exactly what he'd told Maria last night as they were getting ready to meet her sister and brother-in-law for dinner. Maria had been a wreck. "Why did I ever agree to this?" she moaned. "Catharine doesn't want to have this dinner with me any more than I want to have it with her. She only asked us to their house to prove something to my mother, so she could say that she was the one who made the effort. Honestly, why am I doing this? Why are we even here?"

Daniel hadn't replied, merely getting up to rub her shoulders where she sat at the vanity in their hotel suite. Unwilling to be consoled, she stared accusingly at him in the mirror. "I don't know why you're so calm," she said. "It's not like you're going to be the most beloved man in the room tonight."

"Or in the room tomorrow, for that matter," he acknowledged good-naturedly. "I'm calm because I haven't done anything wrong. And neither have you. You need to remember that."

"That's not exactly how my sister and my mother see things. I'm already sick to my stomach. Can you imagine how things will go when I can't even eat the meal I'm sure my sister the martyr has been slaving over all day. Probably to impress you!"

He met her gaze questioningly in the mirror. "What are you talking about?"

Maria looked away. "Maybe she wants you to see what you've been missing all these years. I'm sure she still feels something for you. Evie's told me that it hasn't always been easy for her father. Maybe there's still a spark."

He walked around the chair and knelt beside her, lifting her face until she looked at him. "You're kidding, right? You know that Catharine loves Greg. And you surely must know that I love you. And only you. What are you imagining? That this week is going to end with me in your sister's arms? That a meal I don't even want is going to make me think I got the wrong twin?"

She laughed a little at that, but he was surprised by her fears. As it turned out, the evening had gone surprisingly well. He liked Greg, a quiet man with a dry sense of humor who had them all laughing at themselves and, even more, at Filomena and her hold over all of them. Years before, their alliance against their mother had bonded them together; perhaps it could help them rebuild their relationship.

Maybe this Christmas journey won't turn out to be a complete waste, God willing. Daniel knew they were waiting for his blessing. Maria was looking at him half in fearful expectation of what he might say. If he said he felt blessed by her, Catharine might resent it. If he said he was blessed by this family, it would sound weird and false. Then he remembered their Christmas party back in Sausalito with David, Sandy, and Blossom. He put his arm casually around his wife's shoulders and said, "I'm blessed by friendships old and new, with all they have to offer."

Perfect, Maria thought, looking at her clever husband with admiration. Of course, that meant it was her turn. As soon as Bobby had brought up the Christmas blessings, she'd ungraciously wished that her grandson was just a bit less sensitive and tradition-oriented.

§

The truth was, Maria felt blessed by so many things. Unfortunately, none of them would sound right here. She was, of course, blessed by Daniel, but following his lead, she didn't want to rub Catharine's face in it. She was blessed by the small, tight bud that had formed on the previously barren stem of her relationship with Serena. Thank God she'd thought of doing the book for Serena's Christmas present, though she wasn't sure Serena was completely delighted. Still, it was a start. Maybe the relationship would flower.

She felt blessed by their wonderful home in Sausalito on the bay, but that surely wouldn't go over too well with this crowd. She felt blessed by their decision to donate a percentage of her earnings to the charity for kids in Marin City, but that would sound too pompous. She could say that she felt blessed by the plan to spend tomorrow afternoon alone with her sister, but it wouldn't really be true. Maybe when it was over she'd feel blessed, but right now she just felt a mixture of apprehension and excitement, heavy on the apprehension.

What she felt most blessed by was the fact that in seventy-two hours she and Daniel would be on a plane home. They would celebrate their Christmas on New Year's Eve, and right now it seemed like a bit of heaven waiting for them just a few days away. She definitely couldn't say that.

Or could she?

§

Watching Catharine from the corner of her eye while the blessings were being said, Maria couldn't help laughing at her twin's sarcastic comment about her mother's dual obsessions: food and controlling her family. Hearing Maria snort, Catharine had smiled in spite of herself. Maria hadn't seen that impish grin of her sister's in so long! Catharine had always been sharp-tongued, the funny one, who could occasionally even outwit their mother.

Suddenly Maria knew what she would say: She'd tell the complete truth, for once, in the midst of her family, and hope to see her sister's mischievous smile once again. "I'm blessed," she said, "that this day is almost over!"

There was dead silence, and then Catharine's laughter burst into the room. And then so did everyone else's.

Everyone's, that is, except Filomena's, who, regally ignoring one daughter's remark and the other's reaction, said, "Gregory has already told of his blessing, a good blessing, a *proper* blessing. Catharine, you are next."

Catharine didn't hesitate. She'd had the most time to think about it, but the truth was that she'd known what she would say as soon as Bobby suggested the Christmas Blessings. She surprised herself; she was usually so indecisive, so accustomed to seeing the "glass half-full." But she hadn't even needed to consider her answer, and now she said clearly, "Greg. I am blessed by my husband."

§

Catharine flinched a little when she saw Gregory's eyebrows shoot up in surprise. That was entirely her fault, that he didn't know he was her greatest blessing. Oh yes, she'd known—in her mind, rationally—that Greg was a blessing. At some level, she'd always known that. But it was only over this troubling, tumultuous December that she'd felt it or, more accurately, that she'd opened her heart to the feeling.

She'd noticed how he protected her, helped her, how he structured his whole life around her, how much he'd gone through to make her life easier—dealing with Filomena, dealing with Evie when Catharine just couldn't cope with her stubborn mother and their rebellious daughter. How he'd accepted, not just tolerated, her silences, her moods, her frustration with her mother, her envy of her sister. *How long,* she wondered, as his look of astonishment softened into grateful pleasure, *have I let him think he's second best?*

The reality of him, the gift of him, had hit her full force last night at their dinner with Maria and Daniel. She'd been distressed since inviting them the day before, grousing to Greg, "This is the last thing I want to do on our Christmas Eve. I'm only doing it because my mother will have a fit if I don't. And if she *is* sick, I'm not about to be the one who sends her over the edge!"

After murmuring comforting words, Greg had taken her list and gone for the groceries on the busiest shopping day of the year, braving the Super Stop & Shop as if it were a battleground he was confident of taking, and then helping her chop, sauté, steam, and bake. But it had been his performance once Maria and Daniel arrived that melted Catharine's heart. Greg was welcoming and solicitous in his quiet, funny way until the ice thawed a bit, warmed by the laughter and conversation he created.

What amazed her the most, though, was that Daniel didn't cast even a faint glow next to the sturdy, shining light of her husband. With Greg at her side, she wondered what she'd seen in the tall, pale, gaunt man who now seemed too thin, too distant, too clever for her taste. Again and again, her eyes had gone to her husband, as he shook hands with Daniel, poured the wine, carved the small turkey, joked with Maria to put her at ease, told hilarious stories about Filomena. Had it really taken her thirty years to recognize the treasure she lived with every day?

§

All eyes now turned to Filomena, seated at the head of the table, the tree with the Christmas Glass on her right. It was completely dark out now; the room was lit only by the blaze of candles on the table and the glittering lights on the tree reflected by the twelve pieces of glass. Dressed in her best black silk dress with a bit of jet lace at the throat and sleeves, and with a jeweled cross around her neck, Filomena sat, her back straight and her head high, looking as much the Russian empress as the Italian matriarch.

I must have been wrong, Evie thought as she looked at her. *She looks beautiful, amazing. She's not dying. She can't be.*

Filomena let the moment stretch out, gazing at each of her guests in turn as if she could read their minds. Perhaps she could. It hadn't been a perfect day, but then she'd never truly believed it could be. When she'd issued the ultimatum to her daughters only a few weeks before, she hadn't thought through all that might happen; she'd merely—stubbornly—meant to force them to reconcile. She never really did think very far ahead, unless it was to worry about prospective tragedies. But her ultimatum had taken on a momentum of its own, and it was only recently that she realized this day itself might indeed have become a tragedy.

The fact that it hadn't was a blessing and a relief to her. But had she accomplished her purpose? Had she undone all the damage she'd caused over so many years, she wondered, letting her unreadable gaze linger on her daughters. The only bond they seemed to share was their pleasure in annoying her. Still, that was something, and maybe she deserved it—a little.

They looked back at her steadily, made bold by their alliance. Catharine had lost that cringing look Filomena despised, all the more because she knew it was her own fault that her daughter wore it; and Maria had stopped crumpling and refolding her napkin compulsively as she'd done at the beginning of the dinner. Could she hope for much more in one day? Could she control what happened tomorrow when the twins met on their own, or on every day, every year, every Christmas, after that?

There was a time when she thought she could. But that time was past. As her eyes swept around the room, her great-granddaughter, Mark's little girl Laurie, stared boldly back at her, "You do a blessing, Nana," she demanded.

Quite a live wire, that one, Filomena thought, her lips twitching. The little boy, Bobby, though older, was easily intimidated; he had barely looked at the somber old woman. But the girl—Filomena got a kick out of that one. She'd give her parents a run for their money. Too bad they were leaving tomorrow. But the other family, Serena's family in Mexico, would be happy to see them. She'd done something right in making that possible. Maybe her daughters would realize it.

She smiled faintly at Sarah and Olivia, her old friends, the two who knew her as well as anyone could. Finally, she let her gaze rest on the tree, adorned with her family's treasure. She flicked her eyes over each piece in turn, knowing what it meant to her and to someone at this table. Tomorrow, each piece would again go its separate way, as it should, but today . . . today, they were all together.

Ah, Anna, my dear cousin, she thought, *I haven't done as good a job as you might have, but I've done my best.*

And then she closed her eyes.